GW00472150

Shadowed Passage

Argosy Realm, Volume 2

Al Onia

Published by Al Onia, 2022.

This is a work of fiction. Similarities to real people, places, or events are entirely coincidental.

SHADOWED PASSAGE

First edition. March 28, 2022.

Copyright © 2022 Al Onia.

ISBN: 979-8201760588

Written by Al Onia.

Also by Al Onia

Argosy Realm
Barnacle Passage
Shadowed Passage

Jake Nourth
The Fourth Vertex
The Third Redux

Watch for more at ajonia.com.

Thanks to Sandra and Mike for reading the early version and urging me forward.

Chapter 1

A rgosy Station – *In jumpspace standard, Argosy Realm's nearest hub to the Bohr Confluence, providing Realm-Confluence exchange in goods and services. Jumpship maintenance and refit facility. In accordance with the peace terms negotiated between Bohr Confluence and Argosy Realm, control will pass from solely Realm oversight to joint governance. Transfer to occur with the arrival of the Frigate Rickover under Admiral Wolfe Rowland's command. See hyperlink for evaluation for strategic strengths and weaknesses.*

Confluence Navy Brief.

C arver Denz knew he was suffering a jumpspace nightmare. In reality, the *Rickover* provided barnacle passage for his small ship and the one he'd been commissioned to protect. In the spook dimension dream he struggled to protect himself. The part of his brain in real time and space recognised the illusion but it didn't diminish the primal fear for his life.

He fought back against the knife-wielding attacker. He blocked the blade with his forearms, risking non-fatal cuts over a deadly gut slice.

The attacker's face was hidden behind a fogged visor. Carver pushed away. An alarm rang, distracting his nightmare assailant. Carver drifted up, arms spread like an angel's wings. His assailant sunk lower and away from sight and mind.

Carver's transition from jumpspace dreams to hit-the-deck-moving was sudden. Normal gradual waking from jumpsleep had been bypassed. On his back in the cryo coffin, he recognized acceleration pressure. Disoriented but stirred into action by the continuing klaxon, he pushed up from the coffin as it emerged from its cubbyhole in his ship.

Carver performed an inelegant roll over the edge. The two-person ship's deck frosted his bare knees and palms. The liquid in his lungs crystallized on the icy deck then evaporated within the *Crossed Swords*.

De-barnacling alarms rang with an incessant shrill. A verbal cry roared once. "Under fire." It wasn't repeated.

Who or what was under attack? Not the *Crossed Swords*, or he'd be breathing void instead of pressurized air. Carver pulled himself to the pilot chair and coughed out the remaining deepsleep fluid onto his lap. He heard a repeat of his phlegm-clearance from behind. His shipmate and business partner, DualE, was awake.

"Remind me again why I signed up for this?" she rasped.

"You were bored with naval administrative purgatory." Carver fought down nausea. "I feel like two kilos of crap in a one kilo sack. Now remind me why I'm here."

His colleague braced herself upright, her tall muscular form undisguised by the cryo flimsuit. DualE's military bearing frothed to the surface, cryo-lag or not. She took the second pilot chair and began monitoring. "Where do I start? You were jilted. Your sudden wealth didn't buy happiness."

"Too easy," he said. "As an impartial observer and my partner, forget love and money. What's the real reason?"

"I think you needed to prove to yourself your success wasn't a fluke."

Success? The return journey from Argosy Station to the Bohr Confluence weeks ago had been anything but a success. Except they'd survived. "Nearer the mark. You don't think it was a fluke?"

"Biding my time, Carver. But I wouldn't be here if I thought luck was your sole talent."

Carver activated the *Crossed Swords'* external monitors. The *Rickover* and its two fighter escorts moved away from them. Or they from it. The dreadnaught *Indefatigable* accompanying Bohr's peace-keeping force wasn't in sight. It hadn't emerged yet from jumpspace. Or dropped short to scout Argosy's surroundings. Was it the source of the emergency call? Or the source of the attack?

"What the hell, Carver?" DualE's fingers punched more icons on the monitors.

"We've been cut loose. Admiral Rowland's transport commitment is apparently complete. Up to us to get on to the Eddy."

"Any word from Argosy Station?" DualE toggled a full range of communication icons.

"There was an 'under attack' cry."

An incoming message crackled. "This is *Penance*. Brother Pious speaking. *Crossed Swords* acknowledge."

Carver and DualE's fellow barnacle and clients were in the same situation. "I thought Rowland would provide protective escort into Argosy. Either we don't need it or he's crossed us up." Carver regretted booking barnacle with the navy but it had been expedient and agreed to by their clients. And free, as part of DualE's naval severance.

"We're here, Brother Pious," DualE answered. "Are you free from the *Rickover*?"

"We were barely conscious from cryo when released."

Carver turned to DualE. "The brothers chose not to meditate this time through jump. Cryo's nightmares don't scare them." His attack nightmare before revival bore some resemblance to a past incident but the vagaries of spookspace's time distortion could reflect an event yet to occur.

"They've led less regret-filled lives than me or you." She ramped up another signal. "That's from Argosy. We've arrived at our destination. Admiral Rowland and the *Rickover* fulfilled barnacle commitment."

"Rather unceremoniously," said Carver.

"Rowland's way of clawing back the indignity of transporting civilians."

"Vengeful prick, isn't he?"

"Shush. There's a naval priority message."

"...significant damage to two vessels in dock. Attack apparently confined to one salvo. Jumpfreighter *Orson* in decel."

"Can you raise the *Rickover*?" Carver asked. "I'd like an explanation."

"This is DualE aboard the *Crossed Swords* calling *Rickover*. Acknowledge."

"Get off the comm, *Crossed Swords*. Will explain when situation is secure. Attention freighter *Orson*. Prepare to be boarded for weapon search."

Carver and DualE exchanged glances. "That doesn't help much," he said. He hailed their patrons. "*Penance*. I suggest we navigate toward the station in *Rickover's* wake. The armed frigate should take care of any further attack, if that's what it was."

"Understood. Brother Cardinal has revived from cryo. We will follow you."

"Keep your eyes open," said Carver.

DualE settled into the second seat. "My former bosses only promised to get us this far. Time to start earning our keep protecting the brothers." She manipulated more information eddies on the screens. "Just because the navy won't talk to us doesn't mean we can't listen in."

The frigate's comm chattered on at least two fronts. "Argosy Station, are you intact? Do you require defense? Freighter *Orson*, stand off docking with the station. Hold your position at twenty thousand meters."

"Frigate *Rickover*. This is Argosy Control. Station suffered minor damage. Attack limited to one strike. No indication of further fire from unknown source. We thought it was the Confluence. Can you confirm no fire from you?"

"This is *Orson*. Our fuel tanks were holed by the same projectile which hit your docks, Argosy. We'll need tugs to stop where *Rickover* suggests."

"*Orson*, this is the *Rickover*. Not a suggestion. We command you stop where ordered."

"Just like the navy," said Carver. "Orders are orders. Don't waver for the situation at hand."

"Careful, Carver, those are my former comrades." DualE brought up *Orson's* trajectory. "But you're right. There go the tugs." She pointed through the viewport.

Argosy Station was illuminated by fire and sparks from two of the crippled ships in port. Its rings and spheres rotated about a long central axis. It looked like a necklace pulled straight and stood on end. Vertical was a mere concept in space but the artificial gravity within the station gave it up and down directions which Carver mentally applied to the outside view. They were close enough to see interior lights. "Aim for the bottom?" Carver shone a laser where a gap in a cluster of small ships were docked. Larger freighters docked in separate gantries some distance from the main station. Shuttle traffic moved crew, maintenance staff and cargo between.

"I'm puzzled," said Carver. "Argosy Station could be considered a reckless target. Both sides use its jumpship maintenance and refit facilities."

"The station looks intact," said DualE. "I agree targeting it would be a poor choice for either side. Attention Argosy basal dock-master. This is the *Crossed Swords* out of Bohr Confluence. Permission to lock in for us and the *Penance*. Six passengers total."

"*Crossed Swords* and *Penance*. Hold your distance. We'll send a security team out once we've established you are not a threat to this station."

"We barnacled the *Rickover* from Bohr. If you're looking for a threat, a Confluence naval frigate poses greater danger than two small missionary craft. Check your logs, *Penance* was here two months ago and *Crossed Swords* is more of a danger to itself and occupants than the station or the Realm. We're coming in." DualE's voice was firm.

"I'm impressed," said Carver. "And surprised you never graduated to officer class."

"I've no authority to grant you access. You may approach but don't dock until I get permission." The station master's voice had lost some of its bluster.

"You may board us once we're docked," DualE answered. "The sooner we can make contact with an outgoing jumpship, the sooner we'll be out of your jurisdiction."

She turned to Carver. "I have been an officer. Twice. Both field promotions when our leaders got themselves killed and I took command."

"Didn't stick?"

DualE's grimace held something back. "I achieved mission goals and saved lives. Not every officer can make that claim. Those above me had different philosophies and I didn't complain too much about retreating to my former status."

Would she carry those different ideas into their mission? Carver liked the part about saving lives. He'd trust her that far.

"This is *Penance*," hailed Brother Cardinal. "Are you sure we're cleared to dock?"

"Stay in our target shadow, *Penance*." Carver assumed the pilot duties while DualE continued to monitor *Rickover's* progress.

Crossed Swords crept into the umbilical-laden gantry. Carver decelerated to a final thump and they were docked.

"Cardinal, are you berthed?"

"In twenty seconds, Mr. Denz."

"I see you now, *Penance*. We're underneath you." Carver activated the external lights on his ship. "I want to examine your barnacle mechs. We need to make sure none were damaged when *Rickover* kicked us free."

DualE moved toward the lock. "I'll do the same for us."

"Stay put," said Carver. "No sense in both of us being shot as saboteurs by a station security team."

Carver returned to the station master's wavelength. "Argosy Station. We are docked. One crew member EVA'ing to confirm integrity of hull and barnacle mechs before potential failure points become critical. Our jump transport did a one-way release on us. Acknowledge."

"Remain within your ships until our inspectors reach you."

"Did you suffer casualties?"

"Unconfirmed. Discontinue communication." The speaker went silent.

"Thanks for the warm welcome," Carver muttered.

"I'm sure their hands are busy with more immediate concerns than a half-dozen wayfarers," said DualE.

"I need to move. I can't sit here for days until they bless us with inspection."

She held up a hand. "Hush, I'm listening to the *Rickover*." She'd donned headphones over her short-cropped hair and stuck a throat mic to her tapered neck.

Carver did the same and contacted *Penance*. "Brothers, you heard the instructions from the harbor master? I guess we're staying put."

"I suggest you use the time to find us alternate barnacle transport to Slate's Progress since the *Rickover* seems unavailable."

"I agree, Pious. Easier done in person within the station. I'd start with Phyl's Fill." Carver itched to get out of the ship and stretch. He didn't need to go to Phyl's. He wanted to.

"Can you contact the proprietor from here?"

"Good idea. First, I'm going to EVA and check our locks."

"Is that wise, given the harbor master's instructions?"

"It's wise if I find a broken or frayed anchor cable. I won't set boot on the dock. I doubt they're monitoring every small craft. It's worth the risk. Then I'll look for another jumpship." Carver removed the headset and moved to the airlock to don a suit.

DualE raised an eyebrow and lifted one earpiece.

"I'm going to check our anchors," said Carver. "If there's a jumpfreighter heading for Slate's Progress, we should be on it."

She nodded and returned to the comm monitor.

Carver suited and cycled outside. Beacons lit up glimpses of their surroundings. Three nearby ships were dark inside and out. He attached a line to his suit and spidered to the base of the *Crossed Swords*. His helmet light focused on the six anchor grapples and cable retractors. Carver manually unlocked each one and pulled the cables from their nests. Hand over hand he examined every meter of line. They passed muster. The *Rickover* had turned them loose in a hurry but the sudden release hadn't caused any damage.

He surveyed the docking lattice for activity from the station. It looked quiet. Carver stretched his tether and kicked toward the *Penance*.

He repeated his inspection. Satisfied, Carver returned to his airlock and cycled back inside.

"Welcome aboard, Mr. Denz."

A suited man stood at the front of the *Crossed Swords'* cabin. One glove held a heart disruptor pointed at his chest. In between, DualE sat with her hands behind her head.

"What the hell's this?" asked Carver.

DualE shrugged. "Apparently the spirit of cooperation agreed to between the Confluence and the Realm hasn't trickled down very far in the chain of command."

"Not entirely true," said the stranger. "You were instructed to remain aboard your ship. You didn't."

"We just got tumbled from barnacle," said Carver. "If we're to hitch another ride before we become a burden to this station, I needed to make sure we could hold on through spookspace." He made no effort to raise his hands. "I thought you were all too busy assessing damage from this apparent attack." Carver set his helmet down and leaned against the lock bulkhead. "Wait, you don't think we were responsible?"

"*Rickover's* ballistic backtrack indicates the attack, beam, projectile or whatever it was came out of jumpspace on the same trajectory as the damaged freighter, *Orson*." DualE's voice was calm, she was obviously trying to keep the situation under control.

Carver stared at the armed man. "Satisfied?"

"Well, *Rickover's* on your side, isn't it?" The man pushed a finger to his ear, apparently receiving a message. His focus returned to Carver. "You spent time in the Eddy and around Slate's Progress station."

It wasn't a question. "Fairly common knowledge," said Carver, trying to keep DualE's enforced calm. "Why?"

"A question for the questioners. Put your helmet back on, Denz. You're coming with me."

Carver laughed. "Seriously? An armed escort to customs? Or are you mad I EVA'd without permission. May I remind you a captain's first duty is always to his ship?"

The man didn't share Carver's humor. "No customs inspection required, Denz. You're under arrest. Suspicion of conspiracy and sabotage against Argosy Station."

"You risk creating a diplomatic and military incident before the peace enforcement has even begun," said DualE. "The *Rickover* will hear of this." There was an edge in her voice which Carver recognized. One distracted moment and the guy would be a tangle of messed up limbs on the deck.

Carver said, "DualE, don't. Wait until I'm gone, then contact Admiral Rowland." Carver donned his helmet and proceeded the man into the lock. *Crap, first day on the job and I get arrested. Pious and his fellow missionaries better have patience. And faith in DualE as a solo escort.*

Chapter 2

Admiral Wolfe Rowland studied the *Orson's* exterior scans. His drones had secured detailed images of the damage to the jumpfreighter and Argosy Station. A focussed strike through the *Orson's* outer hull, two docked ships and a dockyard gantry. One shot but the aligned initial wounds were only the beginning; the surrounding material, whether alloy, glassteel or organic began to crystallize further into the target, like a cancer. Station and *Orson* personnel worked feverishly to get ahead of the necrotic growth and remove the scars.

"I did not expect hostilities so soon," he muttered. Rowland turned to the *Rickover's* Captain. "Mr. Siebe, your evaluation."

His second-in-command perused the scans. "Imprecise targeting. The weapon's nature renders surgical aiming unnecessary."

"I agree. In a battle situation, the effort required to cauterize the advancing damage would cripple a ship and crew's ability to continue attack."

"Or mount a defense. An impressive weapon, sir."

"Further analysis and origin?"

Siebe sat down. He glanced at the on-screen summary and nodded. "Analysis. A single shot. Holed the *Orson* in jump and grazed Argosy Station and the two ships along the...projectile's path."

"Projectile or energy beam?"

Siebe shook his head. "Either way, it's beyond anything the Confluence has or is researching."

"Origin?"

"*Orson* jumped from Schoenfeld Eddy. There is the origin. Could be a ship, armed satellite or the Eddy dockyard."

Rowland kept his anger inside. The damn Realm wasn't content with bluffing for more power than they deserved. Independence wasn't enough, they wanted dominance. The Confluence was lucky they'd chosen him for first field, non-diplomatic contact over someone like Admiral Bakken. She'd be talking or retreating. This attack presented him with opportunity to restore disciplined command within the navy hierarchy and respect from politicians without. "This changes our charter."

"Sir?"

"Prepare to accelerate our jump schedule, Captain. The *Indefatigable* will secure Argosy Station and this quadrant. We will proceed to Slate's Progress."

"Why not the Eddy immediately, Admiral? Make our response hard and fast?"

"Swift action must be tempered by intelligence. Slate's is a hive of trade and ships going to and from Schoenfeld Eddy. We stop there."

"Shall I advise the Admiralty regarding our revised agenda?"

Rowland shook his head. "You know me better than that, Mr. Siebe."

"Proceed until apprehended." Siebe grinned. "Anything else, sir?"

"No. I'm expecting a visitor soon. I need to ensure she's ready to acknowledge her true loyalty."

Chapter 3

"**I**s our mission over before we've begun, Brother Pious?"

The pilgrimage leader read more than disappointment in Atone's question and expression. Atone wanted his fears confirmed. The other two brothers' faces were calm but looked to Pious. For guidance? As always, and the reason he couldn't relinquish his leadership yet though it must come.

"Despair is a sin to avoid, Brother Atone. We were interrupted once before at Slate's Progress. The resultant detour brought us the resources to proceed on a grander scale. Mr. Denz's arrest could be another opportunity." He couldn't see how at the moment. Perhaps the added responsibility would transform DualE from soldier to diplomatic commander. Or force Denz to rely more on skill and less on luck. They all had tests. "Don't lose faith."

Penance's interior closed tight upon him with the four pilgrims all awake, their post-cryo odors and the awareness of the vast space outside their hull. Pious tried to breathe deep but his lungs wouldn't cooperate.

Brother Remorse answered the message ping from the *Crossed Swords*. "Give us a few more minutes, DualE. Brother Pious is hearing our confessions after jumpspace exposure."

Pious nodded his approval. "DualE is a woman of action. To remain idle while she perceives the situation deteriorating runs contrary to her nature. Fighting the dual master of emotional response versus patient reason is a test for us all, myself included." Pious served many masters on this trek, not the least in nurturing required leadership qualities in each of them, the three brothers and their two protectors. Qualities which were currently undeveloped, were strong but clung to too many

13

inflexible components or absent. Like DualE's patience. He also needed to fulfill the First Expansion Brotherhood's mission in the Eddy's wilds.

"Can we support her? Or influence the station on Denz's behalf?" Cardinal was the most logical brother of his fellows. His optimism lifted Pious.

"I wonder. The seeds we planted at Slate's Progress would help us there but here I'm not so sure. Being confined to the *Penance* is a handicap but a few electronic inquiries might give a clue." Pious needed energy he didn't have. "Atone, please recover my sermon from Slate's and prepare to broadcast it into Argosy Station. We'll measure the response and proceed from there."

"What about DualE? She's threatening to break quarantine."

"I'll speak with her. We don't want to lose the other half of our escort so soon. We don't know the situation in the Eddy, not with this apparent attack. We can trust in God's protection only to a limit. We must also rely on intuition and caution." Pious squeezed to the comm.

"DualE, this is Pious. Any word on Denz?" He activated video.

Her face strained to control her anger. He wished he was aboard her ship or she here.

"It's a brick wall. I'm not sure where he's been taken or under whose authority. I'm trying to contact the *Rickover* for intervention or information. If I had a diversion, I might sneak into the station and scout."

"Could we be the diversion?"

"You might. I was thinking of debarking my ship on autopilot and performing a crazy manoeuvre or two to distract the station's attention."

"Sounds like a way to have your ship destroyed if those in the station are as edgy as you."

She took a moment to respond. Pious could see the lines in her face smooth.

"You're right. There's more at stake here than my pride. Carver's arrest may be intended to distract me; push me to misguided and negative actions."

Pious was relieved by her verbal de-escalation. "You couldn't have stopped Denz from being arrested without being arrested yourself. That would have left the *Penance* and our mission in limbo. Our worst-case scenario at this moment is to proceed on to Slate's Progress and the Eddy with you as our sole guardian. That's preferable to none, given the potential volatility in the frontier. We didn't barnacle to Argosy Station to stop here." He must not stop here. The church would recall him and send others in their place. Pious couldn't allow that. He knew the Realm balanced on a knife-edge. Fear, reprisal, revolt, all the signs continued. Hope for the church to intervene lay with him; delay and changing missionaries meant changing the message so carefully crafted by his efforts.

DualE nodded. "Agreed. For now. Let me continue to dig from my end. I'll apprise you before I embark on any reckless course." A smile crossed her lips.

She'd backed down from immediate physical action. Good. She and Denz considered themselves protectors but Pious had a reciprocal role as well. "We will make our own inquiries, once we determine if any followers exist aboard the station."

Chapter 4

DualE broke contact with *Penance* and hailed the *Rickover*.

The navy ship's response came quickly. "Clear this channel, *Crossed Swords*. You are interfering with a naval operation."

She knew the voice. "Don't give me that crap, Lieutenant Brienne. I know the protocol. This is a civilian wavelength."

"In case you hadn't noticed, we're surrounded by civilians. Who are at risk. I'm flattered you recognize me, DualE, but recognition won't get you through to Admiral Rowland." Brienne's picture wavered then vanished.

"I don't need Rowland himself. Get me Captain Siebe or an aide with political muscle. I need someone in Rowland's command to run over the bureaucrat clowns running this station."

"Leave your message. I'll see what I can do."

DualE pounded her fist on the chair arm. Brienne was right, Rowland was too busy to take time for an ex-officer who'd already negotiated free passage from the Confluence. Now that she was an outsider looking in, the chain of command minimizing risk looked frustratingly inefficient. "All right, thanks. Message follows." She controlled her emotion and spoke evenly. "This is DualE of the *Crossed Swords*. My co-pilot, Carver Denz, has been arrested and taken off our ship by Argosy Station authorities. They claim the attack came from Schoenfeld Eddy and link Denz's former presence there to the attack. If they arrested everyone in the station who'd been in the Eddy at one time, the brigs would be overflowing. I want the real reason he's been detained and I want him released. I'll stand by." She began reviewing her station knowledge in case it came down to a one-woman retrieval operation.

"Message received. Don't call again. We'll hail you."

The inside of the *Crossed Swords* seemed smaller without Carver. She'd gotten used to sharing the craft with him and being part of a team again after too many months as a lone wolf undercover agent for Rowland.

The months she'd spent haunting Argosy Station had proven fruitless and her mission to determine the Realms' military strength would have failed entirely if not for her second role as Carver's anonymous protector.

While she scrubbed off the post-cryo effluvium, she scanned the messages careening within the station and set the listener program to tag any reference to Carver, herself, their ship or the *Penance* and its crew. She had little doubt she could sneak aboard the station and remain undetected for a day or two. She knew the station's every meter, nook and bolthole. Without knowing Carver's exact location, too much time would be wasted, increasing the likelihood of being caught. And she'd miss any message from the *Rickover*.

"Pious here, DualE. Any response from your former commander?"

"Nothing yet. I've left a message for Rowland. Any answer to your inquiries?"

"Like you, no worthwhile information. We're still searching for an ally if one exists. If this were Slate's Progress instead of Argosy Station, we'd have someone by now."

"Explain." She'd know they'd spent a brief time further out in the Realm. Long enough to gather a congregation?

"We had a successful gathering in Slate's and I believe the faith of one person in particular would be still active."

"There's been enough traffic between the two stations in the weeks we've been in Bohr that your follower could be among them and here now."

Pious cleared his throat. "Excuse me."

She heard another muffled cough then he resumed. "It's unlikely. Our recruit, Chels Harte, was stuck on Slate's. Too many trips through jumpspace had rendered Chels unable to psychologically survive further exposure to the universe's underbelly."

"I understand. I've had colleagues in the navy wash out before retirement because of 'Spook Syndrome'. Hope my time never comes. If it does, I hope I'm not stuck in a rathole like this station. I haven't visited Slate's, but I hear it's even grittier than Argosy."

"It is certainly chaotic. Less geometrically ordered. And the migrant inhabitants are a rougher lot." Pious rasped again. "I will leave you to your task with the *Rickover*. We'll be in touch if news of Denz surfaces."

━━━┼┼╲╲╿┼╱┼━━━

C arver's escort was joined by two more uniforms as they entered the main docking area. Lights flashed, klaxons rang and station staff rushed in all directions. None of it seemed to accomplish anything except creating more panic. Why didn't those who were in one spot stay there, instead of exchanging places with those from another area?

They entered a narrow corridor leading from the main deck. The noise dropped and the light dimmed. Carver ducked when warned by the guard in front and watched his step on his own volition. Conduits dripping station fluids ran within the passageway. "Was this designed for plumbing first and humans as an afterthought?" he asked.

"Shut up."

Carver bit his lip and carried on. He was traversing parts of the station he'd not seen in his previous visits. This was the below-water portion of the Argosy Station iceberg. To complete his analogy, it was also cold. The corridor turned into a steep incline and his boots slipped. The leader grabbed Carver's tunic and pulled him along. They stepped from the tunnel into a public area. Carver tried to picture where they were but his weeks aboard Argosy hadn't brought him here. The odor of bad gin and worse beer told him they had to be close to Phyl's Fill, the basest bar on the station. The lowest geographically and socially.

Two distinct groups were in sight. Three possible patrons on their way to exchange credits for dicey alcohol and questionable goods or services in the tavern, and a pair of armed security officers who gave Carver's company a quick wave then returned to watching the civilians. The station was on edge but a few brave or reckless souls carried on their routine. Crawl from whatever hole one slept in, head for Phyl's and wash away or drown one's demons. Station attack was just another hurtle to get to the next day.

Before he could recognize any specific landmarks, they entered another maintenance tunnel. Ten minutes of ducking and hurtling deck obstacles brought the four to a formidable door, criss-crossed with decades of scars and dents. A knock with a baton spurred an opened slit occupied by a pair of eyes.

"Prisoner you're expecting," said Carver's lead guard.

The door clanged twice then opened. Carver was pushed inside and abandoned by his escorts.

The new guards pointed forward to a barred cell. "Through there." The door grumbled noisily, allowing Carver to squeeze inside. He wasn't the lone occupant; half a dozen dishevelled and tired men met his gaze with disinterest then looked away.

Carver turned around. "How long have you been expecting me?"

"No questions."

No questions from them either. The brig guards were prepared for him. The first escort hadn't contacted anyone in his presence. They must've radioed a heads-up before he re-entered the *Crossed Swords*. Or had someone known of his arrival before they docked? Given the near hour it took to reach here, and the fact there were three station guards ready for his EVA return, it was possible. Old enemies? New?

No interrogation because they didn't need information from him. They wanted him. Isolated from DualE and/or the brothers. Knowing what didn't help him determine why.

Carver mimicked the other prisoners, lowering his focus to the floor and shoving hands in pockets. He slumped on the crude bench to ponder past and present misdeeds.

Chapter 5

Zofie Ked sat in a booth in Phyl's Fill an hour before the bar's usual opening. Phyl granted her off-hours access for the privilege of having a confidant. 'It's us against the universe, girl.' The booth had become Zofie's informal place of business, though business had proved elusive.

The two partners Zofie recruited in the Bohr Confluence a fortnight ago had ditched her once the three of them reached Argosy Station. Her contribution to the alliance had been paying the two men's passage from Bohr to the Realm. More fool me, she thought. The old Zofie would've planned and exacted retaliation by now but the psychologically re-tooled Zofie, courtesy Brother Pious, had no such desire. Their punishment would come or it wouldn't, she would not be dragged into revenge.

Gar Kondradt had at least endorsed a charter to reactivate her brokerage enterprise. No doubt the watchful eye of the Confluence Navy had motivated his generosity. Kondradt had enough on his plate with the peace accord's enforcement not to bother with his former sub-legal commerce and intimidation activities. Rumors indicated he'd avoided conspiracy-to-commit-murder charges in the Confluence through Chancellor Mekli's intervention. His experience and lack of moral compass made him Mekli's ideal choice to deal with the navy's presence in the Chancellor's backyard. She figured Kondradt viewed her activities as a minor annoyance to the Confluence. He hadn't even met her in person; she was too minor a player or he was wary of a direct link. Add enough annoyances together and Kondradt could complete his greater agenda. Whatever it might be.

Kondradt's game was no longer Zofie's primary worry. She scrolled her update screen, looking for opportunities among the arriving and departing jumpfreighters. She tagged possibilities for further investigation. Public data was the first step. She launched her updated worms and burrowed deeper into lading lists. Excise blockers stopped her hacks for three freighters on her radar. She cancelled the inquiries and came in through a backdoor flaw. Two were classified shipments but the profit potential was limited. One had black market possibilities but the legality concerned her. She'd promised Brother Pious to stay legal. Hacking aside.

The lights rose in the tavern. She switched off the table lamp and acknowledged Phyl's arrival.

"Zofie, early bird, eh?" Phyl always looked fresh, no matter how late the customers stayed the previous night or how rowdy they got. The proprietress's red hair spouted like a flame from her head.

"Checking manifests. If I can exploit a few old contacts in the Eddy, I might have some prospects. Wish I had a clone to send to Slate's."

Phyl walked over to her, straightening tables and chairs on the way. "Trust me, Zofie. Neither this cosmos nor spookspace are ready for two of you. Anymore than it could handle two of me. We are unique, girl. I know enough crew who owe me that if you need any confidential messages carried through jumpspace to Slate's, let me help."

"Thanks, Phyl. I'll work up a proposal to send through. I don't mind being in your debt but call it if I overstep my limit."

"We'll stick together. By the way, those two morons you brought from Bohr have already showed their true worth."

"What do you mean?"

"They're in the brig. They picked a fight with the crew from a chartered freighter. You're better off on your own."

Karma showed up quickly, Zofie thought. She didn't have to make it happen. "Yeah. Seems like most days I haven't a choice."

Phyl moved away, humming an old prospector tune.

A new page popped onto Zofie's screen. An audible. She activated her earbud.

"What can I, a stranger in your midst and ignorant of your challenges, offer? I offer guidance, perhaps understanding."

"Pious," whispered Zofie. It shouldn't be a surprise; she knew the brothers were resuming their mission once *Penance* was refitted. She'd departed before them but now they'd arrived. A practice sermon or taking advantage of the stop-over at Argosy? If they were to be on-station for any length of time, she would pay a visit.

Pious' message continued. "Our mission is to task those who seek inner calm to ask themselves, can I do more? Can I make the sphere in which I exist a better place?"

Pious' counsel in Bohr had helped Zofie cleanse her sins or at least accept them and move forward. Jumpspace nightmares of dead lovers and companions hadn't left her yet but the brother's teachings had eased the guilt. The nightmares' presence might tempt her to use Phyl's messenger mule. One less jump for her. But it would mean giving up control, however small. Her guilt might be lessening but her need to be in charge was not. She'd jump regardless.

"If you require our communion, please contact the *Penance*. We are currently unable to enter the station but will listen to any and all through the network. One of our associates, Willie Renfrew, is aboard the station but we've lost contact with him. Help if you can."

Renfrew? It rang a bell then screamed recognition. Willie Renfrew had been Carver's alias. Carver was in Argosy and the brothers had lost him. Carver and DualE, working for the mission.

Over two months ago, in a spookspace-induced psychotic state, Zofie had tried to kill them both. She'd been unbalanced by greed, paranoia and jumpspace drugs. Pious' meditation teachings had returned her mental equilibrium. Perhaps she could add a bit more mass to the good side of the scales by finding Carver aka Renfrew.

She walked to the bar and began polishing the fake wood. She met Phyl in the middle. "Phyl, I need your ears."

Rowland scanned the hourly reports. He needed two brains to absorb the many incidentals. The incidentals added up to major pieces of his puzzle. Captain Siebe was a loyal follower but lacked the mindset to synthesize the disparate data into victory. Rowland's end game was clear in his mind but he couldn't rely on his subordinates to see it. Leadership required filling multiple roles, information analyses merely one. The minutia consumed him.

At least Denz was taken care of for now. His former agent was safer here than in either Gamma Hub in Bohr or Schoenfeld Eddy. Denz's renown as a prospector could create the wrong distractions in the Eddy and in Gamma he'd be too far from Rowland's control. Argosy Station's brig was perfect.

"Admiral, I have the latest repair status from the station." Siebe's entrance interrupted his thoughts. More details to process.

"Thank you, Captain. Anything else?"

"*Indefatigable* awaits orders regarding the station and moving on with us or remaining behind, given the attack seems to be singular and finished."

"No change. We move in increments to Slate's Progress and then the Eddy. Cover our backside as we go. But we do go ahead."

"Understood, sir." Siebe saluted and left.

Rowland considered the decline in quality amongst the next generation of commanders. Few of them battle-hardened like himself or...DualE.

He clasped his hands behind his head and stretched neck muscles. How to deal with DualE? She'd be the kind of aide he could depend on, if only her politics weren't so neutral. He must consider her on the opposite side since she wasn't entirely on his.

Did her loyalty lie solely with the missionaries? How much with Carver Denz? She might be levered into an alliance with Rowland's agenda. A useful tool. He could take advantage of her imbedded training but it would alter his plan for Denz.

Two paths lay before Rowland, his initial direct movement and one with subterfuge using DualE. He would pursue both, his confidence assured him he could modify strategies to suit each situation going forward. The only consistent outcome, no matter what transpired, was the inevitable sacrifice. He reconciled losing human pawns against ultimate victory for the good side. His side.

Chapter 6

Carver recognized two of his cell mates though they didn't acknowledge meeting him before. They'd squired Zofie around Gamma Hub before leaving the Confluence for Argosy. He'd assumed she'd continue on to the Eddy but apparently the partnership hadn't lasted more than one jump.

Argosy Station's brig had all the amenities. Except comfort, privacy and safety. None of the other inmates looked overly psychotic but Carver was a poor judge of mental state, even amongst those he knew. Witness Zofie Ked, for one.

He sat in one corner, munching the worst food ever and studied the cell. Noise from the station's air and water pumps screamed constantly. Carver supposed one would eventually get tired enough to sleep through the howl and vibration. Could he sleep through the smell from the waste recyclers?

He put the unfinished ration back in its wrapper and began the meditation routine Pious had taught him. If he could survive jumpspace without cryo or pharms, he could survive a few days in jail. Longer would be a problem but beyond protesting his innocence, there wasn't much he could do. Rescue would have to come from outside agency. DualE or Pious.

His breathing became even, in through the mouth and out through the nose. Exhalations removed the stress. Inhalations recharged the blood.

"You gonna eat the rest of that?"

Carver blinked, trying to focus on the speaker standing over him. It was one of Zofie's ex-cohorts. The man was young, fit and nervous. Bad strategy to say no even if Carver hadn't had enough to eat. He passed the package up. "Help yourself. I may be more ravenous a week from now if we aren't released so don't consider this a precedent." He wanted to return to his meditation but the fellow prisoner decided he could eat and talk.

He squeezed next to Carver. "What did you do?"

Carver laughed. "Like everyone else, nothing. How about you?"

"Derk and me got into a fight outside a bar. We were blowing off steam after our transport to Slate's Progress evaporated. A similar scrap on Gamma Hub wouldn't have attracted any attention, let alone arrest." He pointed to the sleeping figure Carver'd already identified. "I'm Tommy, by the way."

Carver didn't offer to reveal his name. His notoriety in the Realm wasn't always a positive. "You don't look like prospectors."

"No. We partnered with a struggling broker. We planned to restore her old network and set up commerce between Realm and Bohr but she went nuts and decided a quarter share wasn't enough for her." He sipped his water and swallowed the mash. "We thought it generous since we'd be doing all the work."

"What work? Precisely?" The quarter share was a lie; Zofie'd have kept at least half. She'd already given them passage this far. For what? Protection? She could protect herself.

"There's half the population she can't exploit as well as we can."

Carver took a closer look at Tommy and the sleeping Derk. He admitted both lads were handsome in different ways. "Women traders. Your ex-partner doesn't do well with other women?"

"Not from what we saw."

"You'll be out of here soon, if I know the workings of Argosy. They don't need to board you on their dime. Probably deciding on a suitable fine for damages. Enough to hurt but not enough to leave you stranded."

"I wish they'd hurry up. We've been here three days already."

"There was some sort of attack. They'll get around to you once the threat is over."

Tommy nodded. "I heard the sirens. Who the hell would attack this station?"

"Question of the day," said Carver. "Someone thinks it was me. Which is why I'm here instead of in my ship."

"You could be here for a while." Tommy looked up at the monitor above. "I never met him before," he said to the camera.

"Don't bother," said Carver. "Even if it isn't broken, I doubt anyone is watching."

Tommy rose and walked to the far end of the cell to join his mate.

"Good chat," Carver muttered. There was a third candidate who could free him. How long before DualE got through to Admiral Rowland? Not more than a day or two, given her determination. Unless Rowland was involved in his arrest? Couldn't happen. Cryo had increased Carver's mistrust.

He needed information and the brig wasn't a good source. He needed someone on the outside to dig on his behalf. That's what partners were for. Until DualE cracked the mystery, he'd have to practice patience. Carver rested his hands on his stomach and returned to his mantra.

Zofie burrowed through Argosy's databanks. She focused the search algorithms on cargo and currency exchanges. Any auto-trackers shadowing her queries wouldn't detect anything but a merchanter digging for trade information. The sidebar taking note of names shouldn't raise a flag.

When you were following something or someone, it was always prudent to assume you too were being followed. A lesson she'd learned more than once.

Ping, a Carver Denz reference. She let it pass and continued with her ostensible search. She gave it another twenty minutes, then saved the results. There were some genuine business leads to research further. But that was for later.

She removed the memory wafer from the desk unit and plugged it in to her wrist processor. Denz, audio traffic between Station Central and *Rickover*. Nothing odd at first glance, she thought. She knew Carver and DualE were barnacling to a navy vessel to jump from Bohr with the brothers.

The conversation was one way. That was odd. It all originated from the *Rickover*. She couldn't decipher the actual information but the next mention did surprise her and was more helpful. Carver was incarcerated in an Argosy brig. Then the trail evaporated. Where could he be now? Zofie returned to the desk computer and searched for Tommy and Derk. Good, they were still in jail for the fight Phyl mentioned. 'Confirm current inmate list for visitation', she typed. There was a list of initials, 'CD' among them. Her ex-partners were in the group as well. Three more, unknown to her, made it six in total.

"I think we should make it lucky seven." Zofie's hacking skills easily inserted one 'WF' for Willie Renfrew into the record. Vagrancy. She set his bail at a reasonable number and checked the jailer shift schedule. A fresh guard was due in half an hour, one who hadn't been on duty when Carver was brought in.

Zofie called Phyl. "Are there any Eddy-bound freighter crew in the Fill I can talk to?"

"I'll check."

In ten minutes, a man separated her booth's curtain. "I'm Dawson, purser. Phyl says you're looking to ship out."

"Zofie Ked, broker. What's your next port of call?"

"Direct to the Eddy shipyards. No stopping at Slate's."

She could change her business plan to suit a direct flight, and with Carver in tow. "What's your barnacle profile and when are you leaving?"

"We've no barnacles but for the right price, we can take you on. If your ship is small. We leave once the *Orson* is cleared from our path. They took a hit inbound."

"Yeah, I heard. No embargo complications?" She checked her watch.

"No. we're heading into the fire, not away from it. Captain has a large bonus pending if we hit our deadline. Our ship's the *Ranger*. I'll send you access codes and coordinates once your payment clears."

Zofie synced to Dawson's comm. She blanched at the price. It would stretch her resources but she had an instinct that Carver Denz's luck in the Eddy would pay her back. "My ship's the *Whisper*. It's a four passenger but they'll be just two of us."

"Lock on in the next few hours or you'll miss us."

"I'll be there." She signed off. Time to steal her precious outbound cargo. The less than famous Willie Renfrew.

C arver was shaken from his trance. "Renfrew?" Renfrew? He pretended grogginess while he processed the implications. It had to be DualE's work.

He cracked an eye and slipped into the guise of a spacer at nadir. It was a guard he hadn't seen before.

"Yeah. I'm Willie Renfrew."

"You don't look like a vagrant but you've been bailed. On your feet."

Tommy yelled from the corner. "What about us?"

"Shut up."

The guard escorted Carver outside the bars.

A hooded figure signed the guard's screen. The benefactor, he hoped, was too small for DualE and the wrist too thin for her well-muscled form. The figure passed him a robe and he pulled it over his head. Was it Brother Atone? He was the only one of similar stature. Pious had come through when neither DualE nor Admiral Rowland had. Though DualE might've created the plan. "Bless you, brother."

"Don't talk and don't look up."

Not Atone. It was Zofie. Not whom he expected or was sure he wanted. But freedom was freedom. He dreaded the cost.

He pulled the hood as low as possible and followed her. They moved quickly but not so fast as to raise undue suspicion. Two pilgrims traversing the station to provide comfort where needed. Great, as long as they didn't have to halt to deliver a sermon. Most people ignored them or gave a nod. Carver responded with 'bless you's' and kept pace.

Argosy Station had calmed since he'd been taken to the brig. The human ants had cooled down, the threat of subsequent attack apparently diminished.

Within half an hour, they were at a small docking tube. "It's vacuum and null-grav to my ship, grab a flimsuit." He withdrew the largest one he could find in the EVA locker and put it on over his robe. They cycled into a dim passage and pushed forward to the end.

The inside of Zofie's ship was stark but better than the brig. A good place to hide until reunited with DualE and the brothers. "Water?" She offered a globe.

"Thanks. Jail's thirsty work. I met your ex-partners there. Are you sure you bailed out the right person?"

"Yeah. Those two weren't my best decision. Better ones to come." She initiated detachment and they soon pulled away from the berth.

"Better decisions or better partners?" Carver cinched his harness. "Where the hell are we going?"

"Later." She donned headset and guided the craft forward until Carver could see the growing image of a mid-size jumpfreighter.

"If this is DualE's idea of an escape route, it's elaborate."

"Nothing to do with DualE, Carver. This time, I'm your guardian angel."

Guardian angel of death. "Considering you tried to slice me open the last time, forgive me if I decline." He calculated his chances on escape from this ship once Zofie barnacled.

"You don't have to worry. Brother Pious cleared my head and you're worth way more to me alive than dead. Hope you still like cryo, I don't hold with pharm options in spookspace. Not for me, anyway."

Carver stared at the water globe. He pulled the tube from his lips too late. He fumbled with the restraint and tried to grab for Zofie but the cabin spiraled into blackness.

Chapter 7

D ualE's nudged her hired shuttle into the *Rickover's* supply dock.
"Ellen Fuques to see Admiral Rowland." She showed her i.d. to the armed marines guarding the entrance inside.

"I'm your escort," said one, face hidden by a visor.

"I know the way," said DualE.

"Not a question of guidance. Let's move. The admiral's a busy man."

They paced double-time where possible. The cramped passages inside triggered a hundred memories of her time in service. A life left behind to follow a new loyalty. Marines not on guard duty scrubbed and polished the *Rickover*. She knew when they'd finished, Rowland or his captain would have them start again.

Her diagnosis of Carver's career and philosophical metamorphosis differed from her own. He needed a distraction from the emotional scars in Bohr. She needed fewer extremes to evaluate who she was underneath the warrior mantle. She'd missed growing up gradually. The exposure to the brothers' message reinforced the void in her experience.

She'd witnessed changing their pose from donation mercenaries pursuing Carver's fortune to humble ascetics, intent on expanding their faith base in more dangerous environs. Pious and his mates were willing to risk their safety to spread their gospel. Hence, DualE and Carver as a first level of protection. She admired the faith they had in their message and their God. Her military service always pressed someone else's agenda. The powers above, right or wrong. Time for her to choose what was right.

"Go in." The guard opened the bulkhead and stepped inside Rowland's quarters with her but remained at the door. Rowland passed a note to a yeoman who left.

"What a mess," he said. "Sit, Lieutenant."

"DualE," she corrected. "I'm no longer in your service." It was no slip of the tongue. Rowland didn't make that kind of slip.

"I'm sorry we couldn't meet sooner, I had to make certain the attack was over."

"How can you be sure?" She sat down.

"Good question. I can't. We have determined the source. The energy beam or whatever it was, not a solid projectile, exited jumpspace with the *Orson*, clipping the freighter before inflicting the damage to the station."

"The Realm couldn't, wouldn't be so stupid. Would they? Why would Chancellor Mekli risk the peace so soon? Has to be a rogue faction in the Eddy." Where she and the brothers were headed. She'd do her best to protect them. Who'd protect her?

Rowland spoke with teeth clenched. "I intend to find out. At this stage, I lean toward your suspicions. The Realm isn't exactly unified. But that doesn't mean they don't have an end game in play."

"They seemed unified enough against us while I was in service at the station."

"Economics prevailed over idealism."

There was little room for idealism in Rowland's world. And until recently, hers. "I'm interested in what you do next," she said, "from an intellectual curiosity point of view. My more urgent need is for information and help regarding Carver Denz."

"Mr. Denz is in protective custody aboard the station."

"Protective custody? You've used that already when the *Pollux* arrived at Gamma Hub. He was your operative then. Are you telling me he still is?" Could she have misread Carver so badly?

"No. He created enemies when he turned his discovery over to Bohr, instead of the Realm."

"Old business, Admiral. The Realm got their royalty share and additional Schoenfeldium discoveries with the huge influx of prospectors hoping to duplicate Denz's bonanza. Even the narrowest minded of these idealists would recognize that."

"They recognize what they choose to, DualE. That is why I prefer military methods. We have to look at all the factors and data."

"*The factor you miss or ignore is the one which will kill you*," said DualE in rote. "I remember my training. How do I get him out? If he's willing to accept the risk, and I think he is, we'd like to proceed on our journey with the *Penance*."

"On to the Eddy?"

"Pious wants to stop at Slate's Progress. The brothers made headway there before their rush to follow Denz back to Argosy Station three months ago. We're willing to take the risk. Can you intervene?"

Rowland's face was hard to read. He was in command here, speaking to a subordinate, not a friend.

"I can try. You ask a big favor in a stressful time."

The military boot dropped. "It is a favor. And you want something back."

"I haven't decided our next port of call. I need to know what's going on out there. Wherever you and the missionaries barnacle to, you will observe and evaluate. But get to the Eddy as soon as feasible without raising the brothers' suspicions."

The mask slipped a little. Rowland's need was genuine.

"I'm to be your eyes and ears again, is that it? And Carver too?"

"You'll suffice. Denz has a habit of following his conscience. He need not be aware of your dual mission."

"Divide my loyalty?"

"Your loyalty is to *me*. You owe everything you are to the navy. You'd be a fishwife on Aqueous Prime if not for the service. Old, cold and a drudge. I am your savior." His eyes met hers. "*Once in the service...*"

"...*always in the service*," she finished. "I know that mantra too."

Rowland slid a paper from under a pile and passed it to her. "A formal contract is required for non-enlisted personnel working with us."

"You guarantee to deliver him to me?"

Rowland nodded.

DualE signed off. Service for life. She'd deluded herself into believing her new-found freedom would allow her to make her choices. "Make the call to release him."

Rowland turned his back to her and spoke too low for her to hear. There was silence then he raised his voice. "Gone? What do you mean, he's gone? Find him." Rowland turned back to face her. He tapped a finger on the paper she just completed. "Carver appears to have been misplaced. This doesn't change our deal."

Another boot dropped. "You set this up," said DualE. "Carver's arrest was phony from the outset, designed solely to blackmail me into signing that agreement. Well, stuff it." She whirled and stalked toward the door.

The Lieutenant manning the door stared straight past her. He wasn't part of this. Her eyes fell on one of his battle patches. Tryon's Breach. DualE had fought there, saving and losing comrades in a poorly planned, marginally executed fight.

She stopped and turned to face Rowland. "I will honor my commitment, Admiral. Not because of my loyalty to you but because of my loyalty to those who serve under you."

"Bravely spoken," he answered.

She marched back to the desk. "There's something else you're holding back."

"Someone's trying to re-start the war we avoided," he said. "When we do arrive in the Eddy, I have to prepare to engage in diplomacy or battle. What you discover will help my decision."

"Authorize my full access to the station. I need to find him and book passage to the Eddy." She didn't wait for his answer but heard his voice on the comm before the door closed behind her.

R owland swore under his breath. Argosy Station's personnel were not to be trusted. He couldn't waste time correcting the situation.

He commed the bridge. "Captain Siebe, prepare *Rickover* jump astrogation plans for both Slate's Progress and the Eddy."

"I thought the Eddy was our target, sir."

"That would be the expected route for us. I haven't won my battles by being predictable. I have backup heading for the Eddy. We will get there in good time and with good intelligence."

He opened a secure link to the *Indefatigable*. He calculated his likely timetable. "Maintain surveillance of station and quadrant. Unless countermanded by me personally, jump to Eddy in four weeks. Remain passive there until you hear from me. That is all."

Rowland reviewed the Confluence Naval Brief on screen. *Slate's Progress – Preferred jump-node between Argosy Station and the most popular prospecting quadrant. Alternate stop-off to and from Schoenfeld Eddy for jump vessels more comfortable with two moderate jumps than one full jump between Argosy and the Eddy. A private enterprise overseen by Commander Slate. Shareholders include most of the original settler family consortiums.*

He added his own note. *Military assessment – strategic information and personnel crossroads.*

Chapter 8

Chels Harte stretched and rolled over one last time, luxuriating in a bed which didn't force her to bend her legs to fit. Sharing Slate's quarters within Progress, and the commander's bed, was a welcome change after months of berths and hammocks designed for prospectors and staff a head shorter than she.

Transient visitors didn't complain, prospectors and salvagers came to Slate's Progress to convert their finds into currency and short-term pleasure before returning to their dangerous, rarely lucrative, vocations. She'd done the same in her time but now relegated to this station and non-jump environs, she'd had to eke out a new existence. That meant rudimentary accommodations, even free, inserted amidst Progress' plumbing or structural bones. Regardless, it meant cramped.

She had interacted with Slate on finding accommodation and grunt work for a handful of similarly trapped spacers and they'd connected. He knew the vagabonds could become a problem and pushed her to help them with his support. Now this. Luxury, the best word to describe it.

Chels pointed her toes and raised arms above her head. No barriers to either. What would Pious think of her sensual relief? She'd ask his forgiveness if she saw him again. If not, she'd petition herself.

It was time to rise and begin her daily task of spreading Pious' words within Progress and soliciting donations. Another few months and she reckoned she'd have enough credit to fuel her ship and make a loop amongst the closest prospecting clusters and offer her counsel a person or two at a time.

Showered and coffee'd, Chels made her way through Progress to the small chamber Slate had provided as a chapel for her ministry. Pious had changed her life, given her purpose when she couldn't handle jumpspace any longer and had failed too many times as a prospector. She wasn't certain about God, but she was certain about Pious giving her purpose. If he was God's tool, then the deity had chosen well.

Slate's Progress was a maze of bespoke modifications and specific add-ons following no obvious architectural plan. The station's morphology could best be described as abstract chaos. Chels loved every inch of it, even the inches new and unknown to her. Slate's was alive, an organic construct in constant metamorphosis.

According to Slate, the Realm's brokered peace with Bohr would lead to more commercial and governmental traffic. A caravan hub and an immigration stop-over point. 'Managed well, Progress will rival or surpass Argosy Station in commerce,' Slate had told her. She hoped success didn't destroy its character. She loved the energy which pioneers brought to Progress.

Chels descended a long elevator sling to her chapel's deck. Below her, open to the inside atmosphere, a few hundred meters of infrastructure pumped survival throughout the station.

She pulled a robe from the hook outside the chapel entrance and poked her head through the neck. She crossed herself and entered the small room.

A figure sat on the pew in front of the plain altar she'd scrounged from an old freighter captain's cabin.

She walked to the front and rang a small bell before lighting a candle. "Welcome, space-brother. Don't let me interrupt your thoughts." She wouldn't assume he was praying. The man was a prospector, judging by his attire and helmet-seal welts permanently pressed into his forehead.

Chels sat on the next bench and spoke her morning pledge. "If I can help one person today, I count it as a successful day." She repeated it until it was cellular, then rose to begin her street ministry amongst the passageways, holds and secret places within Slate's Progress. She would return to the chapel at supper shift-change to hold service for anyone who chose to come.

She hoped Pious and his brothers would return. She wanted to be ready for them. She wanted to present them with a congregation. It was time for the Realm to make another step toward a spiritual civilization, not just a technological and economic one.

Chels smiled inwardly at her transformation since meeting Brother Pious. The brash hedonist had become a spiritual messenger. She was able to enjoy physical pleasure with Slate but anxious to help others find peace. Could she be certain the change was permanent? She couldn't. She had to have faith that it was real, no challenge had presented itself thus far to test her.

The visitor lifted his head and turned to face her. His eyes stared past her. What test did he seek?

"Welcome to our chapel. I'm Chels Harte. Do I know you?" She might. He looked like a hundred other prospectors and wayfarers she'd encountered in her rough life in this frontier.

"Maybe. I don't know." A weariness in his voice told her any past acquaintance didn't matter.

"It would help if I know your name."

He focused on her, then swept his gaze to either side.

"You don't need to make a donation to talk with me."

"Perry," he whispered. His hands knotted in front of him. "Do you take confession?"

"Usually over a drink or three in the tavern." Chels smiled. Perry didn't respond to the joke. She mirrored his somber mood. "I listen. I can't absolve you of guilt but I can sympathize with your regrets. Believe me, I've had my share of moral and legal transgressions. I wouldn't be here if I couldn't live with them. Good enough?"

Perry nodded. "I have to tell someone. In confidence, right?"

A sticky question. She wasn't ordained and had no right to confessional privilege. But her commitment to Pious and herself should be complete, no ethical half-measures. "I promise to use my best judgment. If you're planning to injure or kill someone, then I'll protect them if I can."

"My future plans aren't the issue." Perry slid close to her. "No ears?"

"This chapel is unmonitored. I can close the door."

"Please."

Chels checked the passageway. Empty. Any other spacers in spiritual need weren't awake yet. She slid the door closed and sat beside him. "I don't have a proscribed routine for this so just talk."

Perry took a moment, surveying the chapel. "My partner and me, we work the true Eddy. The junk-whorl. Salvage mostly. Ships, satellites, discarded mech; anything which has fallen under the gravitational sink. You understand?"

"Yes." The good and bad. Mostly bad. "I spent too much time there years ago when I first shipped out here. Part of a four-person team looking for heavy asteroids. We found enough to pay for the trip but no more. It takes a patient breed."

"We never found a lode, just tech." Perry gripped the backrest in front of him. "Our last trip we found more than human wreckage. We found something beyond known. Maybe alien."

"I've heard of a few found artifacts no one could identify." Didn't mean alien. "How could you be certain it wasn't manmade?"

"We weren't certain. Not until we used it." His breath was shallow. Sweat beaded his forehead.

"If you could figure the tech out to use it, doesn't that imply human origin?"

Perry shook his head. "My partner was a communication expert. He figured it was some kind of jumpspace beacon. We didn't care about how it got to the Eddy. But we revived it. We wanted to send a test signal when a freighter entered the crackle."

Crackle, the entry point from normal to jump. Chels considered the implications. Getting messages through spookspace consistently was a goal still being chased by the physicists. The researchers couldn't better 50-50 success. She put a hand over Perry's. Why the guilt, then? "What happened? Sounds like you had a grand opportunity."

"We zeroed in on the freighter as it prepped to jump. We fired our message. A light beam emerged from the end of the cylinder. At least we had the right end."

Perry trembled as he breathed deep. "The beam drew matter from near void itself. The contrail was a glowing cylinder thirty or forty thousand kliks long. The recoil tore it from our location. Thank God we weren't attached to it. I don't know what kind of message we sent but it wasn't benevolent. My gut tells me that's a certainty. The jumpspace nightmares coming here confirmed it to me."

"We've not heard any bad news. How long ago?"

"Ten days to sneak back to the Eddy 'yard. It took me a week to get here. I've been drunk for four days since. And took me two more days to decide what to do."

"Would you return to look for the artifact?"

"Not in a thousand years."

"Shit," said Chels.

"Yeah."

"Where's you partner?"

"Last time I saw him at the Eddy shipyard he was severely messed up. Trying to decide whether to retrieve it, destroy it or head for Bohr and anonymity."

"And you? Planning to join him regardless?"

"No. I think the two of us together would push one or the other over reason's edge. I'll stay here for now. Until I need to go out again. But I'll stick to detritus I know." Perry stood; head bowed. "Thanks."

"I don't know if telling me has helped you but feel free to come back anytime."

"I have to go." He left her alone in the chapel.

She wished Pious was here to guide her next choice. Slate should be told, not just for her loyalty to him but for the safety of the station. But Perry had confessed in confidence. Which path took precedence?

Chapter 9

Schoenfeld Eddy – Can refer to the haphazard shipyard or the large of a collection of gravitational anomalies in the Edgecombe system. The whirlpools abound with captured asteroids and human-created detritus. The Eddy's strategic location with respect to exploration of promising worlds beyond it make it ideal for staging.

Rumors persist that the Realm's intended rebel fleet rendezvoused in the system. Confluence Naval inspection teams will survey the quadrant to ensure the fleet has been dispersed and re-assigned to exploration duty.

The Eddy is also home to scavengers preferring to mine the detritus for salvageable tech rather than the high risk, low success mineral prospecting.

Confluence Naval Brief.

Zofie's cryo-mind traversed jumpspace ahead of their transport, racing to escape the spook demons buried in her subconscious. She saw the Eddy shipyard hanging like a confused alloy shard aggregate. Surrounding the jumbled docking, trading and maintenance station were the large and small spatial maelstroms where lurked minor reward and major risk. The foreshortened view in her jump hallucinations magnified the danger.

Over her shoulder, then hurtling past her, was the suited form of another traveler. She didn't need to see the face to recognize Carver Denz, the source of her guilty dreams. One source. She'd betrayed him before on the *Pollux* months ago and now again in pulling him from Argosy Station without telling DualE or the brothers she'd done so.

The rationalization was that she had freed him and both escaped before discovery. Everyone owed Zofie for that bit of trickery. Everyone but her.

As usual in spookspace, the guilt replayed endlessly until she felt the initial warming tingles of cryo withdrawal. She crawled from her coffin, checked Carver's timer and proceeded to de-barnacle from the *Ranger*.

"Ahoy, *Ranger*, this is the *Whisper* bidding you farewell and thanks for the smooth jump."

"Roger, *Whisper*. Good prospecting to you."

Free from the jumpspace transport, she docked the *Whisper* and prepared to go hunting for commerce. She initiated Carver's revival, secured the ship from inside and out. Then she left, trying not to consider Carver's temporary abandonment as yet another betrayal.

———✛✛11✛✛———

C arver tried to run. His feet were too heavy to lift off the ground. A part of his brain repeated he was in deepsleep and the nightmare came from jumpspace, not within himself.

Despite his handicap, he needed to hurry. Helena waited in the Confluence. His regrets magnified with the delay in reaching her. He finally arrived at their rendezvous, exhausted. Helena wasn't there. Instead of his fiancé, a letter awaited him. He didn't need to open it; he knew it by heart. The change in feelings. Her light-hearted dismissal of their engagement. She couldn't be expected to wait for him alone while he jumped across the Realm.

Carver held another paper, his contract with the brothers. He wouldn't keep their rendezvous either. Kidnapped. Zofie Ked. His back twitched. A warning? He tried to look behind but couldn't. Jumpspace held his mind immovable. The cryo coffin held his body firm.

His fingertips burned and he dropped the papers. Toes, ears and nose followed suit. *I hate deepsleep.* His body warmed from cryo back into the real universe.

C arver sat alone in the *Whisper.* The airlock was sealed and code-protected against his exit so he brewed tea and heated food. Zofie's audio monitor was locked on receive only. While he ate, he listened and peered through the viewport.

He recognized the random arrangement of superstructure beams and gantries. The *Whisper* was in a small-craft dock in the Eddy shipyards. This wasn't where diplomats or Confluence naval craft would come. This was where the commerce of frontier settlement took place. The one-sided commerce which drove the Realm to threaten secession. You had to push people past their limits to make them see reason sometimes.

Zofie's barnacle transport had bypassed Slate's Progress or he'd deepslept through it. It could matter if someone tracked them but knowing where he was at this point seemed more important than the navigational details of how he got there.

The communication traffic was all arrival, departure, ladings information and maintenance schedules. Nothing he could use for advantage when Zofie returned.

With nothing more productive to focus on, he chose her as his next item of scrutiny. Why had she freed, kidnapped and now imprisoned him? Why had she taken flight from Argosy Station so quickly? If anyone besides the station wanted him out of the way, then the answer to that was obvious. Still, a keen mind, such as DualE's or Pious' could connect his disappearance and outgoing jumpships to locate him. Eventually.

If Zofie worked alone, intending to exploit his talent or luck to benefit her enterprises, then his disappearance warranted concern only with DualE and the brothers. They'd still check outgoing manifests and unless Zofie had arranged for undocumented barnacle passage, they would follow.

Carver tried the outside cameras to locate the *Whisper* more precisely. They too were locked off. He finished eating and searched the cabin. Nothing useful for a weapon besides blunt instruments and Zofie so far hadn't threatened or acted physically against him, aside from the knockout drug. He needed a plan but questions had to be answered first.

He reclined in the pilot's chair and evaluated. First of all, if anyone in the Eddy knew he was here, was he Carver Denz or Willie Renfrew?

The Renfrew identity shouldn't raise any flags out here. Renfrew'd been a minimal asset persona he'd used on Argosy Station to mask his transport back to Bohr months ago.

The Denz identity could present a problem. His notoriety throughout the Eddy came from a large strike he'd made while working undercover for Admiral Rowland. Carver's guise as a prospector took an unexpected turn when he'd located a Schoenfeldium bonanza. The key mineral used in jumpspace technology was oversupplied for a brief time while every vested party claimed an agreement-specified portion. The share the Realm received hadn't satisfied them. Certain quarters could still harbor a vendetta. Protective custody aboard Argosy Station might have been genuine. If so, Zofie'd brought him from the fire into the crucible.

His thoughts returned to Zofie's motivation. If she wanted him punished, she could have left him in Argosy's brig. Unless the resentment against him had escalated to charges from the Realm. Maybe her new career included bounty hunting. If she'd returned him to the Eddy to collect a reward, the peace accord with the Confluence wouldn't protect him.

Carver checked the *Whisper's* systems. If he couldn't escape from the ship, could he escape the shipyard in the ship?

It was no use; he had no way to see where he was going. External cameras and proximity sensors were all deactivated. The single port was his only viewpoint and that wasn't enough for navigation.

If she returned with company, maybe he could grab her and use her as hostage to get away. There was nowhere to hide except in his cryo coffin and it wasn't an ideal ambush launch point. He scanned the floor, walls and ceiling. Over the door, his muscles might hold him for a minute in the shipyard's minimal induced gravity. Anyone entering wouldn't look up as their first reaction. He climbed up the wall and braced himself between beams. His stomach muscles rebelled and he strained to keep position in the practice run to a target count of twenty.

Carver dropped down to the deck and massaged his gut. It might work if he could push off hard for added momentum. He kept his ear to the lock and speculated on steps to take once he was free. Allies in the 'yard? Unlikely. His best course would be to reverse the jailer-prisoner roles with Zofie and wait for DualE. He heard the outer lock open and clambered to the ambush position.

The Eddy 'yards were relatively deserted. Zofie expected more traffic. It hadn't been that many weeks since the order to break up the Realm's armada had come from the Confluence negotiations. Unless the rumors of that armada were exaggerated. Chancellor Mekli's threat a bluff? She doubted it. Mekli didn't strike her as the type to take that kind of risk. No, the ships had dispersed. Or relocated elsewhere until the peace was guaranteed.

Zofie shuttled to the admin center to clear her paperwork and to evaluate what opportunities were present.

She dug out her registration and charter documents for the initial scrutiny.

"Can I speak to the harbor master? I have intel from Argosy Station. I know he'll be interested."

The clerk appraised her, trying to make up his mind if she was genuine or just wanted special treatment. "What could you know that the captain and crew of the *Ranger* didn't. they were through here an hour ago with a similar story. 'Big information.'"

"Because I'd been to the Confluence before my last three weeks aboard the station, chasing down every rumor and confirming every fact. Because I didn't spend my leave from the *Ranger* getting and staying drunk."

"Leave your contact info, I'll pass it on when he emerges. At the moment, even I can't talk to him."

It didn't seem like a brush off but Zofie couldn't be certain. She keyed in her comm code. "Don't wait too long. If your office isn't interested, they'll be commercial traders who will be." She hoped.

The clerk didn't seem impressed by the threat. "We're a free economy. Do what you must. We'll find out once you pass on anything out here."

She leaned close. "There's always an advantage in being first."

She checked her watch. Carver should be awake by now. One more stop, then she'd return to the *Whisper* and begin her explanations and apologies. Assuming Carver hesitated long enough for her to speak before he did something stupid.

Most of the shipyard passageways were vacuum. This wasn't a place the Realm wanted prospectors or anyone else to linger. Except for one atrium and a trading floor with a bonus. A tavern. The lone drinking, inhaling or otherwise mentally impairing establishment in the station and she expected under surveillance. Hence the encouragement to leave the station or congregate there. She stepped through the lock into Eddie's Dive.

Noise, smells and sights of two dozen spacers even at this time in the second shift assaulted her and it took a moment of scanning the room to acclimate. This wasn't her alternate source of trade. This is where she could make the first of a series of contacts until she finally met a target in one of the off-the-radar carrels which had to exist somewhere in the 'yards.

She took a mild stimulant from the dispenser and perched to one side of the main buzz. Eye contact soon attracted two fellow customers. Male and female.

"I'm Marshall. The *Banshee*," said the woman.

"Higgins," said her companion.

Zofie reciprocated the spacer-condensed exchange. "Ked, The *Whisper*."

The woman carried the conversation. "Watched you dock. You barnacled the *Ranger*? Saw it come in too. Argosy's the rumor. Waiting for news from Slate's." Her speech was clipped in the manner of a spacer who spent too long cooped up in a small ship. Conversation mutated from garrulous in the early weeks to as needed to silence. Higgins and Marshall had been out in the deep for an extended tour.

"Sit," invited Zofie. "I can't stay long, have to get back to my partner, see if he's okay. He had a rough jump."

The couple sat but the man turned away from the two women, constantly surveying the other customers.

"Anything I know about Slate's is weeks old and second hand at the best. I wanted to land here as soon as possible. Before..."

Marshall nodded. "Confluence oversight."

They drank in silence. Zofie returned her half-finished drink to the recycle basin. The woman did the same. She whispered under the noise of the suction drain. "Come see us at loading dock 14M. Next shift. We'll trade."

"Any other traders in Eddie's?" Zofie took a last look at the Dive's clientele.

They moved toward the exit, the woman speaking in normal tone. "Someone's always interdicted and needing a broker. Tread carefully." Marshall left Zofie alone.

A trio in red spacer suits eyed her. One nodded his head.

Zofie circled past them before leaving. Business or pleasure? Threat or opportunity? Her instinct didn't say. Was it worth the risk? She decided. She hadn't come out here, kidnaping a friend along the way, to bide her time. She dropped a comm card on the table among the three.

She retreated to the gantry where the *Whisper* berthed alone. She disliked the quiet. Like jumpspace, silence gave a soul too much opportunity to contemplate the self and find it wanting. She checked her comm before entering the lock. Nothing from either the master nor the reds.

Time to clear the air with Carver. Before he lost his temper, if possible.

She cycled the inner door and braced herself. "Carver?" She couldn't see him through the lock. She'd have to go inside. "I'm coming in. Give me a chance to explain before you do anything rash. Okay?"

Silence. She pulled off her suit and threw it inside. A blur from above dropped on the suit, crushing it to the deck.

Carver bounced once, grunted and rolled on his back, a look of disgust on his very red face.

Zofie laughed. "I can't help it, Carver. I'm sorry. That was a brilliant plan."

He rubbed his stomach. "Yeah, brilliant. Like most of my plans."

"Can I come in without you trying another one?"

He got to his feet and hung up her suit. "That was my only plan."

"Right." She stepped in, still facing him at all times. "I owe you an explanation."

Chapter 10

Slate's Progress rotated slowly against its gas giant neighbor. Illuminated by normal external maintenance and docking activity, it did not look like a weapon staging arena. DualE guided the *Crossed Swords* behind the *Penance* on the station's computer track beams, keeping a vigil for any hostile sign.

The barnacle-jump from Argosy Station had been paid by Pious' brotherhood funds. He was anxious to rekindle support on Progress before moving on to the Eddy. Pious and his order deemed the Eddy was the place to grow their following now, before the Bohr-Realm alliance eroded their solitude with Confluence distractions and mind-candy.

Denz's trail led to the Eddy, apparently in cooperation with someone outside Rowland's control. The mysterious 'who' was solved by a brief message left for Pious from the *Whisper* before she jumped. Zofie. A human barnacle on all their souls.

Brother Cardinal maintained radio silence while the two small craft touched the gantry berths and locked in. DualE'd recommended the silence until she could evaluate the situation. Only it appeared there was no situation to evaluate.

DualE opened the airlock to admit the mechanical sniffers and scanners. Slate kept his overhead costs lean. The sensor 'bots took all of ten minutes to scan her and the *Crossed Swords*. Her comm beeped as they drifted out to perform the same duty aboard the *Penance*. She checked her screen. Entry granted, no taxable items. "I love the minimal bureaucracy out here," she said aloud.

She shut down the drive and activated the dock power input to keep her ship habitable and ready for departure on short notice. Her ship? She was missing a partner. The jump from Argosy to Slate's had been partly to fulfill Pious' flight plan and to ensure the *Whisper* hadn't disguised its destination. Zofie was devious by intent. DualE doubted the woman could fathom a different existence. "I should have killed her when I had the chance," she said, half-seriously.

The dock was pressurized. She donned her robe and went next door.

The sensor 'bots were leaving *Penance* as she arrived. She poked her head inside. "All clear?"

"Come in," said Pious. "Yes, we've passed the security barriers."

Penance's comm pinged a steady stream of notifications.

"You're popular," said DualE. She squeezed between Cardinal and Atone to glance at the screen.

"Outstanding messages from a few followers on Slate's," said Atone.

She looked to Pious. "They knew you were coming?"

"Returning," he corrected. "Not specifically now. These are all posted over time, waiting for us to arrive. No anticipation as to when."

"This one's new," said Cardinal.

Pious leaned in front of DualE. "From our sister Chels. She must be well-connected to know of our arrival. Acknowledge and ask her to meet when she can."

The follower Pious mentioned. "Is she part of your team?" DualE asked.

"Both, I hope. Her jump sickness keeps her here. A blessing to us. Chels broke the ice for us on our previous visit. We created momentum for our mission and it appears she's kept it going in our absence."

DualE ran the sequence of the brothers' previous mission in her head. "This is where you started tracking Carver."

Pious nodded. "As important as our work was here, I made a judgment to interrupt our tour and follow him."

"The right decision by all appearances," she said.

"Financially, yes. Spiritually, I still have doubts. I carry a guilt that we prematurely abandoned Chels and the others."

DualE turned to Atone. "Any menacing messages in the batch? Ones I need to deal with? It's time I started contributing my expertise. Doubly so until we find Carver."

"Nothing negative," Atone answered. "Pledges. Confessions. Encouragement."

"Station news?"

"None worthwhile at my initial glance but I'll go through them and send you any." Atone got a nod from Pious.

"It looks like business-as-usual on Progress." DualE evaluated her next step. "I'm going aboard and talk to Slate if I can. Get first-hand information. Then I suggest we meet this Chels."

"I'll accompany you," said Pious. "Commander Slate was quite accommodating on our previous visit. I'd like to thank him."

DualE changed her approach. A military-style face-to-face with Slate on short notice wasn't the right way to roll here. "You can take the lead and introduce me to Slate. When you've arranged a rendezvous with Chels, I would like to meet her as well."

DualE left her airlock unsealed. She welcomed the fresher air of the station. Not without odor but a magnitude cleaner than the funk in the *Crossed Swords*. She had no luck identifying the most recent arrivals from Argosy. If Zofie and Carver were here, she'd need Slate's help. Pious would be helping her with that, more than she helping the brothers. No guilt there.

She sponged the deepsleep sweats as best she could and donned a clean tunic. Her short-cut hair stood up with a quick brush. She finished buttoning up when Pious rapped. "Ready? I've apprised Slate of our arrival and requested a brief audience. He's available now."

They made their way to the central axis. "Quite different from Argosy Station," Pious commented. He pointed at the open core above them. "It took getting used to on my first visit. Vertigo sufferers wouldn't enjoy the architecture."

"No problem for me. I've been dropped onto planets from a thousand kilometers up and glide-chuted to the surface."

"What did you think about on your way down?"

"Not to land headfirst and to bend my knees upon impact."

DualE noticed the number of residents who recognized Pious and greeted him as they moved. He spoke briefly to each without stopping.

"Thank you, sister...It's good to see you again...We'll announce a service once Slate gives us clearance."

He shook hands and clasped arms, never slowing in their progress toward the central lift system. The route up to Slate's office was an open platform with space to accommodate half a dozen riders or small cargo. The waist-high railing looked frail but it had apparently served thus far.

"The vertigo I was referring to earlier," Pious told her. His hands gripped the open car's rail as they ascended the length of Slate's Progress.

DualE noted the chaotic structure. Decks ending without walls. Walking platforms stretching across large gaps. Pious had been right. Slate's Progress was not for the acrophobic. Her military evaluation kicked in on the trip up. "Strategic structural damage would be difficult with a pinpoint attack on this station," she said. "You'd need a large, indiscriminate weapon to cripple it."

"I'll accept your word. Implication?"

"Whatever hit the *Orson* and Argosy was a narrow, focused beam. Not a weapon which attackers would use to destroy a target in one shot. The cancerous by-product was easily contained." Though in the midst of a dogfight, cauterizing the growth could be difficult. "Implication? I don't know yet. I'm still gathering and processing information."

"You're puzzled."

"More than a little. Why a random attack using a precise weapon? An odd combination. If intentional, then what reaction was anticipated?"

"The naval mind seeks the balance the faithful mind embraces. I must often reconcile contradictions in actions, words and philosophy."

"Add my question to your list, Brother Pious." The lift slowed and DualE's stomach rose. "Remind me to eat," she said.

"My lifestyle prepares me to fast frequently but if time permits a meal here, I will join you." Pious led them along a platform to an open office manned by Slate.

Slate's build reminded DualE of Gar Kondradt, stocky but he differed in his body language. Kondradt used his sturdiness to intimidate, Slate seemed open, not constantly evaluating risk versus profit. Slate's evaluation would place the station before personal gain.

"Pious. Welcome aboard. You left before I could attend one of your sermons last time. Chels recounts your guidance often. Sit. I can't spare much time but I'm glad to see you, especially for her sake. She's kept your words alive to the point of obsession."

"Do you and Chels spend much time together?" Pious asked.

Slate reddened. "A recent attachment. I never had time before. Running this complex is a team job. Unfortunately, I was the whole team."

"And now?" asked DualE.

"Commercial expansion. Queries from the Confluence. I've hired underlings, overseers and accepted a few policy specialists. They'll all be needed for the looming shared governance. There's more paperwork but I delegate up, down and sideways." He studied her shoulders. "And you are? A fellow missionary?" A skeptical note in his voice revealed an observant man.

Her tunic did not hide DualE's musculature. "As you say, Commander Slate, I'm a recent attachment."

"Appearances can deceive. My Chels doesn't look like a spiritual person but her faith is strong."

"I am committed to the brothers and their cause," said DualE. "I'm also committed to their safe passage."

Slate hesitated a moment. "Your jumpship captain apprised me of a disturbance at Argosy, related to the Eddy. Can you confirm? Tell me more?"

DualE wasn't sure what to say. Rowland hadn't ordered her to keep silent and Slate would suspect if she withheld too much. Pious might tumble to her dual role if she didn't say what they both knew. "There was an attack on the *Orson* as it left jumpspace," she said. "Argosy Station and two ships in dock were holed by the same projectile, exact nature unknown." DualE gave Slate time to digest the news. She pointed away from his aerie. "Progress appears busy but not under threat. What can you tell us?"

Pious added, "Faith carries the brotherhood through many trials but no sense in not being prepared. If you can share any information about the Eddy before we jump, we would be grateful."

Slate leaned his elbows on his desk, steepling his fingers. "This is disturbing news. If it ties to anyone on Progress, I'd know. At least I should. We've heard nothing untoward from the Eddy. There've been four ships jump from there in the last three weeks. Not a whisper from any quarter about deployed weapons." He glanced at DualE. "You're welcome to question any crew you encounter but my sources are well informed."

"I believe you," said DualE. "I won't interrogate anyone but I'll see what I can learn informally." What had he said? Not a whisper.

A buzzer rang on Slate's desk. "I'm needed elsewhere. Brother Pious, I hope you're here long enough for a sermon or two, I'd like to attend in person. Get a sense of how the prospectors and crew here react to your message. See how I react." He stood and signaled the pair to proceed back to the lift. "I'll accompany you part way."

When they began the descent, DualE asked, "Have you seen or heard of a barnacle craft *Whisper*? It would have come through in the last three weeks as well, from Argosy Station."

"The name doesn't ring a bell. Forward a request to my dock master. I'll advise him to cooperate."

"Thank you."

Slate stepped off the lift platform as it passed one of many gangway ledges.

"I thought the *Whisper* jumped straight to the Eddy?" said Pious.

"It did. That doesn't mean Zofie and Carver didn't backtrack. I need to be thorough. I doubt we'll get Slate's level of cooperation further out. We are heading into Confluence-unfriendly territory, brother."

The stepped off at the base of the lift. "Where now?"

Pious pointed ahead. "I'm to meet Chels in the atrium beyond the compression plant. Come."

Progress's innards shook and rang with life support mechanicals doing their best to separate from each other and the station. Slate may have a staff of multitudes but DualE wasn't convinced their engineering skills were keeping up with the demands of a randomly growing facility. She made a mental note to double-check the *Penance's* departure readiness.

They passed through a series of bulkheads, finally evading the din and entered a colorful dome twenty meters high and twice as wide. Cloth streamers in red, green and blue hung from the ceiling, creating a spectral garden.

A woman DualE's height walked toward them, her raised arms brushing the ends of the streamers. "Brother Pious. I'm so glad to see you again." The woman's glee faded momentarily when she spied DualE.

I've a self-appointed rival here if I don't diffuse her suspicions. The bodyguard truth or the guise of another disciple? DualE had moments to decide.

Chapter 11

"I await your explanation." Carver rubbed his knee. His landing on the deck hadn't been violent in the reduced station gravity but it hurt enough. Zofie had unsealed the 'lock, then hung outside, waiting for his move. She obviously anticipated some action. At least she didn't laugh long as he writhed at her feet.

She brewed a post-jump recovery drink. He accepted the steaming elixir and sipped. It was better than his tea. He waited for her next words. He'd made his move, unsuccessful as it was, now it was her turn. "Thanks," he said. "Now talk."

"Pious broadcast a general message through Argosy Station. He referenced your Renfrew identity. I interpreted it as a subversive code. I dug into Argosy's security, found you jailed, and added Renfrew to the incarcerated."

"And got Willie released." It was a daring move. Zofie was never to be underestimated. "Why bring me here instead of shuffling me back to Pious?"

She hesitated before answering. Improvising?

After a minute, she spoke. "The Confluence Navy's arrival and the attack wreaked minor physical damage to the station but the reactions threatened its short-term stability. I judged it prudent to get us both away. Pious and DualE will catch up."

"I hope they do before Rowland does. What now? We sit?"

She shook her head. "We have business to conduct," she said. "You and I have a meeting next shift. Maybe one sooner if my second source makes contact."

"The purpose of the meeting and why am I part of it?"

"You're part of it because I need a partner and you're the best available."

"Let's back up and start with shanghaiing me. I made a commitment to the brothers and to DualE which you have voided."

"You voided my last deal with Gar Kondradt and the Realm power brokers. We're even."

Zofie'd rewritten events to justify her current actions, Carver realized. Maybe she wasn't as psychologically healed as he believed back in Bohr. "You were well-compensated, Zofie. By me. This ship is a step above the last piece of detritus you manned." He braced for an onslaught, either verbal or physical.

She dropped her head and sighed. When her eyes rose to meet his, there was no anger. "You're right, Carver. I do owe you. And DualE. And Pious. When they arrive, I swear you can rejoin them. In the meantime, all I ask is your presence and a sliver of your luck. There are opportunities out here. For how long, I can't guess, but I need to act quickly. With whatever happened to Argosy Station and the inbound freighter from here, a siege is imminent. Or at least an embargo. At this moment, only you and I know how serious the conflict could become. I can broker deals with peacetime rates which will look paltry when the gunships arrive. As I told you, I've already made one contact and I expect more within a shift or two."

This wasn't about the money, he thought. This was about Zofie regaining her self-worth. Since he'd been part of the circumstance destroying it on their ill-fated jump to Bohr, he could clear whatever morsel of guilt remained.

"I'll cut you a generous share, Carver. I bet you regret your generosity on the *Pollux* salvage claim."

Pollux. The jumpfreighter they'd all barnacled to which sabotage had left adrift in unknown locales until Carver, Brother Cardinal and the *Pollux*'s late astrogator limped it to Bohr in barely one piece. The barnacles claimed salvage for that one piece by virtue of transport-crew abandonment. The *Pollux*'s captain and officers had been locked into cryo but the claim stood. Incarcerated aboard the freighter, Zofie still qualified for a salvage share. Carver'd signed his portion over to the brothers in a cleansing gesture.

"I'll accompany you to your meeting and judge for myself." He drained the last of the recovery elixir.

"Feeling better?"

"Yeah. Still pissed, but better. How much time before we meet your leads?"

A bang on the *Whisper*'s airlock interrupted Zofie's answer. She checked the monitor.

Carver noted three red-suited figures huddled outside. "You know them?"

"Not yet. Party two might have moved up the priority list." She palm-printed a small screen on the control panel and a shockgun slid free. She handed it to him. "Please don't use this on me."

"Mind reader." A show of trust? Did she deserve it? Carver wondered if it was charged. He hoped he wouldn't find out.

She opened the lock and addressed the visitors. "Come in, this is my partner, Willie Renfrew."

Two of them wadded into the airlock while the third remained on guard outside. Carver appraised the men. Their suits had seen better days but the occupants looked in better than average condition. An incongruence, Carver thought. They were cookie-cutter alike in manner as well. From the bulkhead, the pair scrutinized the *Whisper*'s innards, then Zofie, then Carver.

The first one inside laughed aloud at the introductions. "Willie Renfrew, my ass. Do you know who this really is?" He turned to his mate and then to Zofie.

"This is Carver Denz, the famous prospector. I wouldn't think you'd be needing this kind of work. There's something going on here besides shifty trading. I want in."

Carver fingered the shockgun in his pocket and debated whether this crew was worth the trouble. The man had recognized him but to reveal his recognition showed poor judgment. With what kind of idiots had Zofie got him involved?

Chapter 12

Pious knew he must intervene. Confronted with DualE as his escort, Chels' demeanor changed from joy to concern to emotional turmoil in the twitch of an eye. He recognized jealousy but it so often puzzled him. It sprang forth without genuine justification. Chels needed reassurance.

"Chels, you have done wonders for the cause in my absence." He clasped her hands and kept eye contact. "You have accomplished more than I could hope."

Her pained expression wavered. She hugged him, then stepped back and glanced from his feet to his face. A new look appeared. Chels looked...afraid? No. Apprehensive? Yes. About him. The physical change to his face; the long, hard weeks since his last visit had taken a toll.

He smiled to reassure her. "Jumpspace disagrees with me. If I were a vain man, I'd avoid it altogether or take measures to retain what's left of my middle-age."

"I'm sorry, Brother Pious, the reactions in my heart and my head are in conflict today. I built up your memory in my mind and to see you in person is a shock. To realize you are finally here again." Her gaze flicked over his shoulder.

Could he diffuse at least one of her concerns? "This is DualE, our protector."

"My role might be superfluous on Progress, given *your* work," said DualE.

DualE apparently had recognized Chels' elevated emotion too.

"I'm honored to meet you, Chels. Brother Pious has spoken often of your partnership. I place myself in your service."

"And I, yours." Chels glanced at Pious. "Protection from what? Who?"

"The Realm's environs beyond Slate's can be rough," said DualE. "The Eddy's pioneers tend to shoot first and erase the evidence later." DualE studied the surroundings. "I came to evaluate this place for tomorrow's safety."

DualE reacted as a soldier, a comrade in the cause and as an empathetic soul recognizing Chels' unease. Pious was pleased with his choice. She left them to survey the domed park.

Pious walked with Chels amongst the hanging decorations. "Tell me what your plans are. Where and when do you recommend we offer communion?"

"Give me a day to spread the word and build anticipation."

Chels' manner had blossomed from anxiety into enthusiasm.

"I am grateful for your devotion, Sister," said Pious. "What can I do for you?"

"I'm struggling with a burden, Brother Pious. A troubling confidence I need to reconcile before I decide what to do."

"If I can help clear your decision, I will. I'm free anytime for you."

"I'm still processing it. It could be a threat to all of us or nothing. I'm too excited with your arrival to think about it now. My time will be taken up with preparations for the gathering. After the service, I'll decide. I know your counsel will help me."

"Very well, consider yourself first in line." He signaled DualE to join them. "There is another matter we must investigate. DualE's colleague may or may not have passed through Slate's recently and we need to determine if he did and if he's still here. Would it compromise your plans if she and I were to visit the spacer tavern to inquire?"

"Uh, it would be better if I did the inquiries and you remained secluded."

DualE rejoined them. "What if I accompanied you, Chels?" she asked. "I could be just another nomadic merc you've befriended."

"All right. Keep the robe. I'll show you off as a new recruit." Chels clutched Pious' hand. "I'm so glad you're here. I won't let you down. We will fill this place tomorrow."

"I knew we could count on you Chels."

"Come with me while I spread the word and we can talk." She tugged DualE's robe. "What's your colleague's name?"

"Carver Denz," said Pious.

Chels laughed. "Really? If the most successful prospector in recent history had been near or within Slate's, it wouldn't be a secret."

"He might call himself Willie Renfrew?" DualE asked.

"We'll see."

⸻⸻ ⊬⊬⎟⎟⊬⊬ ⸻⸻

DualE endured the passing nudges and gropes without crippling or crushing bone. The tavern crawled with prospectors, station employees off-shift and jumpfreighter crews. She noted the complete absence of any military types.

She followed in Chels' wake, uncomfortable in the role of a submissive female disciple but almost any pose would appear docile compared to the exuberant Chels. It was a necessary guise for DualE's role as part of the brothers' entourage.

Chels gave each encounter her fullest effort, promoting Pious' appearance. The reception was lukewarm from most but a small number were enthusiastic. Those Chels spent even greater effort upon, judging, DualE assumed, that a fully committed minority was more important than an ambivalent or tolerant mass. DualE agreed with the strategy. A small group of fanatics were much harder to face on the battlefield than loosely-bound large numbers, willing to disengage at the first setback. Pious and the brothers waged war to bring God into these dissolute lives.

From beneath her hood, DualE read the postures and listened to the verbal intonations. Chels was a natural recruiter.

They took a table. DualE was back in a comfort zone. She said, "You're very good. Pious should have you on his full-time payroll instead of me. Assuming your muscles are in tune."

"My life is on Slate's. Even if I could suffer through spookspace, I wouldn't want to."

"Slate?"

"Yeah, that's part of it. But I'd committed to my role for the brothers before he and I got together. This station is my home, my church and will be my resting place."

"No scattering your ashes among the void?"

"No, thank you."

A short, wiry man approached. "Chels? I'm a recent arrival on Slate's. Tarbent's the name. I've been intrigued by your messages but haven't visited your chapel yet. This Pious preacher seems like a big deal for you." He took a seat at Chels invitation.

"Come tomorrow and learn for yourself. We don't convert anyone who isn't ready."

"All or none, eh?" He lowered his head to see DualE's face under her hood.

"Chels is right. I'm all in," said DualE.

"I watched you in the crowd. You're trying not to move like a warrior." He sipped his mug.

"A previous life," she said. "You have better eyes than most."

"What do I reveal?" Chels asked.

DualE was grateful for the deflection.

Tarbent turned his gaze to the acolyte. "You show the strain of too many jump nightmares. You could have been in service too. Or a well-traveled barnacle. Prospector?"

"Anyone here could have told you that."

Tarbent laughed. "That they could have. I've not wasted my time in Slate's getting drunk. You are well-known."

"How many other recent arrivals are aboard?" asked DualE. Her cover wasn't blown but she'd risk the question.

"Not many. I'd say more have left than arrived in my short time."

"We're looking for one of our party who got separated from the brothers at Argosy. A prospector by trade though not a very good one. Still, his astrogational knowledge made a good addition to our mission." DualE felt Chels toe on hers. A warning to go slow?

Chels added, "A patron of ours when his luck was good, a volunteer for the cause when it wasn't. Trading sweat equity for board."

"Name?" asked Tarbent.

"Willie Renfrew aboard the *Whisper*," said DualE. No point in advertising Carver Denz.

Tarbent answered without changing expression. "Never heard of him or the ship. But I will buy you ladies drinks on faith that tomorrow's service will be worth it." Tarbent rose.

Chels laid a hand on his hip. "Save it for a hard donation. Tomorrow, if it pleases."

Tarbent looked to DualE for confirmation. She said, "Chels is right. And anything stronger than tea might impede the rest of today's duties. Thank you just the same. I'll take you up on it another time, I promise."

"Me too," said Chels.

Tarbent left to join two other female patrons having a laughing conversation. With an armload of drinks in his possession, he was quickly welcomed to the group.

DualE and Chels exchanged glances. "Been there," said Chels.

"Been them," answered DualE.

"The crowd's peaking between shifts. It's time I earned Pious' trust."

Time I earned yours, if I can. "How can I help?" DualE asked.

"Watch them. Note the ones with the most visible reactions, interest or skepticism. Then look for them tomorrow at the service."

"In a place like this, I'm more used to holding a fellow marine's coat or having mine held, but I'll do my best."

Chels stuck thumb and middle finger between her lips and shrieked a whistle guaranteed to wake a body from cryo. She stood on the table. "For those who don't know me, I'm Chels Harte. Ignore me at your peril. Those who do know me can confirm I am not to be taken lightly. I won't waste your valuable drinking, flirting or business time but hear this. Those of you who were present the last time Brother Pious addressed the station can vouch for the fact it was a transcendent moment. We're on the edge of civilization for better or worse. We're here for the freedom, for the quest and the chance to make a difference to ourselves and the Realm. But sometimes we need perspective on how to put it all together. What's our next level? What's our end game?"

DualE noted the derisive hoots. They were few and she marked the perpetrators. Most customers were polite and a few in the audience were transfixed by Chels' words.

"It varies for each individual," Chels continued. "It was for me. A forcibly-retired prospector, not much good to myself or anyone else in the Eddy. Pious' message transformed me. It gave me purpose. I can make a difference. If he can change but one of you to the path I chose, then we'll take it. If he can reach more, we'll transform the Eddy into something special. A place to build a new civilization based on respect and trust. We're not building a crusade for God, but for good, in His name. Please join Pious tomorrow at the atrium. Back to your glasses, mugs and friends old and new." She bowed and hopped down.

DualE said, "I'm impressed, Chels. You should be the brothers' fifth column throughout the Realm."

"Thanks. I'm happy with my role here."

One of Tarbent's new friends strolled to them. By her rolling, bow-legged walk, a decade older than DualE at least. As she got closer, the creases in her face and drooping ears added another decade to DualE's estimate. A frontier woman not to be underestimated.

"Coming tomorrow?" asked Chels. "You're a new arrival?"

The woman nodded. "Two days ago. From the Eddy."

DualE tensed. Don't push it, she thought. Let her take or spit the hook.

"You've piqued my interest. The Realm needs a cohesive vision moving forward. I doubt the time required to grow into that choice will be long enough. The Confluence peace might be their way of ensuring we become who they want. Perhaps your man Pious has an answer. I will be there tomorrow." She nodded toward the group she'd just left. "Tarbent tells me you're looking for the *Whisper*."

"I'm curious as to its whereabouts, yes," said DualE, trying to sound casual.

"It's in the Eddy shipyard. Or was when I left. I only noticed it because it was one of the few barnacle-sized craft in the 'yard."

"Any crew around?"

She shook her head. "I couldn't say. Assume someone had to pilot it in but we had to pass by that structure to depart and I saw the list of craft warned not to disembark until we were clear."

"Thank you," said Chels. "I look forward to seeing you at the service."

The woman nodded again and returned to her group.

"The Eddy. They jumped straight there if they were already in dock before this woman jumped." DualE was on her own for the brothers as long as they remained here.

The other niggle surfaced. "Chels, why don't I see any military types on Progress? Even the Realm's unofficial forces must station here occasionally."

"Good question. I hadn't noticed until you mentioned it. I have to think back. It must be a month since our irregulars were aboard."

"A month. Same time as the peace was being firmed up between the Confluence and the Realm. News travels fast."

"There was never more than a ship or two here at the height of the independence rhetoric. I'll check with Slate but I think there might have been two cruiser class and one converted mozzy all here at once, then within a shift, all three were gone. Three, four weeks ago?"

"Hmm. Disbanded or a strategic withdrawal."

"Does it matter to the brothers?"

Chels had almost caught her. DualE's intel gathering mission pushed her profile in the wrong direction. But it was info she needed. "I'm ex-navy adjusting to my mercenary role. It's hard-wired in me to have as much information as possible before I go into a situation. In this case, allow the brothers to be aware of unknown risks before we make our jump into the Eddy itself."

This seemed to satisfy Chels for the moment but the woman was no fool and DualE would need to double down on her bodyguard persona. Her concern was genuine for either mission. Did the Realm's armada lurk in the void, waiting for an indication the Confluence was vulnerable? She had more reason than locating Carver Denz to push Pious to that next jump soon.

Chapter 13

"Carver Denz?" repeated the *Whisper's* second visitor.

Carver grabbed their arms and pulled the two inside the *Whisper*. Zofie for once seemed frozen in shock. Her plans depended that much on Carver's anonymity?

He closed the airlock for privacy. Best way forward? Bluff, indignation and mild insults. "Geez, you guys pretend to be traders?" He sat beside Zofie. "We're trying to run a low-profile operation here and the first thing you do is broadcast my identity. If anyone heard you, our proposed dealings are off and we'll see to it you don't trade with anyone. Got it? Do you think you can be more circumspect going forward?" He glared at each in turn. His anger was genuine. His threat not so much.

"Sorry," one answered when Carver stopped for breath. "You're a legend out here. It was the shock of actually meeting you." He pointed at Zofie. "She didn't tell us you were part of any deal."

"You can see why," she answered.

Good, Carver thought, she'd recovered. He said, "My reputation doesn't affect our dealings here." Not that he knew what those dealings were. Bluff.

Zofie carried on. "We're brokers for Argosy Station and chartered under the Confluence. Peace is coming. Or at least a stand down."

They looked puzzled. Carver pushed. "Argosy Station was fired upon from somewhere in the Eddy. Recently. Any rumors here?"

"Not that it's material to our negotiations," said Zofie. "We'll work through hostilities if we must."

Speak for yourself, Carver thought.

"It can't be true," said the spokesman. "The Eddy'd never attack Argosy Station."

"Someone did," said Carver. "The station might have been an accidental casualty but the *Orson* suffered damage and she jumped from the Eddy." Sooner or later, DualE and the brothers would appear and he wanted to know the risks by the time they arrived.

"This is news to us and I suspect to everyone in the shipyard."

Zofie responded. "Like Carver's presence, I advise you to keep the news private. Listen but don't question. Advantage in knowledge can help us. Now, what do you need moved from here?"

Carver wasn't going to get any more intel at the moment so he let Zofie lead the negotiations. He'd observe her as much as their company. He needed to know as much about her state of mind as possible if he were to end their temporary partnership as soon as he could without pushing her to volatility.

"Artifacts," said the potential client.

Okay, thought Carver, enough of his casual observation role.

"Are we talking pioneer prospector material?" Zofie asked. "Not sure of your market. Family connections? Want to find out what happened to your long-lost ne'er-do-well forefather?"

The two red suits exchanged glances. "Now it's our turn to demand privacy."

Carver suspected the truth behind the need for secrecy. The men weren't referring to any old pioneer relics. This was the prospectors' Holy Grail. Something which rendered his mineral bonanza penny ante.

Zofie stiffened. She'd put it together as quickly as he had. "Alien," she whispered. "Alien artifacts."

No assent or denial from the prospective clients.

Carver didn't trust himself to speak. Zofie'd need more than the partner guise of Willie Renfrew to pull off smuggling alien contraband from the Eddy.

Carver ensured the access catwalk was clear except for their third member before signalling the two Reds to exit the *Whisper*. He returned inside and closed the 'lock.

"Our next visitor-slash-partners will be here in an hour," said Zofie.

"I thought you'd cancel, given what we just heard."

"Too risky to go silent so soon after the Reds met us. We can't reveal this job's manifest. Besides, two shipments would be a perfect cover. Routine brokerage. Nothing worth hijacking."

He could see her mind racing forward, digesting implications and devising strategies. Given his lack of success at hiding his lode's shipment back to Bohr, he should let her do the planning. "Do you honestly think you can keep it secret?"

"Absolutely. I tracked through the 'yard and didn't hear a word about it. The Reds haven't talked and no one else appears to know. We can do it."

"What about your other associates?"

"I have none. Except you." She appeared genuine but Carver couldn't read her well, that he knew.

"You're not working with or for someone? Zofie, I know you. Gar Kondradt knows you. Hell, Chancellor Mekli was your patron."

"All in the past, Carver. I work for Zofie Ked. So do you. For the time being. I mean, aren't you excited? If these guys really found something alien, you'll need a half-dozen false identities to walk down any corridor in Gamma Hub or Argosy Station without being mobbed."

"I've experienced such fame. It's neither what I desire nor need. You take this on, I'll help as much as I can. From this end. My duty is to Brother Pious. When the *Penance* and DualE get here, which I've no doubt they will, my obligation to you is done. You agree or I walk from the *Whisper* now and make my own way in the 'yard." He drew the shockgun from his pocket and hung it at his side.

Zofie had hers pulled. She remained silent in the standoff. She looked around the inside of her ship, then at him.

"Don't think killing me is a viable option," he said. "The Reds have seen me. If Carver Denz disappears, or Willie Renfrew, they will have questions."

"Eliminating you isn't on my mind. Kondradt and Mekli have been exorcized from my psyche. I don't dream in cryo any more going through spookspace. I am clear of entanglement."

"No dreams? No recriminating nightmares? That's a little disturbing." Or a lie. "The deal with jumpspace is to tear those demons from the subconscious and bring them to the fore." Who was this transformed Zofie? A complete psychotic? One who he'd just committed to help change human zeitgeist by introducing the knowledge and reality we were no longer alone.

"Not for me, Carver. I have no guilt. Brother Pious heard my confession."

If true, Carver doubted that Pious realized what he'd created? A guilt-free Zofie Ked still capable of significant mayhem?

Chapter 14

"I'm ready when you are, Chels." Pious sat in Progress' makeshift chapel one row in front of his disciple. He heard her breathing deep, calming her mind, seeking the way. The station's background hum droned like a hive, each individual system performing a task for the whole.

He and the brothers were parts of a greater whole as well, though their independence this far from church headquarters was only physical distance, not spiritual separation. Pious tried not to dwell on the comfort safely enjoyed by the church's higher officers while he and the rest of the missionaries toiled amidst danger. The church needed to ensure its role in the coming alliance. A few sacrifices were acceptable to be part of the Realm's eventual governance, though it would be unaware of the silent partnership. It was the whole which mattered. Drones such as he were critical but not indispensable. There were always new volunteers. Brother Atone was the future, not Pious.

Chels remained silent. Her burden had to be large to stifle her normal garrulity. He probed. "What troubles you? Share it with me and reduce its weight."

"To weigh you down?"

"This is my chosen path." He closed his eyes, still seeing her face before him. "Begin."

"I'm unsure of my role and my trust contract with a man who confessed a possible crime, Brother Pious."

"A long-standing dilemma for any one in my position of confidentiality. The First Expansion Brotherhood adopted many trappings from the Roman Catholic faith centuries ago. Jesuit mission tactics and confession, to name two. By our laws, we can't act or reveal our knowledge of a crime. But some follow their social conscience if more crimes could be committed. It is a difficult question for some; for others, their commitment to the canon of the church outweighs all other considerations. The priest must ask, who do I serve? In your case, both you and the visitor treated the contact as though it was under the protection of the church and priest-confessor privilege."

"I'm not a priest," said Chels. "Though I guess I was your representative when I heard the confession."

"Who do *you* serve?"

"I want to serve the church. But I'm also loyal to this station and Slate."

"The information gained in this sacred trust? Is it material to the station's well-being?"

"Yes, I think so. Definitely the Realm is at risk."

"Was there death by foul means?"

"I don't know. But there could be many deaths to come. It involves hostile action against the Confluence."

"What you tell me, I will hold in confidence. What you do with your information remains up to you. Is your confessor still aboard Progress and does he pose a risk to anyone?"

"I believe he's here. He doesn't pose the risk. What he was involved in created a risk."

"Could you ask him to share his information with Slate? That would clear your conscience and perhaps avoid these deaths you fear will come."

"I can try. I won't burden you with the details. It wouldn't alleviate my responsibility. I thank you for the clarity you've provided. This must remain my decision."

"I will include guidance for such a question in my sermon tomorrow, without revealing what you've shared. I can offer an alternative to those carrying guilt within them."

C hels had two missions. Luckily, they overlapped in execution. She moved through Slate's Progress, publicizing the service and hunting for Perry. She had mixed fortune with the former and none with the latter. Some residents were curious, some anxious and many ambivalent. There was another tension in the station's atmosphere she couldn't define. The whereabouts of Perry were unknown. The salvager had vanished.

She stepped from the lift onto the catwalk approaching Slate's aerie. Progress's commander connected to the station from this spot through all his senses. Sight, smell, taste, sound and the many vibrations inherent in Progress's existence. Slate looked up from his desk and smiled.

"Come in. I hear you've been pounding the corridors and catwalks, priming Pious' audience."

` Chels slumped in a chair. "I've covered every meter of this station in the last ten hours. Twice, or I'm a monkey."

"You're no monkey. You can use the intra-comm to get the message out. Less walking. Touch of a button and whoosh, your message is on every open screen and comm." He knitted his hands behind his head and reclined with a groan. "Though I don't recommend welding your butt to a chair for more than an hour at a time. I lose track."

"I needed personal contact and I needed to find someone."

"Thought you were happy with me."

"Not that kind of search, Slate. I met a spacer from deep in the Eddy two days ago. We spoke in my chapel and I received a confession." She'd come this far for a purpose. Pious' guidance hadn't motivated her to tell him Perry's secret but with Slate, she had to make her choice. "I've tried to rationalize what I'm going to tell you as information for the greater good but I'm betraying a trust in doing so. No amount of justification changes that."

Slate sat forward. "Your conscience should be clear if you share your knowledge."

"Should and reality don't always jive." She took a deep breath. "Recorders are off?"

Slate nodded. "Always for you."

She rested her hands on his and leaned as close as she could. "This spacer was or is, a salvager. Combing the Eddy for detritus to refurbish and sell."

"I know the niche. We buy and trade with a few though lately it's been drying up."

"My confidant and his partner found something not human. A piece of alien tech, he says."

Slate's hands tensed under hers. "Go on." His voice was barely audible.

"His partner had extensive communication experience in freighters before going independent and was convinced the machine was a jumpspace transmission device. They muddled through making it operational and tested it."

"Dangerous. One could be contacting an unfriendly species. Not that the human race has ever been unfriendly to a new tribe of fellow humans."

"Point taken. The danger in this case came from the machine itself. It wasn't what they thought. The spacer claims it was a weapon and they fired it. Once."

"Fools."

"Exactly. It sent a beam of some kind, he wasn't certain in the panic and surprise, through a jumpspace opening following a freighter to Argosy Station. They abandoned it and ran."

"Damn fools." Slate's hands sweated. "I've my own confession to share with you. This hasn't gained full rumor traction yet but it will soon, once the latest arrival's crew circulates. Argosy Station was attacked days ago. I learned about it this morning on a courier packet.

The freighter *Orson* limped out of spookspace simultaneously as an energy beam of some kind tore through a couple of docked ships and a piece of the station. Just before a Confluence frigate arrived from Bohr. The Realm is under suspicion of initiating an act of war."

"I hadn't heard the rumor and I've talked to a lot of people today." The manufactured rationale for her betrayal evaporated. She'd done right. But her loyalty to the church would always be in question going forward. "Now that I look outside my mission, there is a change present."

"Explain."

"Progress is on edge. A week ago, I swear I could have gathered two hundred people for Pious' address. Today I've sense that maybe a quarter of that will come. Something's on their minds whether they know the specifics or not."

"I've been too busy to notice," said Slate. "I need to change that. I'm meeting with the other administrators in an hour to inform them of the attack. I won't share your specifics with them but I'll jump the info on to the Eddy to look for this alien artifact. Did your confessor have any more details about its location?"

"On a recoil path still in the Eddy. Someone else could find it." Chels' stomach sank and wrenched. "What if there's an entire cache of these things in the Eddy?"

"We need to find your man if he's on Progress. The lure of alien tech could start an unprecedented bonanza frenzy. Or worse, the Confluence Navy finds it. The Realm would be under greater pressure than now."

"But it could avoid a war if we got there first."

"Keeping the information tight could also give the Realm the advantage we didn't have before. We'll share it but on our terms."

Chels worried that secrets were dangerous. She'd just betrayed one with good reason. She couldn't see how withholding knowledge from the Confluence was right.

"Who's your contact? Name? Description? Anything, Chels."

"Perry's his name. Little guy, half a head shorter'n me. Weighs maybe sixty kilos standard-gee. Brown hair shaved close to the scalp."

Slate keyed as she spoke. "I've got it in the system. If he's passed by a camera, we'll at least get a picture."

"What about near my chapel. If I give you a time he was there?"

"That'd help. You take over. I've got to meet my team in private."

Slate gave her his seat and rested a hand on her shoulder. "You did well to tell me, Chels."

"I hope so. If not, Pious'll be taking my confessions until they leave Progress."

Slate left her alone on his platform and she started the search. Fifteen minutes later, she had an image. Unfortunately, it was near useless. Perry, if the figure was him, had raised his collar and worn a hood on his way to the chapel. The picture of his back leaving was less helpful. Neither image was good enough for the system-ware to track him further. She'd have to find him the hard way. By covering Progress in person. Again.

Chapter 15

Pious ascended the makeshift dais. His doubts ebbed in this role. The preacher mantle gave him life. In another time, he could've followed the role of priest serving a settled congregation. Nurturing their lives from birth to adulthood, counselling them when requested, offering hope and succor when needed.

His chosen path veered long ago from such a quiet clerical existence. This was his calling, looking for a nodal point in strangers' existences to provide guidance and faith in a moment. It required a special talent. Pious had the gift. Did Atone possess it? Pious must find out soon. He would let Atone try his voice out in the Eddy. Today, the crowd belonged to Pious. To re-engage where he'd left off months before on Progress.

He surveyed the attendees and waited for the nervous chatter to wane. Chels had done well as a place keeper. The assemblage was small, it didn't fill the space but their eyes and posture told him they were keen to hear his words. *Reinforce and recruit.*

"I recognize many familiar faces and thank you for the continued patronage." He'd ask for funds though he didn't need them this time. It made the givers feel they reciprocated his spiritual gifts.

"To those new to myself and the brothers, I welcome you. Whether your attendance is curiosity-driven or you seek an answer to the puzzle of existence on the frontier, you may find solace today or in the future within my words. I address each of you one to one." He ensured eye contact with each person while he spoke.

"I stand before you but not above you. This elevation is purely physical so all can hear my voice without me having to shout or mic."

He cleared his throat to punctuate his point. "Never above you. If you were to hear my sins, you'd realize a man of the cloth has to make many judgments of situational necessity, not always of ethical necessity. My crimes of the soul are neither less nor more than yours, be assured. It is how I choose to compensate which is important. How will you compensate? How will you atone? The answer lies within you." He watched Chels at the edge of the circle nod with her eyes closed. He searched for the other, the confessor she'd exposed. Not present, Pious thought. He hoped the station-wide broadcast of this address reached that man in whatever sanctum he'd chosen.

"My conscience may not be clear, how many of us who've endured jumpspace nightmares can say otherwise?" Pious patted his chest with an open hand. "My conscience will never be clear but my heart is. Because I confide my sins in God, in friends and in colleagues. You have all of those available to you. I returned to Slate's Progress not solely to hear your confessions, nor to pass judgment on your transgressions. I returned to give you hope that you are never too far down the road to spiritual ruin that an act of correction can't reduce your guilt."

He'd given enough stick, now for the carrot. "I see despair in some of your faces." He softened his voice. "Do not be discouraged. Your presence, and those who are not present but listen and watch, tells me you care enough to seek a change. Don't hesitate. Turn to your friend, or to a stranger, or to me and my brothers. Most of all, turn to yourself. Forgiveness starts in here," he touched his chest again, "and here." He tapped his forehead.

The many eyes upon him were nervous, troubled. There was an uneasy current running through Progress. How could he disrupt the negative flow? Most were spacers. A common thread?

Pious coughed and swallowed the last of his water. "Jumpspace taxes the body and spirit. It divides the individual in two, splits perceptions, subverts loyalties. Its dark corners were not meant to be seen by our eyes. But we have opened that enigma and must learn to survive with its revelations. The key is within you." Pious touched his chest again. "Within all of us. Share your nightmares as well as your dreams. Look inside and ask, what can I give the sufferer who walks and ships beside me?"

He ended with a short prayer; an old invocation adapted over the centuries to spacer allusion. He saw DualE moving along the crowd's perimeter. Like him, she never wavered from duty. She possessed the single-minded intensity required for their respective roles. Could hers be transferred to a different cause?

The energy Pious felt when he'd entered the dome ebbed. The mind over matter struggle was always with him. Mind and spirit lost inevitable ground. He stepped to the deck and passed amongst the crowd, touching them as much for his own physical support as reassurance for them. "My brothers' ears are mine, we are one. Please seek them out while I rest for the next stage of our journey to the Eddy."

Atone, Cardinal and Remorse spread through the mass, giving heed to each person in turn. He clasped Chels' arm and escorted her back to the *Penance*.

"I'm weary, Chels. The jump from Argosy Station drained me. Would you man the *Penance's* airlock for me in case anyone comes forward?"

"Of course, Brother Pious. But I can't duplicate the guidance you would dispense."

He sat on a hard cot. "If you listen, that will be enough. I will meet any who wish in the tavern where you and I first met in one shift. We will raise enough funds for you to carry on our mission after the *Penance* leaves."

"You're going to the Eddy? Another jump? You may be reaching your limit. I know. I retired from spookspace a half dozen jumps too late. Don't let that happened to you."

"Good advice, Chels. As with most advice, I'll likely choose to ignore it for a greater purpose. Or greater in my mind. The hardest thing to admit sometimes is when the torch must be passed to better and stronger hands."

"You're not there yet, brother. You can carry on without deepsleep journeys weakening you."

He waved her to the 'lock and stretched out. Despite the personal strain, it had been a good sermon. Where and how would the fruit manifest from his labor?

DualE glided amongst the audience, alert for any threat. She searched for anyone fitting Perry's general description. If she found him, what were the next steps? Take him to Slate? Interrogate him herself? Who'd receive her information? Slate, Pious or Rowland?

Pious' words filtered into her. A clear conscience? Easy to purify through rationalization. Small transgressions in light of a greater good. Maintain truth within her heart? Tougher to weasel away the crimes. How many decisions made in the line of fire had brought greater good? Few. Decisions in those circumstances were about survival. Hers, her squad. Anything greater lost focus in the moment. The greater picture was for people like Rowland. Or Pious. Let them carry the burden.

Pious was right, the only judgment which mattered was one's own. She didn't look forward to her final encounter with DualE the judge.

A figure on the periphery caught her eye. Head covered but the size matched Chels' description of Perry. She lost the glimpse among taller people and he was across the atrium. She retraced her path behind the crowd. When she reached the spot, he was gone.

She chanced a quick look outside but the passageway was empty. If it was Perry, he knew the station better than she.

Pious' voice raised in pitch. He neared conclusion. She returned inside, listening but trying not to be distracted by self-recrimination. That was deepsleep's function.

Chapter 16

The *Whisper* entertained its second set of visitors in an hour. Higgins looked bored. Marshall ran a finger over the airlock seal. She looked disappointed in Zofie's craft. Was their *Banshee* that superior? Judging by their well-worn dockyard suits, Zofie doubted it.

"This is my partner, Willie Renfrew." Zofie invited the pair to sit between she and Carver.

"You spend much time in the Eddy, Renfrew?" Higgins gave Carver an appraising eye. Marshall glanced at him once, then turned her attention back to the interior of the ship.

She was the prime evaluator. Her questions, if they came, would dig to the core of their interest.

"Some," said Carver. "Prospecting isn't my passion."

"What is your passion?" Marshall's attention to Zofie's partner returned in an instant.

Be careful, Carver. These might be clients.

"Maintaining a credit balance above the poverty line. Taking my retirement in snatches when I have surplus funds. I'm a hedonist."

Zofie didn't know if Marshall believed him or not but it was a good answer.

"Let's hope cooperation can allow us all to enjoy luxurious times." Marshall turned to Zofie. "What incentive are you offering?"

"The best rate of return on your goods in either Argosy Station or Bohr. Mister Renfrew and I have extensive contacts on both Argosy Station and on Gamma Hub in Bohr."

"Gamma is primarily a naval hub," said Marshall. "Isn't that a little dangerous? Dealing with the authorities overseeing importation enforcement?"

"Can you think of better camouflage?" Zofie caught Carver's attention.

He took up the narrative. "Depending on your goods, we can run them all the way to Bohr or be content with a reduced but less risky return by passing them on to a middleman in Argosy."

Higgins snorted. "We can get our shipment to Argosy Station as easily as you can. Who cares about Gamma? The *Banshee's* a stout barnacle. I'm not certain this tub has got more than two or three jumps left in her."

Zofie repressed an emotional reply before it left her mouth. Was he negotiating or just rude? Marshall's lips tightened in response to her partner's statement. Higgins thought he was negotiating.

"The integrity of the *Whisper* isn't in question," Zofie answered. "And even if it was, not your concern. As to you getting your goods to Argosy yourselves, that is quite possible. But you won't get the price I can, nor will you be replenishing your stock back here. Which you will be if you let us escort the transport."

"This is all moot," said Carver. "We don't know what you have or how much."

"We need to know if we can work together first, Mister Renfrew." Marshall stood up. Higgins followed a moment later.

Zofie's intuition was confirmed. Marshall ran their show. She could live with that. She preferred dealing with another woman, less emotion and fewer distracting hormones. "I agree, Marshall. We'll both evaluate partnership potential and reconvene on neutral ground or perhaps aboard the *Banshee*. That would give us a chance to appraise your overhead level. Renfrew and I believe in reinvesting our profits in additional cargo and ship fundamental maintenance, not frivolous decoration."

"I'll be in touch." Marshall stopped midway in the 'lock. "Are you contemplating business with the Reds?"

The tone was offhand but Zofie realized Marshall had likely seen the previous visitors to the *Whisper* come and go. It wouldn't do to minimize the facts. "We'll see. It's possible. Having more than one set of clients is often a good thing. Each shipment detracts attention from the other. Especially if your goods walk a fine line between legal and contraband."

"That fine line is a large grey band these days," said Marshall. She and Higgins left with no further word.

Back inside the *Whisper*, 'lock closed, she and Carver shared a drink.

"Do you reckon Marshall figures you're the lead here and I'm hired help?" Carver asked.

"Well, she knows I'm the frontperson, whether or not she underestimates your value, I couldn't tell. Higgins is a wasted suit. I don't understand why she needs him."

"He could be a temporary bodyguard." Carver rubbed his lips. "She doesn't act like a solo operator. I wager there's another partner somewhere."

"I agree. Marshall's the one we concentrate on."

Carver poured a second drink. His recovery from her drugs and deepsleep was coming along. "You're confused about something though. I can tell from the wrinkles on your brow."

"She didn't broach the subject of terms. She's confident whatever they want brokered has sufficient rarity and value that we'll take whatever percentage she offers."

"Higgins' comments about Argosy Station being a possible final destination might be a clue."

"That was a slip. Marshall flinched for a moment. Confluence territory is their goal. What's worth running naval blockades right now? Why not wait for the peace accord to settle and follow the rules?"

"Could be Schoenfeldium," said Carver. "You hear any rumors of a current find?"

"Nothing. Why ship it to Argosy? Worth just as much out here."

"Except there aren't as many jumpships out here as I would expect. Did the Realm Armada evaporate, move or never exist?"

"I've no idea. Could Marshall have a second alien find?"

"I suppose. If there's more than one, there could be a dozen."

"If so, the entire Eddy would know about it. No, Carver, it's something else entirely. I put my head on it. Until we hear from Marshall, I need to find a freighter for the Reds. And come up with a cover story."

"Why doesn't Willie Renfrew invest in surplus mining equipment? We'll ship it back to Argosy Station to resell to the next wave of would-be prospectors."

"A solid cover for the artifacts packed with the equipment, radiation-shielded to discourage detailed human examination." Zofie's thoughts leapt ahead. "I knew you'd be more than a lucky talisman, Carver. You'd best do your buying remotely. If one person recognized you, there could be more. Sorry, you are still confined to ship."

"At least let me get out and stretch my legs. I'll wear a hooded flimsuit."

"Okay. But you talk to no one."

"Not to be paranoid but an alternative explanation for Marshall's circumspection occurs to me."

Her suspicions were not unique. "I know. You're not being paranoid, just careful."

"They could be the authorities."

Zofie caught her breath. This complication so soon wasn't welcome. "Confluence or Realm?"

"No idea. The implication of either baffles. You're small fish, there'd have to be a more important target."

"I don't want to be bait. I'll make more inquiries. I'd like to see the *Banshee*. If they are undercover, Carver, you know what that means."

"Yeah, they'll identify me."

"There's no official bounty but I don't wish to lose my new partner before we begin operation."

"I'm not going back to Argosy with you. The politics don't interest me. I'd rather take the frontier risks in the Eddy than he duplicity of politicians proscribing new rules for their citizens in the guise of peace and prosperity. I'm waiting here for DualE and the brothers. I'll help you set up your transport but you're on your own back on Argosy or Gamma." Carver crossed his arms. "Or I walk into the shipyard and surrender to some actual authorities and wait for DualE and Admiral Rowland to get me free."

"I can live with that. If these artifacts are real, I'm happy not to share the proceeds."

She left the *Whisper* and headed back to the yard's business core, such as it was, loaded with questions. Each answer taking her closer to riches or disaster.

Chapter 17

"I think we should split up," DualE told Chels. "It's the best way to cover Progress. From your description, I've a good idea what Perry looks like. I'll record any possibilities for you to confirm." She wanted to scout the station on her own, not just to search for Perry but to perform her task for the navy.

"I know Slate's Progress from tip to tail," said Chels.

"Your knowledge might blind you in spots. You know it too well. Your eyes can assume a view which isn't real. He could be in the places I would explore."

"Sounds like a military mantra. Four eyes better than two?"

"It's saved my skin more than once. Two fresh eyes can be better than two tired or lazy ones. I'm not saying you're lazy, Chels, in fact I believe the opposite. But we're on a tight timetable."

"Which half do you want?"

"The half you're certain he wouldn't be in? No offense."

"I disagree. If what you say is true, then I should give you the half I'm certain he should be in."

DualE recognized the truth. "You're right. I'm lagged from the jump. Where *should* he be?"

"Perry was on the skids. I know the situation well, having been broke myself many times. If he could afford a berth, it'd be below the life-systems levels. The vibration and noise aren't dampened down there so tube coffins are cheap. Once your credit is exhausted, you hook a sling among the in-between spaces and hope you don't get mugged for your clothes. Be warned, it's not a pleasant place. Nor safe."

"Thanks. Nasty and perilous are in my blood. I'll be in ready-mode." DualE checked her stunners and knife harness inside her flimsuit. "See you in twelve hours. Or less, if we find him."

Chels nodded and moved away from the *Crossed Swords*.

DualE secured her ship and the *Penance* in the brothers' absence. Pious and team were connecting with current and potential followers in the chapel. Her concern for their safety was small with them together. Legitimate danger would come soon enough in the Eddy.

She made her way via dropshaft to the life-systems decks. They were well-manned and brightly lit. A stowaway wouldn't remain undiscovered here for long. Nevertheless, she covered as much as was open to civilians in quick time.

She moved on, descending into the dim levels below. Posters advertising cheap cubbies led her forward. At last, she came to an automated check-in.

"How many shifts?" asked a mechanical voice.

"Three if you have space. Are you busy?"

"Many available, pick from the menu."

The occupied berths numbered four. Unoccupied numbered in the dozens. "Business is slow," said DualE.

"Pick room, please."

"How come you're so empty?"

"Pick room, please."

"I'm meeting a shipmate, any chance he's booked in?"

Progress' minimal security helped her. DualE scanned names of the tenants. She tapped a vacancy closest to the occupied berths. She'd give them a look before continuing her search.

She turned her back to the check-in screen. "Chels, it's me. I know you've probably done this but can you check photo identities of these residents?" She tapped in the names on her wrist screen. While she waited for Chels' response, DualE paid for the berth in cash. The images came back of four varied spacers of various shapes, color and sizes. What they shared was a look of desperation and that none of them were Perry.

"I'll be back later," she informed the machine. "Where can I eat."

"Follow green line to your left and above. Discount coupon for my guests." A plastic tag spit from the check-in panel.

DualE followed the intermittent green indicators and smelled the bistro two turns before she saw it. Inside, two other patrons ate and drank in silence. A serv-bot approached her. "Where's the rest of your custom?" DualE asked, not expecting any better answer than the cube hotel's AI.

"All here. Order from menu please."

"No navy personnel? They always end up in a place like this towards leave-end." She knew from personal experience. Where was the Realm's force which backed up the secession threat? If not near Slate's Progress, then the Eddy must be their muster point.

"All custom here. Place order please."

"Coffee." She nodded at the other two patrons but neither gave here more than a brief glance before returning to their meal. The glances were clear on one point. Don't bother us.

She sipped her coffee and contemplated her next step. Deeper into the bowels of Progress. She slipped out when the other patrons were engaged in ignoring her.

She made her way below the berth level. The illumination on these decks was minimal. She wouldn't make herself an easy target so she foreswore using her suit-light and relied on light-amplifying goggles to see. She scanned ceiling, crannies, nooks and below catwalks for habitation evidence. She found two long-unused hammocks slung on high conduits but nothing else. No food refuse. Progress ran lean but robot cleaners had done their job.

DualE automatically ascended from stand-by to combat mode. In the field, one scanned for threats while simultaneously evaluating strong and weak strategic points in the landscape or fortifications.

Here, she hunted for signs of habitation and noted the station's vulnerabilities. Whether or not she'd ever need or want to pass her intel on to Rowland would depend on future circumstance. If her ex-colleagues were in danger then she'd share. She did not imagine the Confluence attacking Slate's as a legitimate threat. It was a commercial port, and so far as she'd seen, relatively undefended, let alone a staging hub for a mass offensive against Bohr.

Scuff marks caught her eye on a ladder leading up into darkness. She knelt close, noting the worn finish on the rung centers. A regular path for many users over the years. She tilted her head back. Her goggles showed twenty or so rungs above her. She clamped a normal light to the ladder and turned off her night vision. She stood to one side and switched on the light. No response. She was alone.

DualE tried raising Chels on her radio but the interference from the intervening mechanical levels was too great. She switched off the light and climbed in the dark. Halfway up, she paused to listen. Just the station creaking and clanking above the background buzz. She refitted her night goggles and resumed the climb.

At the top rung, DualE saw the boot. She hooked an arm through the rung and prodded the foot. Stiff. The matching leg curled against an unmoving torso. She switched to normal illumination for a better look at the head. The lips pulled back in a rictus grin, distorting the face but she had no doubt she'd found Perry.

Had someone else found him first? While he was still alive, hiding from his conscience or an enemy?

She detailed the lonely cocoon in her mind. Like a wounded animal, Perry'd secluded himself from predators. Slate's people would have to determine cause of death but she wanted to memorize everything she could with a professional eye in case the official version contradicted what she saw.

She descended the ladder, wondering how Chels would react. She hoped the brotherhood's disciple had another soul-confessor to replace

Pious once they'd left for the Eddy. There was a deadly artifact somewhere in the big beyond and one of the two men who could find it was out of the game. Permanently.

Chapter 18

Carver, in his Willie Renfrew guise, searched surplus machinery caches within a week's transport from the Eddy shipyard. He tagged three prospects.

The first was an abandoned ore refining operation near a cluster of asteroids which were tapped out decades ago. The cover might be shaky on that one; if the original owners left the equipment for scrap, why would they have value now? He'd let Zofie work on it.

The second batch were agricultural terra-farming rock weevils never deployed. Near as Carver could tell, they'd never even made orbit around the target planet. They were an open-bid-lot which so far, no one had pursued. Again, the risk of sudden interest in what the majority deemed worthless was a concern.

The last, a century-old observatory, held the most promise. For one thing, the pieces were bigger than weevils and thus better to mask the artifacts. Even in freefall, the masses should deter anything but a cursory inspection. And despite the age, there might be actual value in the equipment. The drawback was the observation complex was mostly intact. It would need dismantling. Again, he'd leave it up to Zofie to decide if she would sub-contract the work. He wasn't going to.

He had other plans. Getting a message to DualE for one, Zofie's assurances aside. Zofie monitored his work so it would have to be something she was unlikely to see. A beacon? If he could access *Whisper's* emergency beacon and code a short signal, he could control the sending when she was asleep or off ship. The *Crossed Swords* should pick it up. DualE was Eddy-bound and would be looking. It was worth a shot. As long as Zofie didn't overreact if she found him out.

While he accessed the beacon's controls, his mind worked on the real cargo. Alien artifacts. He'd been a broker, a fixer in a previous career, so he had no compunction about keeping the artifacts in private hands. Little good ever came out of the military having exclusive right to new technology.

What bothered Carver was why move it? If location held clues to the artifacts' function, then shipping them to the Confluence destroyed part of the key information. And thus, value. A local auction would be the simplest course but less lucrative than the Confluence would provide. The Reds didn't want the Realm to have this. If it did, Chancellor Mekli would use it as a bargaining chip. The Reds weren't Eddy. They were Confluence sympathizers or maybe agents. If Zofie got caught, they wouldn't have their cover blown. Not right away. Zofie would be sacrificed. Carver too if he didn't get away from her.

He needed to get this venture done and hold her to her promise to free him.

Zofie'd snooped in every bar in the shipyard until her legs ached from being pushed around dance floors and hiking the corridors when transport couldn't be found.

She slipped off her boots and rubbed her toes while waiting for the servbot to pour her drink.

"I saw your cross."

Zofie looked up from the table. A woman about her size stood before her, displaying a black and silver cross on a neck chain. Zofie felt the small weight of her own gift from Brother Pious back in Bohr. Pious had not absolved her of her sins but she'd gained peace of mind after her psychological meltdown aboard the *Pollux*.

"A token to remind me of past deeds," said Zofie. "Please sit. Tell me how you came by yours."

"A gift from a missionary months ago on Slate's Progress."

"Brother Pious?" Maybe this woman was the link Zofie needed to penetrate the veil surrounding the shipyards' inhabitants.

"Yes. You know him?"

"I know *a* Pious. Travels aboard the *Penance* with Atone, Remorse and Cardinal."

"Then we are well met. I'm Cassity. I became a follower after his sermon on Slate's. And you?"

"Zofie Ked. Small universe, wouldn't want to giftwrap it, right? Can I offer you drink? I'm avoiding alcohol at the moment but won't be offended if you want to indulge. I've walked from one end of the shipyard to the other and then some today." The servbot placed Zofie's mug on the table.

"Eddy whisky, straight up," ordered Cassity. "Why? If I may ask."

Zofie fingered her cross. "Trying to get the lay of the station and the people aboard. Ships and repair seem at a minimum but I get no sense for the people. Seems a closed shop and no one's inclined to share with an outsider." Zofie exhaled and stared past Cassity.

"It's not as hopeless as *you* look, I'm sure. What do you want to know? Maybe I can help."

Zofie offered a sincere expression while she evaluated the woman. What sins had driven her to Pious? Cassity's cooperation could be like a wild animal, skittish if one moved or spoke wrong. "I'm a trader. A brokerage agent. I work for myself so I deal on a small scale. Transporting cargo to Argosy Station or all the way to Bohr Confluence if required. I take the risk and find the market while my temporary partners in the Eddy can accumulate their next consignment. I cover my costs and take a small percentage for profit. It's slow going but I don't have to worry about pleasing a boss."

"You're looking for clients?"

"No, I've found clients, I want to know if I can trust them. There are too many who'd wear my guts for garters, going on past experience." Zofie eased her feet back into her boots.

Cassity grimaced. A memory in tune with Zofie's painful learning curve?

"Brokerage isn't my line of work. I'm a maintenance analyst. I do hear things though. Anyone specific in mind?"

Zofie knew her approach had worked. "I wouldn't want you to add to your confession next time you meet the brothers so I'm not looking for you to betray a confidence." Though that was exactly what she needed. "I'm dealing with Marshall and Higgins, not even sure what they need shipped but they've approached me and I think we can do business. But I don't want my first jump as an independent operator to go bad due to contraband."

Cassity nodded. "Marshall, I know. Higgins is contract muscle. Doubt he's a partner. I'm surprised Marshall would require your services."

"Why's that?"

"She's a broker herself. Not independent. I'm not sure who she works for but she's not without resources. She has her own ship. The *Banshee*'s good gear."

Zofie wondered if she should ask Cassity's opinion on the Reds. If they were more than advertised, she could give herself away to one of their allies. She needed more time before pushing this friendliness with Cassity too far.

Zofie lowered her head and grasped Cassity's hand. "We should offer a prayer for meeting and keeping Pious' mission alive."

"I pray I will see him again."

"Your prayer may come true."

Cassity returned Zofie's grip for a few moments while each kept their thoughts unspoken.

Zofie released first. "I must return to my ship. Can we meet again. Here? In another shift? If you discovered any more information for me about Marshall, I'd be grateful, Sister Cassity."

"Of course. Make it two shifts. I have to EVA on my next assignment and I don't know if I'll be held over outside for an extra period."

"Then in two. My ship's the *Whisper.*" Zofie parted ways with her new source and headed back to Carver. She'd need to hack the shipyard's systems and find out more about Marshall and her need for a third-party shipper.

C arver heard the rap at the lock.

"It's Marshall. We're here to talk to Zofie."

Her face filled the screen from the 'lock cam. A second pair of shoulders lurked behind her but Marshall blocked the face. Higgins didn't rate even a mention from his own partner?

"Zofie's not here, Marshall."

"She told us to meet here. Do you mind if we come in?"

Carver slid the 'lock open.

Marshall moved past him and said, "I believe you two know each other."

Carver knew her companion but didn't welcome his company. "Gar Kondradt. Argosy Station finally throw you out?"

"Denz," said Kondradt. "Or Renfrew. Which do you prefer? I'd think you'd don a new identity for a liaison with Zofie."

"I prefer liaising with her over any dealings with you."

Kondradt was unfazed. "Nevertheless, we're here. Ready to talk."

"I'd prefer not talking with you, either. You tried to swindle me, then tried to kill me. Me and an entire freighter crew and the barnacles they rode with."

Kondradt maintained his cool. "*Your* interpretation of events, Denz, not mine. I had my orders from the Chancellor to stop your Schoenfeldium shipment at any cost. Elimination was *his* intention. I did my best to turn the operation into a navigational diversion and hijacking. You're the one who forced Zofie over the edge." Kondradt apparently had no secrets from Marshall. Was she his new Zofie?

"She worked for you." Carver ensured his path to the door was clear. He placed himself between the visitors and the escape route.

"No, she pretended to work for me. She was Chancellor Mekli's agent provocateur all along. Frankly, I'm surprised a man of your resourcefulness would allow himself to be tied to her again."

"Let's call it a circumstantial alliance rather than a partnership. Temporary. I help Zofie in return for her aid in my work." Carver turned his attention to Marshall. "In my role as Zofie's aide, are your needs legitimate or was it all a blind to bring Kondradt here? Give him another try at revenge for sending my lode to the Confluence instead of the Realm? This shipyard has a lot of new-looking structures. I bet they were paid for by the discovery royalties on my bonanza."

Kondradt answered for her. "Our need is legitimate. Zofie Ked may have some emotional issues but she is a good broker. And I desire relative anonymity."

"Then why reveal yourself?" A new voice joined the conversation.

"Zofie. Welcome." Kondradt nudged Marshall toward the 'lock. "Make sure we aren't interrupted."

Zofie didn't enter.

"You've no need to fear me, Zofie. I need your help." Kondradt hadn't moved from his seat. "Hear me out. You've spent the last shift combing the yards looking for information about Marshall. Who she works for, what she's shipping? Am I right?"

"You remain well-informed," said Carver. "Now that we know Marshall works for you, can I ask who you work for?" He kept an eye on Zofie. She had calmed herself.

"I work for the Realm. That hasn't changed."

Kondradt worked for himself first. Carver doubted the man's loyalties had changed because of the Confluence-Realm peace accord.

"Why would the Realm need my help?" asked Zofie.

A critical question, Carver thought.

"Because you're not part of the official bureaucracy. There are times, and this temporary peace is one of them, when independent operators function more freely than normal channels."

"Bullshit. You mean we operate more secretively and if caught, are expendable with no harm done to either side."

Kondradt shrugged. "One interpretation. Along with the risk comes greater reward. Zofie, I can guess what you want. A rebuilt network I so callously destroyed in my myopic fervor to serve Chancellor Mekli and an independent Realm. It was a mistake I regret to this day. I won't lie and say I'm trying to make it up to you with this contract. That's up to you to make it work. Your success is a by-product I can accept and welcome. The Realm will ally with the Confluence but we will maintain certain areas of complete independence."

Carver applauded and Kondradt scowled. Marshall tensed, as if ready to pounce.

Kondradt touched her arm, then turned back to Carver. "You remain skeptical, Denz?"

"Not at all, I completely accept your goal for some shred of freedom. And I accept you don't believe it will undermine the peace process going forward. What Bohr doesn't know or suspect, can't hurt them."

Kondradt smiled. "You should work with us. You have a quick grasp of reality."

"No thanks. I've already got too many careers going."

"What do you want me to ship, Gar?"

Kondradt turned back to Zofie. "Nothing embargoed. No weapons, no tech."

"Then you won't need much room?" Carver asked.

"Depends." Kondradt rose and shuffled in *Whisper's* small cabin. He tapped walls and the deck and pulled out one of the cryo coffins. "Are you going back with her?" he asked Carver.

"No. I'm waiting for my clients to show up from Argosy Station."

"Excellent. Zofie will have room for a passenger."

"You're shipping an information courier," said Zofie. "Marshall?" Zofie glanced outside.

"Smart guess. I knew my renewed faith in you was not misplaced. She may be disoriented when we bring her aboard. You put her in standard deepsleep. Upon arrival in Bohr, you will escort her to a rendezvous which she will reveal."

"Info-mule," said Zofie.

An unfamiliar term to Carver but he inferred meaning from context. A shadow subconscious filled with confidential data. He scanned the *Whisper's* cabin. How many snoopers had Kondradt planted on his inspection?

Kondradt stood in the 'lock. "You've two shifts to accept. Don't turn me down, Zofie. I can accelerate your recovery and enhance your future success. And don't run. This is a golden opportunity. It would help if you have a material shipment to accompany you aboard whichever jumpfreighter you choose. Denz, good to see you alive and thriving." He turned and left.

Marshall poked her head in. "I promise I'll be no threat."

Once the two were alone, Carver put a finger to his lips to indicate silence. After five minutes he went outside the *Whisper*. Kondradt and Marshall were nowhere in sight. "Come out," he called to Zofie. He closed the 'lock from the outside. "We need to review in private."

"The bastard bugged my ship," she said.

"He planted it in the coffin. I'll deal with it later. Right now, I need to summarize your options for the Reds' camouflage."

Chapter 19

Pious repeated his evening mantra with difficulty. The breathing exercise wouldn't cooperate. The doctor in Gamma Hub had been right in her diagnosis. The treatment would've taken him well past the *Penance's* departure date so he accepted the medicines he could transport and an uncertain life expectancy.

"Good news," said Cardinal. "I've found us barnacle to the Eddy shipyards leaving tomorrow. Not a direct jump to the Eddy but it's cheap. It's a small freighter and has room for one more ship. Do we draw straws to see who stays behind to barnacle *Crossed Swords* later?"

Pious considered the alternatives. *Penance*, though refitted and upgraded, still only had room for four passengers. DualE made five and he would not leave her behind. He wanted security and more time to evaluate her. Another decision driven by time pressure rather than logical compromise. Use it to advantage, he realized. "It's an opportunity for one of you to stay here and build our mission on Slate's." An occasion to demonstrate leadership. "Brothers, I wish DualE to accompany the *Penance* to the Eddy. Cardinal, we need you as well for potential astrogation once we reach the further frontier. Atone and Remorse, I ask you to decide between you." Avoiding the final decision, he'd lowered his stress from command, if only by a small bit.

Remorse looked unsure. A good follower, not a leader. Atone spoke, "If Brother Remorse doesn't object, I embrace the challenge."

"I won't object," said a relieved-looking Remorse.

"Very well, Brother Atone," said Pious. "In addition to building followers here, you must counsel Sister Chels through her grief and guilt at Perry's unfortunate death. Whether by his own hand or another, we share the blame."

"I'm prepared to provide guidance where I can, Brother Pious."

"Thank you." Was Atone ready? No, not yet. One rarely was ready. But neither Pious nor the brotherhood had the luxury of waiting until he was. "This will test you. When you're overwhelmed, and it will happen, do not choose that time to barnacle aboard DualE's ship. Stay and soldier through. Join us when you judge Chels is capable of maintaining our message on her own. Then go to Slate and search for passage to the Eddy."

"Understood. Thank you for your faith in me." Atone's voice cracked almost imperceptibly.

Pious placed a hand on Atone's shoulder. "You have faith within you which is as important. Brother Cardinal, we have departure preparations to make."

Pious shut the airlock and sat. He waited for Cardinal to send the message then signalled him to shut off the comm. "Please sit, brothers. I have some news of my own to share." The three took their places while he considered his words.

"You have no doubt noticed my increased frailty and frequent exhaustion. I dismiss it publicly as a bad jumpspace reaction but that isn't the case. While we were on Gamma Hub, I had a medical to ensure my increasing shortness of breath was nothing for concern. Unfortunately, it was. I have a cancer in my lungs which is aggressive and far-progressed. I am on medications which provide small relief but do not forestall the inevitable. I will survive our mission to the Eddy, this I have vowed. You needn't worry about my strength to carry forward our work but all things have a time limit. Brother Atone will assume a leadership role on Slate's and Cardinal and Remorse will carry more of the mission's load in the Eddy as needed. We have each other for support and we all serve the same God. This is not to be discussed outside our group. I must exclude DualE and Carver Denz; they are protection from without, not within. I see no change in our routine, though I'll need more rest than normal."

"Your courage inspires," said Atone.

"Not courage brother, faith."

Cardinal opened his mouth but no words came forth. He would take it the hardest, Pious thought. He was their navigator but relied on Pious for all other guidance.

Remorse, to his credit, regained his composure first. "Do you know when?"

"The end?" Pious shook his head. "Health, like faith, is not always definable in hard numbers. I'll know before any doctor does, I'm sure. Alert DualE that she will join us aboard *Penance* for the jump to the Eddy."

———————✠✠✠✠———————

DualE stared for a moment at her comm. Then she stood and packed her kit. She was bugging out aboard *Penance*, and being the prepared soldier she was, she didn't stop to ruminate over the change in plan. Adaptation was a key to survival in the corps.

She resisted dividing their force further but Pious was determined to reach the Eddy. She was too, not least to find Carver.

Jumping to orders was ingrained within her. But she wasn't in the navy anymore. Pious needed to move quickly for some reason and she would question his motives before the jump. She added Atone's identity to the *Crossed Swords'* control link. He'd better look after her ship when he jumped solo. She put the *Crossed Swords* into sleep mode, locking off her personal records. Atone could bunk aboard and barnacle it but access to files wouldn't happen. Not that she didn't trust him, he was a man of the cloth. But who knew what boredom could lead to?

DualE walked the gantry to the *Penance* and spoke into the external comm.

"One moment, if you will, DualE." Cardinal's voice sounded strained. The brothers were surprised at their sudden departure too? "A bit crowded in here while we sort out Brother Atone's gear."

"Take your time." She stepped back and turned to scan the spiderweb of dockyard connectors. The small number of ships in port still bothered her. Were the Realm's forces concentrated in the Eddy? There were lots of questions and few answers. Perry came to mind again. The salvager's death weighed on Chels and Pious, yet Pious was willing to leave Chels with Brother Atone to reconcile her guilt. DualE admired all the brothers' dedication to their cause but in her estimation Atone wasn't ready for this field promotion. Who ever was?

Her discovery of Perry's corpse would repeat in deepsleep. As much as she wanted to catch up to Carver, DualE continued to wonder what pushed Pious to jump to the Eddy so soon.

The lock opened and Atone joined her on the gantry. His face was ashen. The task before him had started to sink in? He said, "I'll stow a few jump essentials aboard the *Crossed Swords* for now but I intend to bunk within Progress. Chels is fragile over Perry's death and I want to be accessible to her and other followers."

She admired his choice. Maybe Atone had more potential than she thought. "The ship is commed to your command for habitation and navigation to barnacle."

"Thank you. Good luck on your journey to the Eddy. I hope you find Carver well."

"If not, you'll have another soul to pray for when I'm finished with Zofie."

"Revenge is a sour recompense, DualE."

"I'm used to its taste, brother. Good luck on your mission here." She heard the klaxon from within the *Penance*. "Sounds like we're ready to leave."

DualE entered the *Penance* and cycled the airlock. Cardinal huddled over the control console. Remorse was checking the cryo coffins and Pious sat cross-legged on the deck in meditation. All three looked glum. Leaving Atone behind or female intrusion? How could she mitigate the change in dynamics within *Penance*? Prove her worth. DualE stepped around Pious and began her own survey of Atone's coffin. On the occasions she'd used drugs to endure jumpspace nightmares, she'd wished for cryo. On the cryo jumps to here, she'd wished for drugs. Had she reached her spookspace limit like Chels? DualE would hate to be exiled to the Eddy if she was. If she had to retire from space, she'd prefer to live within the Confluence. On solid ground. A mountain retreat. She'd had enough water, growing up on Aqueous Prime and enough freefall and artificial gravity since leaving her home world for the navy.

The *Penance* jolted free from docking and Cardinal piloted her away from Progress towards a lighted spiderweb some kilos distant. DualE peered over his shoulder, searching for their transport. They were almost upon it before she could discern details. "Not much bigger than a tug," she said.

"You can see why there was no room for your ship." Cardinal manoeuvred their ship between two other barnacles and *Penance* jolted again as the clamps extracted.

"I'll EVA to check lockdown," DualE volunteered.

Pious opened his eyes and stood. "Thank you." He braced himself as he moved to his coffin. "I will see you in the Eddy and receive your cleanse there."

He climbed into the cryo sleeper, closed the clear lid and the coffin retracted into the holding chute. The status panel on its end flashed orange signalling cryo initiation sequence, then glowed solid green. Pious was under.

What sins and nightmares haunted him through spookspace? DualE wondered. She slipped into the EVA gear and exited. The curvature of their transport's hull was noticeable and she had to triple check each anchor before she was satisfied *Penance* wouldn't be flung away during accel or decel. She eyed the two other barnacles as well. They appeared solid. She could feel the pull of the transport beginning its run away from Slate's Progress in prep for jump. From the size of the ship, she'd guessed its jumpdrive occupied the majority of space inside. She returned inside to see Remorse's coffin activated.

"I can remain awake until we reach max accel, Brother Cardinal."

"The *Penance* is on shutdown sequence but I leave it up to you to decide when you want to go under." He climbed into his berth and she envied his calmness before the jumpspace ordeal.

Alone amongst the unconscious brothers, DualE evaluated her new career choice. Partnering with Carver had seemed the best way forward from a dead-end desk job in the navy, punishment for providing unexpected results from her last mission. Carver was of a like mind, his commercial endeavors losing their appeal and the lure of adventure an attractive option to purge internal greed. And the chance to distance himself from the woman he'd wanted to marry, only to discover her true intentions were far less serious than his.

Making it clear in their business association that emotional involvement was not on her agenda, DualE'd been relieved that Carver felt the same. Now, with no partner in sight, she was lonely. Would she waver in her commitment to keep their hormonal and companionship drives in check? Great, more mental fodder for her deepsleep haunts.

DualE checked status on the three occupied coffins. Satisfied all were functioning, she slipped from her bulky suit and lay down in her flimsy with a light blanket covering her. "See you on the far side of hell." She muttered the naval saying with the memory of a hundred jumps into battle. This was easy. They were going to the Eddy to look for converts. She was going to look for Carver and signs of unrequited rebellion.

She heard a voice through a fog. Cardinal's? Couldn't be, he was in cryo. "The *Rickover* has arrived. With company."

Who spoke? Reality or the first of her spookspace nightmares? Too late for her to react as the deepsleep chill engulfed her.

P ious raced beyond the carrier ship. His mind existed outside normal dimensions. Jumpspace freed the brain from physical limitations but imposed guilt from repressed memories.

This immersion differed. His inner disease wasn't in the forefront like it had been jumping from Bohr to Argosy Station and then to Slate's Progress. His eyes witnessed the brothers streaming their individual vortexes. Atone moved amongst potential believers in Slate's. Cardinal guided the *Penance* through the Eddy's backvoids. Remorse toiled in diligent secondary service, tracking their funds, following up with past donors, critiquing Pious' sermons. Pious spun beside them but couldn't interact. Each was alone. Did he not exist in their timelines?

Jumpspace illusions haunted those who allowed it. Pious knew this but it didn't soften the impact of what he was for his brother priests. Abandonment. Failure. He tried calming routines. This wasn't what had to be, just one thread of a million possibilities. The emptiness left by his death would be filled, how and who had yet to be determined.

The time-space ripples left in his wake and stretched out before him repeated the failure over and over. A part of Pious knew this spookspace effect was his mind processing the vision he hadn't wanted to see. It didn't necessarily represent future certainty.

The mission would continue and he would continue. His body would support him until the circumstances boded success. Faith would come to the Eddy.

As he spiraled forward, another realization disturbed him. He couldn't see DualE yet she traveled inside *Penance*. Carver touched his side briefly then was lost to another stream.

The sin of pride had created this vision. He was replaceable and refused to admit it. The disease overtaking him wouldn't destroy the pilgrimage and where pilgrims walked, new followers joined.

Chapter 20

"Aren't you suspicious of your popularity?" Carver asked Zofie. They stood outside the *Whisper*, a handbreadth apart. He repressed memories of their past intimacy aboard Argosy Station.

Zofie flushed. Similar romantic memories or anger at his question?

"I'm a good businesswoman. I generated this interest. I've covered as much of the dockyards as possible soliciting business. Give me some credit."

"Look, I know you've scoured the docks here but these clients found you early on. I hate being skeptical but a businesswoman should be asking more questions about her cargo. Especially these so-called alien artifacts."

"It's gold Carver. Better than Schoenfeldium in my opinion. Your aid in getting them through is all that I ask. You call it suspicious; I call it Denz luck." She headed inside her ship. "We have a lot to arrange."

He tugged her arm and whispered. "Remember, Kondradt bugged your ship while he pretended to examine it."

"I'm not blinded by greed, Carver. If he's that committed, then I can trust him."

"How much?"

"He's trusting me with Marshall."

Carver stopped her. "He entrusted the *Pollux* with another of his associates. He made certain said minion didn't make it alive to the jump's end."

"Old news, Carver." She dragged him into the *Whisper*. Kondradt would hear what she wanted. "It's your privilege not to trust Kondradt but I've an insurance policy. He won't double cross me. If he tries, Mekli will ensure Kondradt suffers my fate. Before the Realm implodes."

Carver doubted her reasoning. "You play a dangerous game against dangerous people, Zofie. I'm not convinced the severity of the reaction can be justified. But you and Marshall will be far away from me by then. I'll be in the protection of the brotherhood, for what that's worth." He realized the irony of role reversal as he spoke, he'd been hired to protect the brothers.

"Better'n alone. Let's finalize my camouflage shipment. I want to go with the refining equipment, slag though it is."

"Are you sure? Its questionable worth could raise suspicion."

Zofie nodded. "I know. But that very argument could deflect interest from what it's disguising. And the danger of an inspector actually risking their safety by going inside to look will keep the artifacts safe."

"Your call."

They worked in silence. After an hour, Zofie stood to leave. She touched a red LED on the control panel long enough for Carver to get the message. She was going to meet the Reds and didn't want Kondradt to know.

The surplus machinery would be dockside within two days.

"I'm off to inspect potential barnacle transports. Monitor any incoming as well, please?"

"You got it. If you've time, find me a cubby that's cheap while I wait for DualE."

"Kondradt will cover your bill. After all, Marshall's kicking you out of your cryo bunk. It's the least he can do."

Carver knew it was for the listener's benefit but he didn't relish being indebted to Gar Kondradt for any sum, no matter how small.

━━━━✚┼╲╲┃┃┝┼╀━━━━

Z ofie spied Cassity in Eddie's Dive. The woman drank with a few prospectors and beckoned Zofie to join them.

"This is Zofie," introduced Cassity. "The *Whisper's* captain, owner and chief mechanic,". "Anything you need brokered in the inner Realm or the Confluence, talk to Zofie."

Cassity looked like she walked the edge between lucidity and complete impairment. The first might promote business, the latter wasn't good for Zofie's confidentiality. She might've chosen a poor intimate.

One of Cassity's companions said, "Forget about trading with Bohr. I hear they've sent a force through to Slate's Progress. We'll be next."

Cassity gave a private wink to Zofie. *Run with it.*

"Not an invasion force, surely," said Zofie. "The void rumor-mill has transformed a single frigate overseeing the peace accord into an armada? Misinformation can be more dangerous than information."

"So can a fleet," replied the man. "Not a rumor. News from a private sub-freighter who left Argosy Station the same time as a dreadnaught and escort showed up from Bohr, ready to skip on to Slate's. The privateer had three drops before the Eddy, didn't know if the news had reached us yet. Arrived two hours ago. The harbor master has been locked up with the command crew since they revived."

Zofie was skeptical. If anything like this had happened, Kondradt would know about it. Maybe he did and chose not to share it with her. If so, he'd be pushing for the *Whisper's* quick exit.

"Let's get you a drink," said Cassity and drew Zofie away. "I thought you should hear that. It's the latest rumor."

"Okay. Any other solid news?"

"Marshall works for Gar Kondradt." Cassity looked at her expectantly.

"I guessed as much." Zofie wouldn't confirm it in case Cassity was fishing both sides of the river. Time to check the other mystery. "What can you tell me about the Reds?"

Cassity didn't answer immediately. After a minute of examining and swirling her drink, she spoke. "Very little. They don't socialize and if their agenda is prospecting, I've not seen any evidence. I can dig but don't think I'll learn more than that. What's your next move?"

Okay, Cassity was too curious or peddling info to whoever paid. "I'm waiting for confirmation of a big shipment. Nothing exciting, just low-tech, bulky salvage machinery." That much Zofie did want publicized, if Cassity didn't already know.

Cassity handed her a tumbler. "I'd arrange barnacle soon, if I were you. Before whatever force from Bohr shows up. Less paperwork."

"Thanks, I'm close. What's next for you. Stay and watch the fireworks?"

"There's a chance the crew we just spoke with might need a backup communications officer. Their last one turned to salvage months ago and they've been running with only one. She's showing signs of jumpspace burnout. They're going deepvoid."

` "Seek far refuge until the fallout from the peace accord settles," said Zofie. "Not a bad plan, if you're not in business. Me. I'll barnacle upstream."

Cassity clinked mugs. "To the brave."

"You mean foolish." Zofie joined her in a toast.

"Like there's a difference?"

Chapter 21

Chels stared at the deck above their bed. Slate stirred in his sleep. Her slumber wouldn't come. Perry's death haunted her. Brother Atone had tried to help but his wisdom lacked the seasoned experience Pious brought to any conversation.

Time would heal a part of her regret but she didn't seek whole exorcism. The guilt would help direct her and the tough knowledge she acquired would help those who came to her for guidance.

Slate's comm beeped. He woke instantly. "Slate here."

The speaker boomed. "A navy frigate and two escort fighters have emerged from jumpspace, commander. Thought you should know. They're asking for all administrative staff to be on standby for Admiral Rowland's briefing."

"Not unexpected with the peace accord so recent. You sound concerned." Slate was half dressed by now.

"I see no reason we should welcome this sudden intrusion, despite your prediction. They don't sound very diplomatic."

"On my way."

Chels padded beside him to the door. "Do you think Pious got away?"

"I'll know soon enough."

"An admiral-toting frigate. The Confluence response to the attack on Argosy Station?"

He kissed her. "Most likely. Bohr using it as an excuse to claw back concessions. We're outgunned but not surprised." Slate left.

Chels stared at the closed door. Not surprised? Slate's tone hinted 'not unprepared'. Were Realm forces arrayed to respond? Not here. In the Eddy?

Suddenly her problems seemed small compared to what could come. She and the rest of the Realm thought they had won their rebellion in the negotiation room, not in battle. Now the conflict had arrived on their doorstep.

People would need assurances. She and Atone would be challenged. A trial by endless fire would test their true mettle.

She dressed in her coverall and commed Atone. "Brother, it's Chels. We need to talk. There is a development from the Confluence. Can you meet me in the chapel?"

He mumbled a groggy, "I'm there."

Twenty minutes later, she joined him. He looked alert and ready to dispense comfort.

"We have customers waiting, Sister Chels."

"First I must tell you what's happened." She gave what little information she had in two sentences.

"Have you heard from *Penance*?" he asked.

"No. That's a good thing. I think their freighter got away just as the navy arrived. Slate will confirm when he has a chance. His staff have more pressing matters at the moment."

Atone nodded to the gathering spacers in and outside the chapel. "So have we." He laid a hand on her arm. "Brother Pious had enough faith in you to rely on your keeping our message alive in our absence. I share that faith and would be grateful for your partnership today."

He didn't ask if she was ready for the volume of unburdening souls but the brotherhood didn't wait for one to be ready. One served.

"Of course," she said. "I think you should start with a communal address to calm nerves."

"I agree. We can deal with the more serious worries one on one, after I've reduced the general anxiety." Atone pulled his robe tight and beckoned the throng inside the chapel.

Chels lit candles while Atone composed himself at the front. A dozen spacers in various stages of sobriety sat and stood within.

"One of the faculties which separates man from animal is our ability to imagine," he began. "At this moment, our imaginations create scenarios which may be false. When we lack information, the brain fills in the blanks with whatever fears and misgivings we carry with us."

Chels watched their faces. Some nodded understanding. Atone was off to a good start.

"We know little about the current situation. What I know, Chels has shared with me. A Confluence representative has arrived in the Realm. A peace-keeping force or an aggressive one? Have they fired upon Slate's Progress? No. Have they taken prisoners? No. Have they blockaded the station? Not officially. I'm not a military strategist but my brothers and I have threaded our way through more than a few similar situations. My interpretation is to allow them to reveal their agenda in their time. Meanwhile, we carry on." Atone walked among the supplicants. His stature didn't rise above many of them but his voice carried well.

"I'm not a military man but I am a bit of a military historian and I can see the motive behind the Confluence's precaution. To allay *their* fears. The Realm has many advantages in an armed conflict. The sheer volume of space you occupy. The lack of concentration of critical infrastructure. The Eddy would not be an easy target from what I know. Any battle would be fought asteroid by asteroid by small moonlet by tiny refining stations. The Confluence might win such a war but it would take years and what would they have won in the end?" He returned to the front.

"Are you defeated at this moment? I don't believe so. Look to the person beside you. Do they appear defeated? I want you to leave here with a confident heart. The station will need your positive resolve. Spread your knowledge that the unknown will not induce panic but give you time to reinforce your commitment. For those who would stay behind and speak to me or Chels, I welcome you. If it can wait for another shift or two, I encourage you to circulate within Progress and share your confidence with those dealing with their imaginations."

Chels was impressed. Atone showed more insight than she expected. He'd calmed some of her fears.

A man close to her asked in a loud voice. "What about our livelihoods? We can't survive an embargo for long, whether our imaginations are dampened down or not."

Murmurs of agreement rippled through the crowd.

"No, you can't survive," said Atone. "Not on your own. If it comes, you won't be alone. Many of you will be in the same financial situation. You can't change that. But you can band together. Pool your resources. It won't last forever. What meagre means Chels has managed to accumulate for the brotherhood will be shared to those most in need."

Chels repressed a sigh. The credits raised during the brothers' absence weren't huge but were ear-marked for her own mission off Slate's. Needs change. She would approach the richer followers and build a war chest for the poorest stranded spacers.

Another voice spoke. "The brother is right. We must avoid panic. The Confluence wants to destroy our confidence and our resolve. If it's peace they're trying to subvert, we won't let them."

Atone raised his hands. "I'm not preaching violence. Cooperation to survive is my message. The Confluence has shown no signs of unwarranted aggression. A security blockade may be in everyone's best safety interest. Don't give them provocation to raise the stakes."

"What about our stakes? When starvation hits."

"The station will provide in the short term. They can't sequester us forever."

"Doesn't need to be more than a few weeks."

More murmurs. Chels wasn't sure if Atone had convinced them. His face flushed. His mouth opened but no words came forth. She moved quickly to the podium. "You know me and you know Slate. Do you trust him to take the right action?"

"Slate's only one man and he's not in sole charge any more."

"He's the most experienced hand on Progress. In our situation, I'm convinced his opinion will carry the most weight."

"He's up against a fleet."

"You exaggerate." She had to downplay the speculation. "We're up against three Confluence ships. Bohr and Slate both know how important a functional Slate's Progress is to the Realm and the peace accord. I know his mind. He will do what's best for the Realm and you." She hoped she was right. Slate was the most experienced in administration but would reason prevail amongst the entire governance board?

The station public address hummed to life. "This is Admiral Rowland aboard the *Rickover*. Until further notice, for mutual safety of the Realm and the Confluence, a selective embargo from Slate's Progress to Argosy Station and Bohr is in force until inspection teams are deployed."

The assemblage broke up, each man and woman rushing to protect themselves. Chels couldn't blame them.

"I failed," said Atone.

"Their panic won't last. They'll see the wisdom in your message. Give it time."

Chels' earbud pinged. She listened, then acknowledged. "Speaking of messages, you and I have been summoned."

C hels and Brother Atone waited within the *Rickover*. Slate had preceded them into Admiral Rowland's quarters.

"Why us?" Atone asked. "We're not strategic pieces to this action. We're not even pawns."

His nervousness grew visibly while they waited. The service hadn't gone as they'd hoped. The questions raised about details on how the embargo would affect individuals weren't satisfactorily addressed. Chels knew it wasn't their function to minimize the impact but Atone's inability to address specifics didn't help the cause.

She wondered how Pious would have handled the anxious crowd. Her own attempt had some effect. At least the spacers who knew Slate trusted him. Now he was secluded with the naval commander. Apparently, the Confluence also knew how influential Slate could be. Were they trying to draw him to their side?

"We may be pawns in another game entirely, Brother." Chels shared his puzzlement but she had a few ideas and tried to prepare herself for any interrogation along those lines. Whether the man beside her was up to the pressure, she didn't know.

Chels started when the door clanged open and Slate strode out. His worried look didn't surprise her. His words did.

"Rowland might be more interested in talking to you than me. I'd wait but have items to relay to the board. I'll see you back in Progress. By the way, *Penance* got out." He leaned in on her open side. "Tell Rowland the truth and we may get out of this. "

"Don't I always?" She tried to lighten the mood.

"Hah." Slate cracked a weak smile. "Let her do the talking," he told Atone.

"Come." A junior officer guided the pair inside.

Admiral Rowland stood before a hologram of Slate's Progress. He was alone. He was also younger than Chels had expected. She estimated he was in his late forties. An admiral that age was either very good or very ambitious. Or both.

"Fascinating complex," he said. "I'm Admiral Rowland. Thank you for coming. You are Chels Harte. Brother Atone, good to see you arrived safely from Argosy. I won't keep you long. My time here is compressed."

Atone locked eyes with Rowland while Chels scanned the room. It was stark aside from the comm center and a cryo coffin panel against the far wall. Rowland didn't deepsleep with the crew in jumpspace. She stepped closer to the hologram but really wanted a look into his eyes. Was he a non-sleeper? Did this commander risk the waking hallucinations rather than the torment of deepsleep nightmares in order to stay in control? His temples showed the strain of something. A fine network of wrinkles webbed around his eyes. She added a decade to her age estimate. A vain man who used skin rejuvenation products to deny life's natural ebb.

"Why are we here?" asked Atone. "We have no political or strategic value."

To corroborate whatever Slate had told Rowland? Chels had no other inkling. Unless...Perry? But she didn't know him other than the single encounter. And she'd told Slate. And he knew about the beam hitting Argosy Station. Could she betray the confession in front of Atone? Or at all?

"Don't underestimate the power of the smallest pieces of information. I do need your help. Please sit. I will get to the point. Ms. Harte, what can you tell me about the deceased Realm citizen Perry?"

"How much do you know already?"

Rowland's eyes pierced. "Don't task me. My time is limited."

Chels matched his gaze. She was a Realm citizen and a civilian, not some Confluence junior ensign.

Rowland grinned. "Slate told me you were tough. Fair enough. The *Rickover* arrived at Argosy Station right after a particle weapon had been deployed against a jumpfreighter coming from the Eddy. The beam also damaged the station and two ships in dock. On my instructions, the navy treated the attack as a potential act of war. We arrived here, not knowing what threat could be present in the Eddy."

He tapped a finger on his desk. The solid wood top muffled the sound. "I understand you have information which contradicts my interpretation. I'd like to hear it."

"My information was given in confession and I can't betray that trust."

"You've already told others. I'm not asking for details. Not yet. But tell me about Perry. Besides his words."

"A salvager. They scour the Eddy's flotsam for recyclable material. It's a grind of a living but less risky than prospecting. He claimed he and his partner found an alien artifact." She glanced to Atone. "How far can I go, brother?"

Atone's resolve had evaporated. "Follow your conscience, sister."

A platitude. No concrete guidance from him. Pious' words would have to determine her next reveals. Or did they? Slate advised her to be truthful, to mitigate the navy's potential threat.

Rowland spoke. "I honor the pact you share with Perry but I remind you he is dead. Possibly because you didn't reveal his secret with the right authorities on Progress. This is a chance to redeem that oversight. You could stop a battle, Ms. Harte. A battle the Realm can't win."

She'd argue that point but another time. "Perry and his partner thought the device a jumpspace communicator."

"Why would they think that?"

"His partner had been a comm officer."

"Private or naval service?"

Chels shook her head. "I don't know. I don't think he told me. I don't have a name either. Perry was consumed by his own guilt. They believed they were sending a message as the jumpfreighter opened the gate. The recoil revealed the artifact's true function."

"Where is it now?"

"Again, I don't know for certain. Neither did Perry. They abandoned it in the Eddy." Her voice dropped to a *Whisper*. "It's still out there."

"A trajectory specialist might recreate the beam's path along the *Orson's* jump coordinates. We can back-track it."

Rowland spoke to himself as much as to them, she thought.

"Did you ever doubt his story?" the admiral asked.

"That's a strange question."

"Perry might have been playing a larger game. An accident is too easy an explanation. I can't accept it without questioning its validity."

"I don't question his honesty."

"You're not in charge of a peace-keeping fleet. I wish I could interview him."

She had a disturbing insight. Did Rowland intend to keep the peace or to shatter it? "Like you said, Perry's dead. Either by his own hand to still his conscience or by another's hand to shut him up."

"His partner may be aboard Progress. Slate is checking for me. Ms. Harte, in my eyes you haven't betrayed Perry's trust. You may have helped avert a war."

She was surprised at Rowland's quick retreat from the suspicion Perry lied. Had the admiral slipped up? Revealed more than he intended? If he didn't want war, then why did he have a hologram of Slate's Progress on display? And why have the station in lockdown?

"Brother Atone, I'd like to know the status of your shipmates."

"Uh, they've barnacled, sir."

"When and where?"

"They left just before you arrived. Jumping for the Eddy shipyards."

"Why didn't you go with them?" Rowland's attention focused on the brother. Chels no longer held his interest.

"I have a mission here, sir. To keep our message alive with the spacers here. We must build our congregation piece by piece, go from strength to strength."

"Hmm. And your companions? DualE and Carver Denz. Where are they?"

"DualE took my coffin aboard *Penance*. We have no certain knowledge of Denz's whereabouts though a rumor placed him in the Eddy."

"Did DualE leave any message behind?"

"No, not as far as I know."

"You have access to her ship and its records?"

"Limited, sir."

Rowland pressed a button on his desk and the junior officer entered. "You will escort Brother Atone to the *Crossed Swords* and scan its databanks for any messages left for me."

Chels said, "Wait a minute. DualE's working for you?"

Rowland shook his head. "No. But she's ex-navy and she'd note anything unusual she thought might be of interest to us. Hard to break the habits of a long career."

Chels watched Atone's face. He didn't seem alarmed about a possible conflict. Hell, she'd just crossed the confession protocol and he'd not protested. Shock or timidity before the admiral? She didn't think Pious would've cooperated so readily.

"Thank you for your help," said Rowland.

They'd been dismissed. She needed to talk to Slate. But she wanted to see what, if anything, DualE left behind. She didn't think the woman could serve two masters but Rowland believed she'd message him.

Chels also wanted to warn Pious but how? The mission in the Eddy could make the brothers a military target in Rowland's universe. How long before the embargo extended to the Eddy? Either she or Atone had to jump. A huge psychological and physical risk for her but was Atone's capacity any better? He'd been eager to stay behind. Maybe it was more than his desire to lead on Slate's. Maybe his spookspace demons mounted.

Chels kept her thoughts to herself as she and Atone shuttled back to Progress with Rowland's marine. DualE had dual purposes. And she'd allied with the brothers. Did Atone serve the Confluence as well? She couldn't accept Pious having any master except his mission but the young acolyte with her was an unknown.

This was how battles were won. Divide and conquer. Sew mistrust and crumble a disunited front. How could she stop it?

Chapter 22

DualE's jumpspace traverse wasn't pleasant. Her past misdeeds overprinted present and future sins. The Confluence force arriving at Slate's Progress as *Penance* readied to jump seemed real, not a pre-cryo hallucination. It repeated over and over in deepsleep, along with her betraying the brothers in service to a second master, the Confluence Navy. More distress overlaid those nightmares. Zofie betraying Carver. Rowland betraying her. Rowland betraying the peace accord.

Her chest warmed from the inside out as lung fluid was displaced by oxygen. Pins and needles attacked her extremities. Cryo dreams crept back into the blackness of her subconscious.

She was first to revive, body before soul. She checked arrival coordinates and de-barnacled *Penance* when satisfied their transport had fulfilled its charter. She scanned the commlinks, relying on her naval-based algorithm to reveal military messages. It was quiet. At least the fleet hadn't jumped immediately from Slate's. They would come; she knew Rowland's tactics. He would use the attack on Argosy to disguise his own agenda to secure what he thought the Confluence deserved.

She activated the remaining coffins' revival routines. She wasn't here to protect Argosy Realm and the Eddy. She was here to protect Pious and his brothers. And to find Carver.

DualE hunted through the shipyard's registry for record of the *Whisper*. Her naval routines couldn't decrypt the location but the *Whisper* was in dock. She scanned visual recognition bases but nothing certain pinged. She changed her comm scans to a longband modulation only one person would use. Tagged. "Thank you, Carver." An automatic signal but she could triangulate its source as she approached the 'yard.

Coughs and splutters signaled more activity within *Penance*. The brothers woke. She heard them rustle while cleaning up then Pious spoke. "I will take my brothers' confessions from deepsleep, DualE. You are welcome to participate."

She turned away from the controls for a moment. "I'll be okay, thanks, Brother Pious. My nightmares were more external this jump. I want to dock us on the lee side of the shipyards." Any incoming hostiles would arrive jumpside. Every second of warning and cover opposite could make a difference in survival or escape. She'd contact Carver once they were locked on.

"As you wish," said Pious. "You are a full partner here."

She studied him for a moment, his frailties enhanced by cryo. He'd aged on this voyage. She returned to her navigation task and tuned out Cardinal and Remorse's voices as they cleansed themselves before Pious.

"Permission to dock on gantry twelve," she hailed. "We need basic service only and wish to observe the Eddy unobstructed by the bulk of the station. Our funds are limited and the remote gantry's fees are acceptable to our mission."

The automated harbor-master responded after a minute. "Granted, *Penance*. State your business."

"Our business is non-commercial. We're on a religious commission to offer a message of faith to the Eddy."

There was no emotion in the mechanical reply. "Non-commercial business is subject to duty. A tithe on your fund-raising efforts with minimum to be determined based on length of occupancy. Proceed to gantry twelve."

Damn. It had mentioned their identity. If Zofie was watching for them, she knew.

DualE didn't wait for docking to locate her target. Using Carver's signal, she found the *Whisper* and flagged its location. Carver may or may not still be with it. Zofie's ship was a long hike from gantry twelve but DualE wouldn't change her first priority. Protect the *Penance* and its crew.

Thirty minutes later, she docked. Umbilicals from the gantry responded to her invitation to connect. They would have air, heat and water for their fee.

She cracked the inner lock and adjusted the air circulators for four. She was about to EVA to check her anchors when the comm pinged.

"Welcome, *Penance*." A man's voice, not the automaton. It was familiar but she couldn't place it. She turned to Pious. "Recognize the speaker?"

He shook his head.

"This is *Penance*. Are you the welcome wagon?"

"I can be. You're a long way from the normal docking gantries for ships your size. I will be at your door in an hour. Please be present."

"Identify."

The screen flickered and DualE got a visual. "Don't you recognize me?"

"Gar Kondradt."

"One hour, DualE."

"I'll put the kettle on." DualE's job to ensure the brothers' security had begun in earnest.

"Do what you need, brothers," she said. "I have preparations to make for our visitor. Especially if he's not alone. Then, I need to find Carver."

———————— ✝┼╫╢╞╪ ————————

Pious remembered Kondradt from Argosy Station. At least by reputation. DualE returned from her external inspection.

"You don't have to prepare on your own, DualE," he said. "The brothers and I are schooled in self-preservation. You must consider us another resource."

"I will. Arm yourselves. I doubt he'll be aggressive on this visit. He's looking for information. But that doesn't mean he won't return or won't send a physical message at some point."

"Rumors on Argosy Station pegged Kondradt as a financial threat." Pious tried to recall anything else he'd heard while he and the brothers searched for the elusive Carver Denz and his mining fortune months before. Kondradt might not have even been aware of them. He would be aware of Denz. The high profile from his lode discovery was known throughout the Realm. How well did Kondradt know DualE? Was she the reason for his visit?

"Do you think he can help us find Denz?" Cardinal asked.

"Good question," she answered. "I prefer to find Denz on my own. I won't ask Kondradt to lead me to him." She looked to Pious and then the other two. "I'd rather you not mention Carver in Kondradt's presence. Not yet."

"But the sooner we locate Denz," said Remorse, "the sooner we can be on our way to the outer settlements."

"True," said Pious. "Our mission is paramount but a small delay won't hurt. We have a message to deliver to this facility. As for Mr. Kondradt, DualE is right, we must rely on her expertise when it comes to dealing with men like him." DualE believed she could find Denz. Had she already found him? If so, why not share? Then again, he hadn't chosen to share completely with her. "We will listen to Mr. Kondradt and evaluate our next steps from there. In the meantime, Brother Remorse, you will announce our presence and locate a suitable location for my address."

"Make it as soon as you can," said DualE. "And have more than one possibility. I'll accompany you to scout the locations after Kondradt leaves." She spoke to Pious. "Before scouting venues, Remorse and I will track down Zofie and our MIA." She leaned over Remorse's shoulder. "Confirm the *Whisper's* location and how we get there."

"I will accompany you, DualE. I need to get a sense of this place." He retrieved his last sermon from Slate's. He pulled DualE away from the console. "You know these outposts as well as I do. Any hints you'd suggest when it comes to my first message?"

"This 'yard was an embryo the only time I was here. That'd be six years ago. But one 'yard's pretty much the same as another. Different from Gamma Hub though."

"I assume this reflects the frontier attitude of the Eddy in general. An independent mindset. Resource-based economics and living strike-to-strike."

"You got it. They are used to protecting themselves, not relying on authority for support and not asking them to interfere." She read his notes upside down. "What's your message?"

"Self-reliance is a virtue but don't shut out your fellows who may need your aid or support. They did mount an armada, ready to engage the Confluence, a much larger and better-equipped foe. There is some degree of cooperation latent within these pioneers. I'll catalyze it if I can. A spiritual alliance doesn't mean the end of independence."

DualE called to Remorse. "Find anything?"

"Yes. Three potential sites. Two public areas and a bar. And *Whisper's* location is confirmed, though a barnacle is scheduled in three shifts. Its jumpfreighter is waiting for a barge from an Eddy pocket to arrive and then she'll be away."

"Break your station link. Kondradt may have a scanner."

Their protector anticipated. Pious asked, "Won't it look suspicious to be inactive? After all, we just ascended from jumpspace."

"Brother Cardinal, start plotting outbound courses for *Penance*." She glanced at Pious. "If you agree?"

"Certainly. I want to cover as much space as we can in a timely fashion."

They settled into their respective tasks and thoughts.

Remorse broke the silence. "Brother Pious, we have company."

DualE faced the 'lock. "Kondradt."

DualE's tone implied strong emotion. Hate? Fear? Mistrust? All the emotions Pious fought hard to cleanse from himself when he got the cancer diagnosis in Gamma Hub. None were helpful in moving forward and completing his missions. Could he rely on her? They needed Denz to balance her instinctive fight reaction.

"Show him in, Ms. DualE."

Carver saw the incoming jumpfreighter dislodge three barnacles. He couldn't get into the shipyard's log to identify *Penance* or the *Crossed Swords* but if it was among the new arrivals, he hoped Cardinal or DualE would recognize his signal.

He could ask Kondradt or wait for Zofie's hacking expertise but he didn't relish being indebted to either. A manual search-and-locate crossed his mind. Carver weighed the risk of being seen versus finding the brothers and decided to wait a shift or two. Zofie wasn't due to leave for at least three more shifts. He'd use the Willie Renfrew identity to book lodging. He ran a hand over his itchy stubble. Another few shifts and the beard would make an effective disguise. Patience was hard to swallow. He needed to act. He needed to fulfill his commitment to Pious. He had to get away from Zofie and commerce.

A message from the incoming cargo ship hauling Zofie's camouflage machinery pulled him out of his frustration. He guided them to the pre-arranged location the Reds were using as their storage. "This is *Whisper*. I'm Zofie Ked's authorized agent. Payment will be transferred upon satisfactory inspection."

"Inspection? Don't make me laugh," answered the shipper. "This is salvage. If it passed inspection, it would still be in use."

"Nevertheless. It requires confirmation that it is what you claim and not mining slag."

"Then get someone out here in a hurry. We've got our own schedule to maintain and you paid extra for quick delivery."

"I appreciate it." Carver switched contacts. "Reds, this is *Whisper*. Can you verify the incoming shipment's contents? Zofie's tied up somewhere in the 'yard. The shippers won't release the cargo to us until we pay and I won't pay until the cargo is confirmed."

It took a moment but he got an answer. "We're on our way, tell the shipper to dock and we'll let you know when funds can be released."

"Thanks." Before he put out a general call for Zofie, he'd try a direct contact with *Penance*. "Hailing barnacle *Penance*. Come in. *Penance* come in."

A 'fail' light flashed on the screen. Interdict word *Penance* disallowed.

Zofie'd anticipated his attempt and programmed *Whisper* to block him.

"Hailing Cardinal."

Interdict word Cardinal disallowed.

Damn.

Zofie entered the *Whisper*. "Having trouble?" She dropped her pack on the deck and scrolled back through his attempts on screen.

Carver didn't hide his work. "Yeah, I think *Penance* docked with a few other new barnacles and I'd like to reunite. Your camouflage shipment for the Reds is here and they are inspecting it now. I suggest you get out there if you want personal confirmation before you make payment."

"*I'll* talk to *Penance*. Once I've looked at the machinery we're using to disguise the artifacts."

"Zofie, if I were you, I'd have a look at those so-called artifacts as well."

"You don't trust the Reds?"

"It isn't me who needs to trust them, it's you. Why should you trust them? Marshall turned out to be a front, why not these guys?"

"Because these guys are dealing on a whole different risk level. They've trusted me."

Their first mistake, Carver thought. "I'm saying there's more than one Gar Kondradt in the Eddy."

Zofie chewed her lip and nodded. "You make sense, Carver. Are you sure you don't want to chuck the brothers and partner with me officially?"

"No."

"Just the same, come with me. If *Penance* is here, I'll get you to her after we do the inspection."

"I shouldn't be seen."

"We'll scooter. I've got one parked outside. We can avoid the inside of the station."

He looked around the *Whisper*. "Can't say I'll miss this one." He donned a visor with drop-down anti-glare specs. "Recognize me?"

"You'll return those when we find the *Penance*."

Chapter 23

D ualE put her arm across the inner 'lock at Kondradt's neck level. "Indulge me, sir. My job is to protect the brothers."

Kondradt raised his hands and spread his feet, a smirk on his lips. "If I wanted you dead or injured, you'd already be casualties."

She frisked him and lowered her arm. "And you'd be collateral damage. Come in." She poked her head outside and scanned the nearby area. One person, a woman DualE thought, stood a hundred meters away. Beside her was a two-person scooter. One of those would help DualE cover more of the shipyard looking for Carver. She shut the outer door and joined the rest.

"Why are you here, Kondradt?" DualE observed his body language more than his lips. The man didn't betray any inner emotion or discontinuity. He was good. Better than a politician. "I'm genuinely puzzled."

"How so?"

Answered with a question. She'd play up to a point and then go beserker whether Pious approved or not.

"We're not a source of income," said Pious, "we're a recipient."

Good pick up, she thought. Pious was a strategist at least Kondradt's equal.

Kondradt alternated his attention from DualE to Pious and back, finally settling on Brother Cardinal. "Income? No, you're right. There are more valuable things than credits. Information for one. I'm not a dealer in information but merely the middleman. An agent, if you will. You've just arrived from Slate's Progress and before that, the Confluence. My own time in Bohr was cut short when Chancellor

136

Mekli requested my early return to the Realm. We need to prepare for the detailed work to come in enacting terms of the accord. I've interviewed the other barnacles and the captain of your transport. You're the last, so don't overreact and believe you're unique."

"What can we tell you?" asked Pious. "I'm not sure anything we'd notice would be relevant to your questions."

DualE continued to monitor Kondradt for any give-away tells.

Kondradt stretched his legs out before him, brushing an invisible mote from his knee.

He was about to lie, DualE concluded. She studied his hands. Thumb and forefinger of his left hand rubbed. She had him. Maybe. She glanced to Brother Remorse. He too watched Kondradt's hands. Confirmation? They'd debrief once Kondradt left.

"I piece together all the information I can gather," said Kondradt. "A small item you provide could support or bely a critical assumption. You're a judge of people, Brother Pious. An expert one. What were your impressions of the overall mood aboard Slate's? Are the people satisfied with the Confluence accord outcome? Do they regret a peaceful, perhaps disadvantageous, solution? I spent the last number of years aboard Argosy Station, an unofficial steward."

A borderline criminal boss, according to DualE's naval briefing before she traveled there the first time.

"The mood in Slate's was one of uncertainty," Pious answered. "We were there months ago and were warmly received. This time, the reaction to my message was less enthusiastic. I left one of my brothers behind to try and restore a larger following."

Interesting, DualE thought. She hadn't noticed disappointment in Pious after his sermon.

"Why do you suppose your message didn't get the expected reactions?"

"I think the second last time we were there, the occupants' immediate future was in question. Would they face battle? A war they might not have chosen to fight? Slate's was a privateer. Now it's part of the Realm proper, I gather from speaking with Slate. He's no longer the sole administrator but one of a group."

"The future is more defined with the accord," said Kondradt. "Your counsel may not be needed. Not right now. I wouldn't despair, these things swing back before you know it."

Too right there. DualE guessed the uncertainly returned to Slate's in spades with the arrival of Rowland and his fleet. She wouldn't volunteer that information to Kondradt. Not yet.

"Your impressions tally with what I've put together from the other two barnacles." Kondradt stood, smoothing the wrinkles from his flimsuit legs. "One other thing. The barnacles claim a number of ships arrived at Slate's immediately prior to your jump. What did you see?" He made eye contact with Cardinal. "You're the astrogator, right?"

"Yes. There was a ship. More than one I couldn't verify."

"Freighter?"

Don't tell him, don't tell him, don't tell him, DualE tried to telepathically influence Cardinal.

"No. A frigate, maybe the *Rickover*. It transported us to Argosy." Cardinal looked at Pious. "What do you think it meant?"

Kondradt didn't seem surprised. "They'll be here soon enough and we can ask them."

Kondradt already knew. He wanted honesty from the brothers. Maybe it was a good thing Cardinal did spill. DualE asked, "If we think of anything else, how do we contact you?" She might trust him after all to locate Zofie.

"The frequency I used to hail you. Don't be too specific, just say you'd like to meet and we'll arrange it. I thank you for your time and cooperation. Good luck with your mission, Brother Pious. If you're going beyond this shipyard, let me know. I can direct you to some of the more lucrative operations."

He gave DualE a nod. "Don't let your guard down. This 'yard can be dangerous."

A warning or a threat? "Don't worry," she said, "I never do."

Kondradt left and DualE closed the 'lock. She put a finger to her lips and moved silently about the cabin. She examined every spot Kondradt had been near or touched. No bugs.

"We can talk," she said. "If he planted a snooper, I can't find it." She spoke to Remorse. "What do you think of our information gatherer?"

The brother glanced at Pious for a reassuring nod before answering. "I believe he has many agendas but he was here as he claimed. To confirm the navy's arrival at Slate's."

"He has power," said Pious. "He is discrete in using it. I will be grateful to leave this 'yard and commune with those beyond the stain of intrigue."

"Then let's get your venue sorted and Denz repatriated."

Pious locked his hands together around DualE's waist. If he could see his fingers, he knew they'd be drained of blood.

"Lean with the scooter," she instructed. "If you try to stay upright, you'll throw off our balance."

They accelerated away from *Penance* toward the denser spiderweb of shipyard struts and gantry-ways. He closed his eyes and repeated a prayer. Despite the queasiness from her piloting, he did trust DualE's physical capabilities. He just wasn't certain about her loyalty to their mission. At times, she looked backward, focused on what she had no control over. Back to her pre-gun-for-hire career?

The scooter slowed and he dared a glimpse. They approached a small ship anchored alone at the end of a long docking strut.

"The *Whisper*," she said.

"Denz? You found him quickly."

"He or the ship broadcast a message. I logged it as we arrived. I wasn't certain it was the right ship until now. There can't be two like it." She leaned the scooter back and they stopped a hundred meters away.

"What are you waiting for?"

"A sign we're welcome." A beam flashed from the scooter three times on and off.

There was no response from the ship. "I'll move closer, behind the protection of the dock. Hang tight."

Pious' guts stayed behind as she zipped above and circled from a long distance until they were hidden from *Whisper's* view. Then she moved them up to the strut. She parked the scooter and dismounted. "You want to come or stay with the rig?" she asked.

"I'm not up to piloting on my own. I'll join you."

"Suit yourself. Driving is better than pillion, trust me. You get secure in holding onto the control bar. Let's try knocking."

She led them over the girder mesh to the main platform where he could see the *Whisper's* airlock. DualE put a hand to his chest. "Give me a head start."

She moved close and fiddled with the 'lock controls. The door didn't open immediately. She unzipped her sleeve pocket and plugged in a cable from her suit to the panel. The red light flicked to green and the outer door slid open. She turned, waved and entered.

Ten minutes later, the door re-opened and DualE exited. "No one home," she said.

"I'm surprised you got in so easily. Zofie's faith in her fellow spacers is substantial."

DualE patted her sleeve where the connection cable had been. "My resources are unavailable to a casual intruder. Nothing worth stealing inside and the controls are locked to her command. Even I couldn't get around those failsafes."

"Any sign of Denz?"

"Yeah, he left a few telltales for me. But didn't indicate where they were going." She led the way back to the scooter.

"Where to now?"

"Let's check out your potential sermon venues and look for Zofie. If no luck, I'll return here and wait."

"You could ask Mr. Kondradt to help." The man seemed to be well informed of the happenings here and in the Eddy in general.

"I could but I'd rather not be indebted to Gar Kondradt. The price might me more than I'd like to pay."

"Your call. But I remind you we hired you *and* Carver Denz. I will make the call to Kondradt and take the risk."

She hopped aboard and waited for him to settle behind her. "You also hired my judgment. In this case, give me more time before you make that call."

He didn't like the prospect of DualE returning to the *Whisper* and leaving he and the brothers unguarded. He closed his eyes again and locked arms around her. "I give you one shift."

DualE secured the scooter and she and Pious entered the station's central hub. Flimsuits unsealed, she recognized the odor of machine oil and burnt...plastic? Aside from systems' hum there was little noise. And no spacers.

If Rowland wanted an assessment of the Eddy's military readiness, she'd advise he wouldn't find much here. So why the rumors of a rekindled secession by force? The malcontents, if in numbers, were out in the void well beyond this shipyard. It made strategic sense; they were less vulnerable if not gathered in one place. Also, less powerful. The *Rickover* alone wouldn't pose a huge threat. Rowland was securing one beachhead at a time; a series of surgical strikes could soften resistance for the next phase. Perhaps his reserves would make the next jump in greater numbers.

"Here," Pious told her.

They passed through a pressurized 'lock into a garden dome. The humidity and smells hit her immediately. "The plants are real," she said.

Pious took a deep breath. "This is refreshing. I should instruct Chels to recreate something like this on Slate's. I think a portion of our funds could be channelled into such a project."

DualE was fine with that as long as it doesn't come out of her remuneration. She said, "It lifts the spirits. Makes me think I'm surface bound."

"Planets are hard to tame but I understand the Eddy has more than a few on the easier side. Once they settle who owns them."

"Bohr agreed the Realm shall continue possession with our side taking a profit share only if and when said planets become net exporters."

"My brotherhood looks forward to the day we can set root upon real land again. Imagine, DualE, an entire world to guide and assist."

"And tithe?" her skepticism was borne from too many economically-based battles.

"Only for the continuing benefit of our congregation."

DualE strolled across the paths and lawn, checking access and overhead. "This isn't bad. I can monitor the entry easily enough." She hiked to the opposite side. "This door can be used as an exit only."

"I can address the audience from the hillock near center. Remorse can handle lighting and sound. Cardinal can mingle and evaluate the crowd." Pious marched to the knoll. He turned full circle. "Yes, I'm very pleased. Do we need to look at the others?"

She needed to. "We might as well. No permission has been requested or given as yet. We should prepare for an alternate."

They left the atrium and hiked to the other locations identified by Brother Remorse. The first was empty, a temporary live cargo hold which reeked of not-quite-effective disinfectant.

DualE heard the last venue before they saw the flashing EDDIE'S DIVE light.

DRINKS

GAMBLING

ENTERTAINMENT

"Sounds like our kind of place," she said.

"One is called where one is called," said Pious and accompanied her inside.

DualE kept Pious in her periphery while she hunted for Zofie and Carver. A silhouette rang a bell but it wasn't either of the *Whisper's* crew. She studied the figure closer and recognized Kondradt's scooter pilot. If the woman worked for Kondradt then she knew who DualE and Pious were. It wouldn't hurt to approach her.

"Someone we should meet," she told Pious and guided him past the few customers.

The woman was younger than DualE and thinner. DualE hated her on sight. "Hi. Recognized you from Kondradt's visit." DualE extended a hand. "I'm DualE from the *Penance*. This is Brother Pious." She didn't give the woman a chance to deny the Kondradt connection but moved along. "Pious is scouting for a good place to speak to anyone who'd like to listen to his message of gaining peace of mind."

Pious jumped in on cue. "In this chaotic time and place, I preach a path which can help the confused learn to guide themselves through the turmoil, whether it be internal or external. You look tense. Are you troubled?"

"That's one question too many. My name's Marshall. You did well to recognize me, Kondradt told me to remain at a non-threatening distance from *Penance*. I was doing him a favor by shuttling him to you."

Pious was right, Marshall's face was lined with tension. DualE doubted Kondradt would rely on a casual acquaintance to escort him to the *Penance*. Not with DualE's reputation. He'd want someone he could trust backing him up if things went sideways. Publicly, DualE would take the woman at her word. "We've scouted the Atrium and one of the pressurized cargo-holds."

"Now you're here," said Marshall. "Frankly, I'd choose this place. The spacers and 'yard workers know it and frequent it. You might have to split any funds raised with the owner." She drained her glass.

"Can I get you another?" DualE asked.

"No, thanks. I'm not here to drown non-existent sorrows. Purely refreshment, non-alcoholic and I've had enough."

She looked strained but not someone who fought it with drugs or booze. Like DualE, Marshall needed to stay in control. Stress had to be endured. For the moment.

"How do you fit into the 'yard society?" Pious asked.

"I deploy spacers, prospectors and equipment where they're needed in the Eddy."

DualE wanted to ask if Marshall worked alone or for a greater concern but held back a direct query. "That must take some organizing." She'd build up to the real questions.

"If you mean 'do I have an organization?', say so."

Marshall would clam up if DualE pushed.

Pious said, "I'm always interested in someone with those skills to keep my message current when the brothers and I move on. I deliver God's guidance but can't be everywhere at once. Are you a woman of faith, Ms. Marshall?"

"I adhere to my own set of principles, brother."

Pious laughed. "Honest and well said. I would welcome ten of you over a hundred self-deceiving souls looking for the wrong answers."

"Or the right answers to the wrong questions?" asked Marshall.

"That happens all too often. You may have more in common philosophically with DualE than my brotherhood."

DualE wasn't sure she liked being categorized with a woman she barely knew. "What do you think?" she asked Marshall. "My principles can be compromised externally if I let them. Do you control your external pressures?"

Marshall's smile was one of confirmation not amusement. She knew what DualE asked. "Not often. I collaborate with those who hold similar goals."

The end justifying the deeds. The juncture where loyalties divided but rewards assembled.

"A freedom we all aspire to, I'm sure," said Pious. "If I choose this place to speak, would you help spread the word in advance? It sounds like your connections could be more effective than any publicity we mount."

"I'd hate to lose my partners to the fold. I need to keep them hungry for the next big strike."

"Are there any left?" DualE asked. "Or does the lure of one more undiscovered moonlet full of Schoenfeldium drive the dreamers forward despite the overwhelming negative odds?"

"If we believed the odds, none of us, including you and Pious, would be here." Marshall rose. "Here's my contact link. Tell me when you wish to make your address and I'll pass the word. Use your own announcement as well. I wouldn't want people to get the impression we're allied."

But they would. Marshall wouldn't offer unless she wanted to link with Pious.

"Very gracious of you." Pious stood to bid Marshall goodbye. "You'll hear from me within a shift."

"Nice meeting you," said Marshall. She walked out.

"Her manner changed during the conversation," said DualE.

"She's balancing agendas, I suspect." Pious sipped his drink. "I agree with you, she became more transparent at the end of our exchange. She doesn't believe there's another Carver Denz-size lode to be found but is sending the hopeful out anyway."

"Following the Gar Kondradt model. The prospectors aren't the ones who get rich. It's the outfitters and the transporters."

DualE replayed the conversation. "Marshall is more than Kondradt's chauffer. She's an ally, a partner."

"We should depart the dockyard before we're too involved with either. I considered asking her recommendation for our tour."

"It could put *Penance* at risk if we followed her suggested route. Assuming Kondradt wishes you to fail and fade away."

Pious sat and sighed. "I don't have time to fail. His influence is double-edged."

"Double at the least," said DualE. "We must find Carver in a hurry."

"I think this is the most likely place Zofie will come. I will return to the *Penance* and prepare my sermon."

"I won't let you leave unescorted. We'll go together."

"You think I'm in danger?"

"Don't look over your shoulder but two men in rust-colored flimsuits have been watching us since we came in. I can handle them but I'm not sure you could. Best get you to *Penance* where I can secure you from prying intruders."

"I defer to your judgment. It's unfortunate you have to do this alone."

"Yeah. I'll take it out of Denz's share."

Chapter 24

C hels stood in the *Crossed Swords'* airlock, watching Atone and the marine delve into its databanks.

"There are no entries since we arrived here," said Atone.

"What about the arrival itself? Did DualE leave a pilot log as you exited jumpspace and de-barnacled?"

Atone keyed the screen. "I'll go back to pre-jump." It took a moment before shaking his head. "No, I'm locked out there. Here's a navigation log." He leaned out of the way so Rowland's man could see the screen.

The officer spent some time scrolling the data. Chels stepped inside and looked over his shoulder. He hadn't ordered her not to. *...general absence of ships, commercial and naval, here. Docking routine. Locked down. Check Swords and Penance.*

That was all the electronic message DualE'd left for prying eyes. Chels looked around the inside of the ship for anything else. She shuddered at the cryo coffin control panels. Her last deepsleep nightmares stayed with her to this day. More than one night she'd woken up shivering and fearful. They said spookspace laid bare your sins. The images she saw in her sleep aboard Slate's were not her memories. The deeds witnessed in those dreams weren't hers. As far as she remembered. Maybe they were and she'd sublimated them too deep to consciously access.

The officer parroted Chels' examination of the interior. He pulled storage panels open, dug into DualE's hardsuit pockets and finally opened the two coffins. The odors from the cryo fluids lingered, turning her stomach and dredging bad memories. Chels couldn't look into them and moved back into the 'lock.

"Excuse me, Ms. Harte, I need to check the airlock as well. The Admiral will have my guts and braid if I overlook anything."

"Got it." She stepped onto the gantry.

He joined her a few minutes later.

"Going back empty-handed?" Chels asked.

"Looks pretty bare. I've sent the log to the *Rickover*. If there's a hidden message, they'll decode it but I doubt there's anything to find. DualE was looking out for the brother and his mates first." He nodded toward Atone, still inside the *Crossed Swords*. "Her obligation to Rowland came second and hadn't become operational yet." He called inside. "Thanks for your help, Brother Atone. I leave you to your mission."

Chels stepped into the ship. "She left nothing?"

"He got all I could find." Atone tapped his temple. "If DualE was gathering data for the Confluence, she kept it up here. Not to be shared until required and in person."

"I wonder what made her agree to provide intel for Rowland? I got the sense she was bitter how her service ended in Bohr. Which is why she joined you."

"Loyalty to the corps?"

"Not to Rowland? Could be. Seems one and the same to me."

Atone shook his head. "If I had to choose between my loyalty to the church or my brothers, I would choose the latter over any figurehead."

Her choices cascaded into her existence. Slate, Progress, Argosy Realm, Pious, the church. She'd compromised her role for the church once. Slate's Progress was a small part of the Realm but it was the only part she cared about. How could she align her duty to all? Pick the most important and pray the others weren't betrayed.

C hels sat in the dark. It was two hours since shift change. Slate should've been back by now.

She'd spent an hour doodling notes for Brother Atone's next address but wound up categorizing her own fears. How could that help the rest of Progress? She turned the light on and reread her ideas. Maybe this was how it should be done. Maybe her anxieties weren't unique; a path for Atone to connect with Progress.

How had Pious spurred such interest? Their first meeting. She pictured him in the pub, sipping the cheapest wine. He was more than one of them, he was *less*. The semblance of poverty wasn't an act, it was honesty. Now the brothers travelled in a well re-fitted ship. They had bodyguards, or at least one. They still lived frugally and their mindset showed. But now fund-raising didn't drive this mission. Spreading a message of self-discovery leading to a balanced life drove them.

The door to their suite clunked open and the motion lights came on with a background glow.

"You're up late, Chels." Slate plopped face down on the bed.

She scrambled to her knees and pressed her thumbs into his shoulder blades. He groaned under her kneads.

She asked, "Who do we work for now? Mekli or Rowland?"

"I always strove to keep Progress as free from singular control as possible," Slate mumbled. "Rowland's here. Mekli's still in the Confluence, for all I know. Kondradt's jumped to the Eddy."

"The Admiral has spies here," she said. "Or did. He expected DualE to leave him a message. His man escorted Atone and me back to her ship to check."

Slate rolled onto his back. "Did they find anything?"

"Very little that I could see. The officer left empty-handed. Except for the docking log. I saw some of it on screen and nothing which seemed compromising to us or the Realm." Chels replayed it in her mind. "DualE commented about how few combat-capable ships were in port."

"Not much secret intelligence in that." Slate spread-eagled his arms. "Rowland can see for himself the commercial nature of most of our clientele."

"I'm disappointed with DualE if she really was Rowland's spy. She either works with Brother Pious or not."

"Not as simple for her. An ex-marine is never really 'ex'. And missionaries frequently acted as spies across human history. If Rowland hadn't recruited DualE, he might well have engaged Pious."

"Or Atone." He hadn't protested the *Crossed Swords'* intrusion by Rowland. "Why risk it?" Chels curled on her side next to Slate. "Why risk the peace before it's begun?"

"Rowland's a soldier. Fighting is his career. His job. Maybe he doesn't like the idea of a peace he didn't win by battle. He told me he believed there were some officials who wanted the Realm's armed fight to re-start."

"Did he say which side?"

"I assumed the Realm's. Your suspicions are too devious, Chels. You should have spent more time with Pious while he was aboard."

"It's Rowland who's devious. How much sense would this make if he were the one? He knows the beam attack was an accident, right?"

"That's what I told him."

"And I reinforced it but he seemed quite skeptical that Perry and his unknown partner could have found, restored and deployed alien tech." Chels had believed Perry. His death added weight to her belief.

"Rowland could be using the attack to put himself in the right strategic position to launch a quick, decisive assault and claim victory for the Confluence, in spite of his political masters' agenda."

"Or with their consent. He'll head for the Eddy."

"The Eddy needs to be warned. Pious too. Chels, can you convince Atone to leave Progress and join his brothers?"

"I'd have to overcome his desire to prove himself ready to lead their mission here. Then find someone to hold his hand through a jump."

Her anxieties welled up with a vengeance. "I wish I could do it but the next jump would be my last plus one." Was she being as selfish as Atone? Pious needed them.

"I can't leave here either. Atone will have to gut up or we force him into cryo."

She propped up her head with an arm, staring past Slate, past Progress' shell into the frightening void beyond her shells. "Let me talk to him first."

"Chels, we don't have much time. My sense is Rowland wants to jump to the Eddy soon."

"I'd reached the same conclusion hours ago."

"Then we'd better be ahead of him."

The inevitable conclusion could test her loyalty and her sanity.

Chapter 25

Z ofie appraised Carver with a side glance. "The beard changes your look, Carver. Not sure I like it esthetically but it's a fair disguise, coupled with a cleric robe." Zofie checked her wrist screen. "Almost there. We'll suit up at the next outside access 'lock."

Carver walked in step but remained silent, hands folded in front, aping Pious' stride. She doubted he was meditating over ecclesiastical matters. More likely, counting the hours he had left as her situational partner.

She halted at the EVA station. "Let's see what goodies you bought for the cargo deception. If they're as good a mask as your new look, I'll be happy."

"So will the Reds. Are they joining us?" Carver quickly exchanged his robe for a hardsuit.

Zofie donned hers. "I want to inspect first without them. I'll call them now and put them on standby." She tagged a message and closed helmet visor. "We're on suit comm," she said.

"Receiving," Carver answered.

The pair cycled outside the pressurized shipyard passageway into the barge holding area. Carver attached their tethers while she located the machinery shipment pod. She pointed to a cocoon-shaped lozenge above and counter-spinwise.

He nodded and strapped to her. She guided them with an airjet to the pod's inspection door. Navigating in three dimensions plus adjusting for the slow movement of her target brought back memories of an early life amidst the jumble of a small salvage whirlpool. Raised in a constantly changing environment, where a small mistake cost you credit or your life, she'd mastered the skills before she was ten.

They intercepted the pod cleanly and she keyed in the ownership code. Carver anchored the tethers outside the 'lock and followed her inside. Zofie's suit light reflected from a myriad of metal and synthetic alloys, jumbled in a cat's cradle of assorted surplus equipment.

"What a mess," she said. "Looks like none of it was locked down for transport."

"Couldn't have harmed this crap much. It's perfect for your use. Safely secure and protect the Reds' material on the opposite side and let this rubbish float free. Few inspectors would risk suit integrity digging through the deadly shards and pointed refuse."

"Good point. You did well, Carver. Thanks." Her earbud pinged. "The Reds are here."

"That was quick. They must have followed us." Zofie returned to the 'lock and opened it for her clients. "Private frequency," she said. She didn't want or need shipyard chatter distracting her focus.

"Got you," answered the newcomers.

"Have a look inside but watch your suits. The stuff isn't anchored." She drifted with them to Carver's side. "When can you deliver your goods? I suggest we use this pod. It's small enough to barnacle or slide into a jumpfreighter's hold intact."

"Tomorrow. Give us the access code and we'll load up."

"I'll meet you here. No one gets my codes." She wanted to see the shipment for herself as Carver suggested. She hoped Carver would join her.

"We'd prefer to load in private."

"I've got Gar Kondradt as my other client. I doubt he'll rely on second-hand confirmation." Maybe Kondradt's name could do her some good.

"Kondradt doesn't concern us. His influence won't draw water against this shipment. I suggest you worry about what he's shipping and leave us mind ours. You'll be well compensated."

"I don't move goods I haven't seen with my own eyes."

"Not part of our deal. We're prepared to walk away. Good luck with your other shipment."

Zofie couldn't afford to lose this. Not just for the credits but to divert attention from Marshall. Kondradt would be disappointed and he didn't suffer well people who let him down.

"We understand," said Carver. "Zofie had to try, right?"

The Reds turned to him as one. "Naturally. The code?"

Did Carver have a get-around strategy? She had to trust him. Not easy for her with anyone, let alone a one-time lover who she'd tried to kill. Zofie gave them the code. It wasn't as though they'd steal anything valuable.

"Find transport and we'll deposit your first installment." The Reds left.

Zofie changed the comm to Carver-only. "What do you think?"

"I suggest you find someone to hide in here before they return."

"Are you volunteering?"

"No thanks. I'll bet they'll be watching both of us to ensure we're not in the pod."

"I don't get why they didn't seem worried about Kondradt." She replayed their reaction.

"One scenario is they work with him. Or for him."

"Or they're bigger than him," she suggested.

"They might think they are and that could be your advantage."

"I hope so or I'll be the one holding the pod if anything goes wrong."

"Marshall is your protection, Zofie. Now, any ideas for a spy in here?"

"Yeah. Cassity. If she'll do it."

"The spacer you met? If she's not working for Kondradt as well. If she is, you're no further behind."

"I'm starting to regret doing business with him."

C arver sat unnoticed in the pub's shadows while Zofie prowled. After an hour and three of the worst-tasting beers he'd experienced, Carver was ready to return to the solitude of the *Whisper* prior to Zofie's departure. There was an anticipation in the atmosphere he couldn't pin down. As per Zofie's and his choice, he talked to no one and no one talked to him.

Zofie came back to his table, a guest in tow. "Willie Renfrew, meet Cassity."

Cassity stood a head taller than Zofie and was as fit-looking as the formidable DualE.

"Renfrew. Hi." Her grip was firm but friendly. "Here for the show?"

"Please sit," Carver slid deeper into the booth. "What show?"

"I won't spoil it," said Cassity.

"I've told Cassity what I need," said Zofie. "She's not convinced I should mess with the Reds."

"One part of me agrees with Cassity." He spoke to the woman directly. "I'm Zofie's partner and I've a strong interest in this shipment. Since she's already committed to the Reds, it's too late for second thoughts. We need to prepare for the other end of jump. We'd like to see their cargo first hand. Obviously, they're aren't going to let us near it."

Cassity accepted a drink from the serv-bot and looked to the partners.

"I've had enough," said Carver. "Any more and I'll need to reline my stomach."

Zofie declined as well.

"Count me out for personal inspection. If the Reds are watching you, then they've already tagged me."

"I don't see them here," said Zofie. "I've made certain."

"Maybe not today but we've spoken before in public, Zofie. We're a mutual risk." Cassity swirled the drink in her glass. "What do you expect to see?"

Zofie glanced at Carver. He wasn't going to be the one to convince her. She had to make that decision herself. "The Reds claim to have artifacts. *Alien* artifacts. We're shipping them with an aggregate of surplus refining machinery. A real prize. Our thoughts are customs won't dig too deep with a loose collection of sharp and massive garbage."

"A good plan. I see only one flaw," said Cassity.

"Only one?" Carver had to laugh.

"Yeah, the main one." Cassity lowered her voice. "If any amount of alien artifacts had been found, this whole shipyard would know about it. Hell, the whole Eddy would know about it."

Zofie didn't laugh with Carver. "How can you be sure? Secrets have been kept before."

"Not lately. You should've been here when the big Schoenfeldium lode was discovered months ago. An entire moonlet full. It came into the Eddy's claim office and with light speed, every prospector in the Eddy knew about the confidential strike. Within a week, the Realm buzzed with the news."

"The famous Carver Denz," said Zofie. "I agree a secret's tough but we're talking a magnitude difference here."

Cassity upended her glass on the table. "I say it with confidence because there's already been one artifact found. A weapon. By accident."

"The particle beam?"

Cassity stared at Carver. "You know?"

"I do now. An attack on Argosy Station not long before we jumped. Hit a jumpfreighter coming from here. The *Orson?*"

"That would fit."

"How do you know?" asked Carver.

"New arrivals from Argosy Station via Slate's Progress. Lightspeed gossip once again."

"Maybe the Reds are shipping that," said Zofie.

"Uh uh," said Cassity. "It's lost. The salvagers who found it are gone. I'll tell you this for free because I like you. The Reds aren't known to work with Gar Kondradt but it doesn't rule out a temporary alliance. Whatever they're shipping in disguise, it isn't alien. It's probably Realm-ware and it isn't necessarily harmless. Or a new Schoenfeldium lode, denying the Realm its share."

Cassity rose and nodded to them. "The good news is Kondradt doesn't like to waste resources. That includes you, Zofie. This may just be a trial run. I'll see you around. If not before you jump, when you get back. Nice meeting you, Renfrew."

Once Cassity was beyond ear-shot, Zofie said, "Kondradt. Why not just hire me for both this mysterious shipment *and* hauling Marshall's wet-wared body?"

"He's letting you create the diversion. If you're caught, the suspicion falls on the Reds. And Marshall still gets through with whatever she's carrying in her brain."

"Do you think Cassity's right about Kondradt not wasting resources?"

"I can't answer that, Zofie. Take what precautions you can. Make sure you revive before Marshall and have the *Whisper* fuelled for a quick escape post-jump."

"I'll do..." Zofie's expression changed in an instant from concern to shock. "Holy shit. Look who just walked in."

Carver turned to look. His unshaven jaw dropped.

Chapter 26

Pious smoothed his robes as he walked beside DualE. Comparing her stride to Remorse's ahead of them he was struck by her economy of movement. It was as though her body used mind meditation techniques to guide it through space and time.

She said, "I didn't think you'd be ready to appear so soon, Brother Pious."

"We must not rest. This shipyard has fewer spacers than I expected. If the potential converts scattered throughout the Eddy can't come to me here, the *Penance* will go to them. Today is a humble start."

"What about the ones yet to come here? This 'yard could get a lot busier if hostilities rekindle."

"I'll repeat what we did at Slate's Progress. This time Brother Remorse will assume responsibility for this facility." The *Penance* would need Brother Cardinal to pilot their way around the Eddy's small outposts. Remorse would pass or fail his test.

Remorse turned. "The message looks successful," he said.

They joined a straggly line of men and women heading in the same direction. "The promise of one free drink might be the lone incentive," said Pious. "I'm still uncertain that was the best advertisement."

"You can afford it," said DualE. "I'll bet you recoup triple your investment. I know these people. Their type. They claim to be loners, solitary prospectors wanting to be left to work without interference. But get them together and they're suddenly grateful for company. For a short while. You'll reach them at a good time."

Pious accepted her evaluation. Once again, he thought DualE's potential as a missionary was substantial. He saw the gaudy light identifying the pub and squeezed through the portal. He pulled back his hood and sleeves as he followed his brother to the elevated deck on one side. Pious activated his collar microphone and adjusted it for the size of the space. "Will you look after the drinks, Remorse?"

DualE stopped and stared across the room, holding his arm. "I'll be damned. Sorry, brother. I'll be double-damned."

He followed her gaze. Carver Denz and Zofie Ked sat in a booth. They appeared in earnest discussion and unaware or uncaring of the growing crowd. He didn't recognize the woman with them but she had the survivor look DualE projected. "Our luck improves."

"I'll circulate then join my partner." She drifted away.

Pious straightened his back and strode confidently to the platform. A few spacers leaned on the railing. He greeted them. "I am your host for the next half hour. You are welcome to remain with me or descend to the main floor. The brotherhood would be honored to buy you a refreshment." He pointed to Remorse. "My associate arranges your fare. My only price is you loan me your time."

"You got it, mate...Sounds good as long as you're not preaching war...Not preaching peace, you mean."

Fractious opinions. He'd watch his step here. At least until he overcame their reluctance to listen. Pious gripped the railing, now vacated by the retreating spacers. He cleared his throat, testing the volume. He should've grabbed water for himself. He coughed again and the crowd quieted.

"Thank you all for joining me today. I realize notice was short and your time is valuable."

"You promised drink," hooted a voice. "More valuable than time and enough to lure me."

Laughs rippled through the pub.

"The promise is kept," said Pious. He scanned the faces. "I recognize a few of you from Slate's Progress when my brothers and I communed there months ago. I hope your presence today indicates a continuing curiosity in my message. You are pioneers, replicating the perilous journeys our ancestors made across a half-unknown, vastly-unexplored planet called Earth. They embarked on wind-powered sailing ships across oceans of water as opposed to the starry void and jumpspace cheats. But they didn't know what lay on the other end of the trek. They struggled, they died, they eventually prospered."

DualE passed below him and handed a water globe to him before heading toward Carver's booth.

Pious sipped, the cool liquid soothed. "You of the Realm, specifically the Eddy, carry this spirit alone within mankind's sphere. What kept those first explorers from giving up? What strength reinforced survival? Not physical resolve but mental resolve. Their indefatigable spirit was most fundamental to success. I submit it was *faith*." He walked to one side and made eye contact with a small knot of men. "A faith in the knowledge their hardships and sacrifices meant freedom. They earned freedom. As you have. You are bound by the laws of the universe. Captains aren't free to vent your ships. You're not free to do harm to one another. You *are* free to live as you choose." He transferred his gaze to the entire room. "Until your choice brings harm to another. Isn't that the ultimate freedom? Free to make a choice which helps your own kind? The choice is easy when you carry God with you."

Pious drained his drink and set the globe aside. Remorse joined him. "Faith," said Pious. "A single word with so many layers." His throat dried up again. He signalled Remorse to continue.

"Reflect upon your own set of standards. Are you free because of your faith in how you live? Or are you constrained by sin? By greed? By lust? All the limiting lures preventing you from reaching your spiritual potential."

Pious hoisted himself onto the railing, relieving the pressure on his lower back. He indicated his readiness to speak again. "Thank you, brother. External forces may dictate your immediate future. I heard some of you voice grudges against Bohr Confluence." He tapped his head. "Here is where your freedom and your faith reside. Keep it whole whatever short-term aggression you face." Pious shifted his body but the nagging pain continued. A petty distraction not worth his notice but it was a lesson to be shared. He inhaled deep. "Don't equate physical boundaries with loss of liberty. Look inside to determine how you can help even one person less fortunate than you. Lead them by example." Had he gotten through? He couldn't read the mood. His failing or some deeper issue?

Remorse spoke. "We thank you for your attention. We travel to your comrades out there." Remorse pointed above and to the sides. "Any gift you make will help our ship reach as many as possible and help those who are in desperate straits."

Pious clapped a hand on his confederate's shoulder. "Well spoken, brother. Would you return to the *Penance* and begin broadcasting our message to the Eddy?"

Pious navigated through the crowd toward Carver Denz and company. He gripped hands of those who stopped him to talk. The weariness tested him but the response bolstered his spirit. He must keep up the strength until they completed their chosen task.

Carver stood to block DualE's direct access to Zofie. He said, "Before you say or do anything, I'm intact and here voluntarily, though we didn't know about the sermon. I've been locked out of the *Whisper's* comm and Zofie's been to busy with business. I'm also ready to rejoin you and the brothers."

DualE pushed him aside with ease. "Give me one reason I shouldn't do you damage, Zofie. No, give me multiple reasons."

Carver regained his position, leaning into DualE as hard as he dared. "She got me out of Argosy's brig. That's more than anyone else appeared to be doing."

DualE backed off a step. "I made a deal with Rowland to free you. An arrangement I'm still committed to, despite Zofie's interference. That's how I roll."

"You're angrier at yourself than me," said Zofie.

Carver interrupted before it escalated. "She got me away from Argosy Station and from whoever decided I should be separated and confined."

"Rowland told me is was for your protection," said DualE. "Did she tell you to grow that ridiculous beard and shave your head, too? It looks...awful."

Eyes and ears in Eddie's Dive had taken notice of their escalating exchange. DualE sat down. Carver made sure he was between the two women. "It's not awful. And it's a good guise for Willie Renfrew, prospector."

"Rowland's so full of bullshit," said Zofie, "his blue eyes are turning brown."

"I agree," said Carver. "I think he's been disingenuous from the start of his mission to the Realm."

"He admitted he had you arrested," DualE confirmed. "He told me why and it seemed logical."

"What else did he tell you?" Zofie asked.

DualE hesitated, as though weighing options. Or how much to tell. "He said there were factions in the Realm, particularly within the Eddy, who weren't satisfied with the peace accord. He used the attack on the *Orson* we witnessed out of jump as evidence."

"If it was an attack, it could've come from anyone or anywhere," said Carver. "It might have been an accident."

"The admiral wouldn't believe that," said Zofie. "It doesn't suit his agenda."

"Meaning what?" DualE whispered as Pious continued to speak from across the pub.

"Admiral Rowland's the one who doesn't like the peace accord. What else has he got you doing besides spreading misinformation?" Zofie signalled the servbot for more drinks.

"Not your business," DualE answered.

"It is mine," said Carver. "We're partners, remember?"

"We'll discuss this later. After Pious finishes. We're on the job, *partner*."

Tempers cooled for the moment, Carver turned his attention to Pious. DualE slid from the booth and moved amongst the crowd in Eddie's Dive. Carver did the same, taking the opposite side. All the while he listened, to the mutterings from the assemblage and Pious' words.

Carver had to admit the crowd was more respectful than he would have guessed. Living on the edge of survival against the void, the lure of wealth which never appeared and the growing military danger created an audience willing to listen for any optimism. Pious' theme was that the optimism started within the self. Pious' God wasn't the only deity in town but the First Expansion Brotherhood had arrived first and remained persistent.

Carver let his hood shade his face, in case a more observant spacer connected the acolyte collecting funds for the brotherhood to the prospector who'd found the lode they all dreamed about mere months before. Carver Denz, wealthiest prospector in the Realm. Until he divided his undeserved fortune amongst his fellow survivors aboard the jump-sabotaged *Pollux*.

The nightmares in spookspace couldn't be bought off but he'd tried anyway. At least the nightmares were less debilitating than if he'd kept the fortune. Carver murmured his thanks as credits filled his hands. The brotherhood didn't need the funds, not after Carver's generosity, but the act of giving reinforced the listeners' faith.

He admired Pious' optimism. If the Eddy was Shadow Death Valley, Pious walked unfearingly through it, confident in his protection. With Carver and DualE for backup.

DualE let Carver gather funds while she monitored body language. There were few side conversations. Pious had the crowd's attention. She swept the room continuously but as if looking for something or someone specific. She tracked Carver to see if anyone took special interest in the collector guised as Willie Renfrew.

Her conflict with Zofie was undisciplined. Had she learned nothing from Pious? When heat-of-the-moment moments arose, her 'fight' instinct had saved her life many times where 'flight' would have been fatal. She had to adapt; follow a third reaction, conciliation. The current situation demanded a new role, protector, not company soldier. She contemplated the differences while she moved.

Peripherally, she noted two new arrivals suited in red. Her gaze didn't stop as she swung her eyes past them but they were different than the majority here. They were military, trying to mask their identities as much as Carver was. Their training to the point of inbred carriage couldn't be entirely masked any more than hers. Whose military? Knowing they'd recognize her posture for what she once was, she moved toward them. Would the pair leave, divide or stand their ground? DualE had no reservations about her ability to carry a fight but she was here in a defensive role for the brothers. Rowland's task was in limbo until she digested Zofie's accusations.

DualE halted two paces away. They hadn't moved. "Here for the show?"

"We heard there was a message for all," one of them said. The other had turned his gaze away after first eye contact. Dismissal?

"That's true," said DualE. "Is there a particular message you seek?" Displaced anger rose quickly. She fought down the instinct. She served Pious.

"Have to listen. Always interested in news from the Confluence."

She had it. The unique pronunciation and the flutter of the left hand. They were Confluence Navy. "I hope Brother Pious has something for you." She nodded once and moved away.

She shouldn't be surprised. A good commander never went in without backup, if they could help it. She'd infiltrated outposts and planets herself for the navy. It was safest to assume they knew who she was and whose orders she was under. It wouldn't do to discuss it here. They'd message her at some point and she'd respond. Or not. Pious was first priority now. And he wanted to leave the 'yard soon. She made a decision and circled back to the pair. "One of you, outside."

DualE did another circuit, then left, confident Carver would keep Pious from danger. The Red waited in an alcove beside the main entrance.

They exchanged code identifiers and she spoke. "I've little for Rowland. You see what I see. The Realm's forces aren't in evidence. Not here. Nor at Slate's Progress."

"Appreciate the intel though we're not duplicate task forces here. Our assignment is unrelated. We're deep cover. Can't move. If you have contact before us, tell the admiral it's in motion. He'll understand."

She hated riddles but it's how the game worked. "We're going the other way. Out to the mining operations, pre-settlement stuff. You'll see him before I will." She thought of his arrival at Slate's. Rowland wouldn't stop there. The Eddy was the heart of the Realm's resistance. "Tell Rowland I'll keep watch for any signs of armada buildup but my sense is there's nothing to fear." Except the admiral's paranoia. "I have to go. Don't contact me."

"Good luck." He gave her the service handclasp and they parted.

Pious wrapped up his address as she re-entered the bar. Carver stood before him. She glanced to the rear. No sign of Zofie. DualE joined her partners, suppressing guilt over her dual role here. She shouldn't have left Pious. This time it was okay but she wouldn't do it again. Damn Rowland.

Chapter 27

Zofie, Carver and Kondradt squished inside the *Whisper*. Marshall stood watch outside the closed airlock. Zofie wondered if she and Kondradt were audio-linked.

"If she's listening in," said Zofie, "I hope your encryption is tight so no one else can."

"She isn't. Who else would?" asked Kondradt.

"Navy," answered Carver.

"Which one?"

"Does it matter?" Zofie asked. "If you want me to get Marshall to your end point. I want to know what I'm carrying besides one info-mule."

"I heard you're shipping some salvage junk. Likely some sort of smuggling cover. It doesn't matter to me as long as it distracts anyone from paying too much attention to Marshall."

"You mean it isn't for you? Please don't lie, Kondradt. I hold Marshall's fate. If I think you're twisting me, I'll cut and run at the first sign of trouble."

"You're trusting Zofie with valuable goods, Kondradt," added Carver. "We think it's time you trusted her the whole way. Do the Reds work for you?"

"I thought we were going to be subtle, Carver." Zofie had planned to get to this point slower. But it was out now. She turned to Kondradt. "Well?"

"No, they don't. I've been busy with Realm matters and I can't tell you much about them. Word is they've been here for six months, buying and shipping inconsequential goods back to Argosy Station and smaller Realm settlements."

"To answer your question, we have information they are Confluence Navy." DualE's appraisal had shocked Zofie at first but it might fit.

Kondradt didn't seem surprised. "It's nothing new. I suspect the navy has had agents here for a long time. I've no idea what advantage they're gaining for Bohr. This shipyard is non-military. Usually. Realm forces haven't been near since before these three arrived. If they're Confluence agents, I'd prefer them here, where I can watch them and where they are unlikely to learn anything valuable. It drain's Confluence resources, however minute."

"Confluence Navy's command prepares for the long game, " said Carver.

"What are they shipping?" Kondradt asked.

Zofie didn't like betraying a trust but this was her life in the balance. "What have you heard about alien artifacts?"

Kondradt didn't laugh or smile. "Little. A myth. There's rumor of a weapon out in the void but my contacts haven't found it."

They *were* looking. He didn't lie. The information from DualE about the weapon was known outside Argosy Station. Cassity for one and probably everyone in this 'yard by now. "Is Marshall's information related?"

Kondradt brushed invisible dust from his sleeve. "No. I would share any knowledge about such a weapon with the Confluence."

"Isn't that a risk to the Realm?" asked Carver.

"You think too small, Denz. It's that important and potentially dangerous to everyone. Zofie, if you want a long business relationship with me, we have to accept each other's word."

"You're right. I know Carver's not part of it and you wouldn't tell me in front of him anyway."

"Treat me as a priest in confession," said Carver. "Whatever you say doesn't leave my lips. To DualE, Pious or another."

"An honorable goal, Denz. You worked for Admiral Rowland before, how do I know you're not working for him now?"

Zofie had a sudden revelation. Had Kondradt known Carver's twin role as prospector and spy when Kondradt had sabotaged the *Pollux* with Carver barnacled? Maybe Kondradt hadn't been after Carver's Schoenfeldium shipment after all. He'd been trying to stop the intelligence from reaching Bohr. She asked, "Are you trying to start a war or stop one?"

Kondradt took his time before answering. "We have an accord. Why would I want to rekindle hostilities?"

"Why would anyone?" Carver stood to peer through the porthole.

"Ask yourself who has the most to gain from a victory?" Kondradt stared at him, then Zofie.

Zofie couldn't figure it out. The Realm needed Confluence markets and support as much as the Confluence needed the Realm's raw resources. "Who has the least to lose?" she said.

Kondradt rolled his head. "That is a better way to examine it. You confirm my faith in our association, Zofie."

"The Confluence has the least to lose," Carver answered. "They will ultimately gain access to the resources required on their own if need be. The Realm provides a more timely, efficient solution."

This was too much politics and strategy for Zofie. She focused on what she could control. "I get your info-mule to Bohr. Then what?"

"She engages the politicians on both sides. While the accord holds."

"Can you find out what the Reds are shipping?" Zofie asked.

Kondradt stood, the meeting finished. "If I can find out without alerting them, I will pass the information to you. In the meantime, I suggest you arrange for transport. Direct to Bohr if you can."

"The Reds' shipment is destined for Argosy Station," she said. "They'll know if my jumpfreighter bypasses it."

"Nothing they could do about it from here. More important is timing. The sooner you leave, the better."

"It limits my options but I'll make inquiries."

"I already have," said Carver. "I had time on my hands while confined here."

Kondradt said, "You and I should have been partners too, Denz. I apologize for arranging to attack you on *Pollux*."

"I'll decline," said Carver. "I can't twist my morals quite far enough. I'm happy to wish you both luck on your mutual dealings."

And be well rid of us both. Zofie couldn't blame Carver for the sentiment. Her homicidal tendencies in the past had mitigating circumstances. Spookspace demons had sent her into a third, entirely delusional, dimension.

"Thanks, Kondradt. For trusting me this far." She watched the two men leave. Marshall, to Zofie's surprise, entered.

"I need to look at your coffins. Ensure I'm going to wake up on the other side. Objection?"

"Not at all, A second set of eyes would be welcome." *What the hell is locked in your subconscious to be so vital?*

C arver hitched a lift with Kondradt as far as the central hub. He could make the remaining trip to the *Penance* on his own.

"I'd've bet my former fortune the Reds worked for you, Kondradt."

"Then you'd've foolishly lost it again, Denz."

"That's my curse, making and losing fortunes I don't deserve." Luck could be a sin. He wondered if Pious ever worked that concept into a sermon.

"In my experience, luck is something you earn, whether you know it or not. It's like inspiration, the harder you work the more likely it is to appear."

"I never worked less hard in my life than when I discovered the Denz Lode."

"If you say so. In that rare case, take it and run. Do the hard work later. You did on *Pollux*, right?"

"Not work, *survival*." Denz battled the twisted universe and the human obstacles to get *Pollux* to Bohr. "Never thought of it that way. Makes me feel better."

"Your preacher wouldn't begrudge your hard-earned 'luck'. Stay in one piece in the Eddy, Denz. One day I might need some of your good fortune." Kondradt shot away.

Carver had much to ponder while he made his way to the *Penance*. The next stage of Pious' pilgrimage would take them away from the relative comforts and security of shipyards and transit stations. Out to frontiers where security often meant firing before being fired upon. It would be up to all aboard *Penance* to ensure they got into each small settlement safely. And back out. Word would eventually spread, making their visits marginally safer but once landed, Pious would still rely on him and DualE to keep the brothers safe.

He scanned the dock surrounding *Penance's* berth for watchers. None he could see. He announced himself at the 'lock.

"Carver, come in, glad to have you back with us." Pious offered a steaming cup of something non-alcoholic.

Carver took the hot vessel in both hands, warming his fingers before sipping the brew. "The shipyard doesn't worry about heating the atmosphere provided." He nodded to Cardinal and Remorse. DualE gave up her seat for him and stepped halfway into the airlock.

Carver took a swig. Warmth spread through him. The closeness of the three brothers added to the interior's coziness. "It's going to be a tight fit for the five of us beyond the back of beyond."

Pious drew his legs in tight. "Brother Remorse will remain here to continue our work and await Brother Atone when he arrives in the *Crossed Swords* from Slate's Progress."

Carver glanced at Remorse. The brother paled. Not his first choice to remain, Carver thought. "Why didn't you bring both ships together?" Carver nodded to DualE. "I see more safety in separation when we visit some of these outposts. One thing solitude generates is paranoia. Not that many of these prospectors needed any nudge to get there."

"Our jump transport only had room left for one," she answered. "We wanted to leave Slate's quickly."

Pious said, "It was always my intent to leave one or two of my fellows in reserve."

"We need to learn how to lead a congregation," said Remorse.

Carver studied Pious. The jumps had taken their toll on the leader. He'd aged unnaturally since he'd recruited Carver and DualE. Or rather, they'd convinced him to recruit two bodyguards. He'd ask DualE in private for her impressions. "When do we depart?" He'd hoped to see Zofie safely away but the puzzle over the Reds' real content slowed her down.

DualE spoke from the 'lock. "I recommend as soon as we can finalize our initial route. Expedience over efficiency."

Carver wasn't sure what pushed her until Pious illuminated it for him.

"Get away before the navy shows up," said the brother.

"You should warn Zofie the same, Carver," said DualE. "The *Rickover* showed up as we left Slate's. Once Rowland's satisfied it's secure, this shipyard will be his next port of call."

"Doesn't that contravene the peace terms?" asked Carver. "I understood no mutual inspection was to occur until Chancellor Mekli and his counterparts in Bohr agreed."

"Rowland pushes his own agenda. The navy isn't always in sync with the politicians. I suspect the Realm is doing the same. I've yet to see any of her armada. They're not here nor at Slate's. That could mean they're further out. A deep void muster point could complicate strategy but it's safer. Or they're near the Confluence trying to gain their own advantage. Either way, we need to move on before an embargo is put into place."

Carver drained his mug and slid to the console. "Zofie? It's me. Good luck with your jump." He listened privately to her reply then disconnected. He looked over his shoulder. "I'm ready when you are. Zofie won't waste time leaving the Eddy. DualE and I will plan defense contingencies given one ship instead of two." One basket, four eggs. Fragile eggs.

Chapter 28

Zofie accepted her departing partner's good wishes. "Thanks Carver, Kondradt's already put me on short notice to get the hell out of here with his human shipment." Zofie heard the rattle from her airlock. "Sounds like they're here."

Zofie cut the connection and spun in her padded chair. "Marshall, come in. I thought Kondradt was coming with you."

Her cargo dropped her duffle onto the deck and sat on it, legs crossed. "He's finalizing some arrangements with your jumpfreighter captain." Her speech was slow, as if every word was an effort to match the next.

"I prefer to make my own arrangements. Not that I don't trust your boss, but I suspect his priorities may not match mine."

"In this case you're wrong, if your priority is reaching the Confluence alive. My life is matched to yours. You have contacts he needs and you're as non-aligned with Realm or Bohr as he can find on short notice." Marshall exhaled a long breath.

"I also like to finalize my own barnacle details." Zofie studied her passenger, not for the first time. Marshall was nothing out of the ordinary yet acted as though she was more than a mere vessel muling intel for Kondradt. A memory cube could hold so much more volume of information, why risk the fragility of human storage? Was Marshall to bring something back from Bohr? Observations? More data?

"You will, he's just adding a rider to your other shipment."

"I knew it." Zofie slammed a fist on her thigh. "The Reds work for him. DualE was wrong."

Marshall shook her head, eyes unfocused. "No, they work for Rowland. And you won't like what they're shipping."

Zofie knelt before Marshall. "Are you going to tell me? Or do I back out of the deal with Kondradt?"

Marshall's head snapped upright. "Arms."

"Why the hell would Admiral Rowland send arms back to Bohr?"

Marshall's lethargy receded. "He isn't. He's equipping his own partisans in the Realm. He wants sorties to break on more than one front. He'll initiate small firefights from Argosy Station to Slate's Progress to here. And blame it on Realm insurgents." Marshall tapped her head. "I don't know the details locked inside me but it's all there. Rowland's duplicity revealed. You're going to get me to the powers in Bohr who can recall him before he starts a larger war the Realm won't win."

"Why would Rowland choose me to smuggle the arms?"

"Same reason Kondradt chose you. Who'd believe you're anything but a lone operator, trying to eke a living shuttling meagre wares between sides? A void opportunist."

Zofie returned to the console. She hailed the *Procyon*. "This is the *Whisper*. Permission to barnacle my ship. Update my cargo pod's status."

"Cargo pod locking on now. You may approach and barnacle. Sending your hull position. We depart in four hours. *Procyon* out."

Marshall stood and slung her pack into a locker beneath the cryo-coffins. "I'll seal the airlock."

Zofie waited for confirmation the *Whisper* was sealed tight then released the dock anchors. She followed the instructions and boosted toward the *Procyon*. The jumpfreighter was underway, clearing the shipyard and Zofie's intercept course carried her small ship quickly away from the 'yard and the only allies she had.

She heard Marshall buckle in behind her as she navigated closer. The *Procyon* grew rapidly in size through the front portal and soon she could make out the other barnacles. The Procyon had seen a lot of space, judging by the pocked surface. The steady glow of jumpdrive ignition shone from the front of the ship, anticipating the transition from normal. Whatever the cosmetic condition of the freighter, the propulsion systems appeared in top condition.

Zofie's cargo pod bulged near the stern of the freighter. Her signal pushed the *Whisper* forward and on the opposite side. "Whatever arrangements Kondradt made for my pod, I'm glad we're not located close to it."

"It won't arrive at the Reds' contracted destination. *Procyon's* captain's been well compensated for the change."

"I hope Rowland's agents don't feel the same about you and your destination, Marshall." *If the captain could be bribed once?*

Marshall didn't respond. No doubt the thought had crossed her mind too.

The *Whisper* matched velocity and clunked onto the *Procyon*. Zofie activated her anchors, then donned her EVA suit. "We're going outside to double check all the lockdowns." She didn't want to leave Marshall alone with the coffins. Zofie had only the woman's word that Kondradt needed her on the other side of jump. "We'll be back in plenty of time for you to prepare your coffin then."

It took a moment to orient outside the airlock but Zofie soon got her bearings. She left Marshall cabled to the hull and pulled herself down to the bigger ship's surface. Zofie tested each anchor cable twice until she was satisfied *Whisper* would jump with *Procyon* as one through spookspace.

The increasing acceleration was noticeable and Zofie climbed to the 'lock. Back inside, Zofie pinged a short farewell to the *Penance*.

She extruded her coffin. "As captain, I go under last." She watched Marshall recline and seal the lid. The coffin slid back into its space. Green telltale lights flashed to orange and finally blue. Marshall was now frozen alone with the coming nightmares of jumpspace.

Zofie climbed into her cocoon and initiated deepsleep. Processing the information about Rowland and his rogue war would provide all the nightmares she could handle.

Z ofie knew she was in cryo yet her mind processed the timetable stretched before her. The pod containing Carver's junk and Rowland's armaments wouldn't be dropped by the *Procyon* at Argosy. What if Rowland's insurgents missed their shipment and took action against the *Procyon*? Timing was on her side. *Procyon* would be back in jumpspace before Rowland's undercover team could respond.

There were no guarantees. Zofie and Marshall were flotsam in the void. Not intentionally expendable but too insignificant in the physical sense to matter in a fringe fight.

The agenda repeated over and over in her dreams. She couldn't escape the endless loop. She tried thinking of Brother Pious. It calmed her for a short time but then Ellick's ghosts began to circle. Her former lover's spirit haunted spookspace in all time directions. His past, her past, her future. The guilt from his death was on her.

The options tempted her. Ditch Marshall instead of the arms. What did she care for the Realm's preservation? For her, the Realm had provided squalor and betrayal, but a home. The alternative under Confluence rule would be worse.

Zofie retreated from jumpspace, cocooning within the *Whisper*. She pictured herself sitting on the deck, legs crossed, eyes closed. She exhaled and slowly rose from the deck to a mid-air position. No pressure from outside her core. Pious' mantras coursed through her nerves. Tranquility didn't follow but tolerance did. She would make it to the next drop.

Chapter 29

Chels dosed in the chapel. She'd stayed all night, spelling off an overstressed Atone, ready to counsel visitors to the makeshift church. Uneven footfalls nearby woke her fully. She smelled sweated alcohol.

A man stood in the doorway. A spacer. He trembled and licked his lips. His eyes darted from side to side; looking but did he see? Knees were bent in the station's artificial gravity. Another spacer far from his element.

"Hi," said Chels. "Could you use a bite to eat?" She reached in her robe and drew out an energy wafer pack. She rose and stepped near, holding the package in front. "Here." She set it down on the last chair and stepped back. He wasn't ready for soul cleansing. Not yet. "Some wine as well? It's pretty bad stuff but might help you through the next hour." She moved to the front of the chapel and poured a small cup of sacramental red. She wouldn't force him to endure withdrawal if he wasn't ready.

Chels returned to the man, now seated, chewing the wafer. "Bad jump?"

He smirked. "Is there such a thing as a good jump? No, jump wasn't the issue." He gulped the wine and set the cup down, not asking for more. His hands shook as he finished the wafer. "Thank you."

"It's been a few years since I jumped but I doubt they've refined the process. How long have you been on Slate's?"

"Two, maybe three, shifts. Not sure. I came looking for a friend. Heard he's dead. Carried too many demons in his head." He looked around and seemed able to focus on what he saw. "Thought he might've come here before he passed."

A chill passed from her head to toes. He didn't say more. Chels stared forward. She'd have to tease his story from him.

"It's possible. What was his name?"

"Perry. Though he might not have given it." He described her confessor.

"I met him. Once." This man couldn't know with certainty what Perry had told her. If she revealed what she knew, he might bolt. If he would confess to her, she might learn the location of the artifact. The weapon. If the Realm could get it before Rowland, it might balance the scales back to even. "Not well enough."

"My name's Altman. It won't mean anything. Not yet. Maybe never."

"Why don't you tell me?" Chels rose and closed the chapel door. She sat three seats away from Altman, turned toward him, but without eye contact. If he moved closer, she'd react appropriately. "I don't see you. To me, you're a voice. An unknown voice, if you like. I'm not your conscience, I don't judge. I listen and if I can guide you to the next step of recovery from the demons chasing you, I will." Her guilt, posing as a confidant, disturbed her. But greater good, or greater harm potential, had to be considered. She'd crossed the line once with Perry, this second time was as difficult.

He was silent for a while and she considered pouring another cup of wine. She was about to move when he began.

"Me and Perry. We're salvagers. *Were.* We found something. I used to comm on a short-jumpfreighter and I'd never seen the like." Altman sneezed.

Chels felt the spittle on her hand but didn't react, though she wanted to wipe it clean. "You found something you didn't recognize? Mineral lode?"

"Nothing like that. Nothing like anything I'd ever seen. But I thought I knew what it was for." His voice dropped to a *Whisper*. "It was alien, you see. Alien or some piece of equipment from mankind's future, dropped out of spookspace into our laps. Who can tell what time or dimension eddies we've stirred up in jump?"

"A perceptive thought, sir. You saw this object as a gift."

"Yeah. Make us rich. Richer if we could make it work. I was sure it was a comm device. I figured the aliens or our future selves had uncovered a more reliable tech."

"A marvelous breakthrough if successful. You acted on your assumption. What then?"

"Perry never told you this?"

"Continue *your* story, Mr. Altman."

"If overconfidence is a sin, I sinned. I bulled ahead, thinking I had it all reckoned. We needed the opening of a jumpship to send a test message. That's what I theorized. I was a great scientist. Thought I knew more than those who wrote the textbooks and rendered their imaginations in elegant equations. This was hardware. Solid machinery you could touch." He fell silent again. His hands caressed a phantom shape.

"Your arrogance deceived you. The universe played it's trick."

He sniffed and rasped a wet cough. "That it did. We sent our message but it wasn't a radio beam. It was a particle beam. The recoil tore the machine away from us. We fled. Perry came here. I tried to lose myself in the Eddy but my conscience caught up to me. He and I need to set it right."

"With Perry dead, you're alone. Your goal could be difficult." Chels turned to face him. She was no longer the anonymous listener. She was involved. "Perry's dead. You need to show someone where you lost it. Don't let Perry's demons catch you before you've made amends."

"How can I make amends for loosing death and destruction?"

Chels slid closer. She stretched a hand to his shoulder. Altman's head hung forward, shaking.

"This machine is a gift," she said. "You were right. Help find it again. Are you Realm?"

He raised his head a fraction. "Never thought of myself as anything but a spacer. But yeah, I've no attachment to the Confluence. I don't want sides, I want forgiveness."

"If you're prepared to be a guide, you shall have it."

The chapel door rapped softly.

"Will you trust me, Mr. Altman?"

He nodded.

Chels cracked the door. Brother Atone huddled outside. "Sorry, Brother, I was in counsel with a spacer."

"A new recruit? You should have left him for me."

"Forgive me. This man's not a recruit; he's a confessor. I don't think he'd have waited. It was me or no one." She stepped aside. "Brother Atone, this is Altman. He and I have an appointment with Slate."

She hustled Altman away before the brother could protest.

———————+H∏\\∠+——————

S late listened as Chels relayed Altman's story. They both watched the rumpled spacer sip Slate's worst whiskey.

When she finished, Slate held the bottle just beyond Altman's reach. "Could you find the place where you and Perry last saw the device?"

"I think so." Altman's hand was steady now, despite the dissipation in his face.

"Think harder." Slate moved the bottle fractionally closer.

"My nav'cube's safely stored with a friend in the Eddy shipyard."

Slate poured him another drink.

"Where's your ship?" asked Chels. She didn't like bribing the man with more temptation but Slate's method so far had provided results.

"Same place. Eddy shipyard. Mothballed and in hock." He sipped, stretching the liquid out. "Used the funds to get here. Thought maybe Perry had raised a new grubstake and we'd go back to salvaging manmade detritus."

The opportunity was obvious to Chels. Could she condone it? She was glad Pious wasn't available to counsel her, she had a feeling his advice would be contrary to what was needed here. Some missionary she'd make. *Sister Compromise*. Chels made eye contact with Slate. He nodded. It would have to be unofficial so she would be the conduit.

"What if I staked you?" she asked. "Would that get you back in salvager harness?"

"I'd still need a working partner."

"I'm sure you could have your pick," said Slate. "One of the refining settlements, any possibles there? Someone wanting a change? A youngster looking to escape from the endless routine?"

Altman put his half-finished glass down on Slate's desk. "One I remember. The youngest son of the manager. He'll be an old man before taking over the family charter, if ever. If I could get back there, maybe I could convince him." He dipped a finger into the drink and wet his lips. "There's a likely aggregate two days push from them we could start sifting on our own."

"After you locate the alien weapon," said Slate.

"I'd need more than a grubstake. I'd need to ransom my ship."

Chels made up her mind. In for the lot. "You only need your nav cube. Any ship will do." She paused to consider the implications of the next step. "We have a ship."

Slate looked at her, shocked.

"The *Crossed Swords*," she said. "Atone isn't going anywhere."

"He's not going to allow a stranger to pilot her." Slate nodded at Altman.

"Atone will allow me," said Chels.

"No, no, no." Slate banged a fist.

Altman darted his eyes back and forth between them.

Slate pointed at Chels. "She's jumpbust. She can't do spookspace anymore."

"That was me once," said Altman. "Found a cure."

"If there was a cure, don't you think I'd know about it?" Chels bit her lip at the psychological damage she'd face. "I'll just have to take my chances. Forget about trying to partner with some rock rat's kid. This is too important to the Realm's survival not to."

"It's mental discipline," said Altman. "I came from the Eddy without cryo. Look at me. I admit I'm less than whole yet I made jump. Without deepsleep."

"Without nightmares?" Chels was skeptical.

"Without nightmares?" He chuckled. "No. Never without nightmares."

Altman's fingers rubbed his knees. Part of the discipline or nerves?

He continued. "The mental discipline keeps them from overprinting."

"You don't have to do this, Chels." Slate whispered in her ear. "Look at him. That isn't damage? How do we know his wonderful discovery didn't leave this residue?"

"Who else have we got?" The lure of being able to jump again coupled with the desire to aid the Realm pushed her.

Altman stood, lifting his head high. "You can do this. I can teach you."

"I want Atone involved," said Chels. "The brothers have jumped without meds or cryo when forced."

"And you're taking his ship," said Slate. "Though technically I can commandeer it if necessary."

"You watch Altman. I'll convince Atone."

———

"It comes down to value," Chels argued. "I'm more valuable in the Eddy and you're more valuable here." The last phrase was an exaggeration but she had to convince Atone of his worth to Slate's Progress. "Pious trusted me as a place holder until the brothers returned. Now he trusts you to build on the momentum created on your previous visit. The converts and the listeners waited for you."

Atone wrung his hands, fingering the mala hanging from his neck. "I'm not Brother Pious. I don't know if I can duplicate his success. *You* pushed us over the top on our first visit."

"The sentiment was there to be pushed. Pious left you here to test your faith in yourself, Brother Atone. He believed in you as I do." Time was wasting. She was almost ready to take the *Crossed Swords* and disappear into the Eddy with Altman. But she wanted Atone's skills first.

"The ship is my responsibility." Atone added to his protest.

"I'm returning it to her rightful captain, now in the Eddy. I can pilot her as can Altman. Pious must be warned about the Confluence Navy." She gripped his cold hands. "I need your help to traverse spookspace without losing my mind. I know you've meditative techniques I can try. Altman says he learned them from a nomadic savant. Maybe one of your predecessors. I'm trying to prevent a war. Peace is your goal. You can train me and I can make a difference, Atone. How often does that happen in a lifetime?"

He looked past her through the porthole behind her. Then, without preamble, he began. "Sit on the deck, your back pressed to the wall. Close your eyes and focus on a point beyond your chest. Picture a cone of energy radiating from your core to that point."

Chels followed his instructions. Her fears bubbled up but she imagined the cone springing from her chest.

Atone said, "Breath calmly. With each exhalation, relax. Feel the ship pressing your buttocks and back. You join with the ship. It remains constant in the transfer to jumpspace. Your sins twist in your mind but you concentrate on the contact with the ship."

But Progress isn't a ship, she thought. Ships traverse the universe's black heart. Chels gasped and opened her eyes.

"External distractions are the enemy." Atone knew and verbalized her fear. "You fight the enemy with calm. Let the nightmares wash through you, pass over you like a warm stream but you can't drown in this stream."

She repeated his advice silently. Her breathing normalized and deepened.

"Your head and mind are one with a safe haven, Chels. A haven drawn from your memory. Have you such a place?"

Chels drifted from her body. "Here. Slate's. This chamber."

"Imprint this moment, this space."

Atone drilled a mantra until the very thought of the word recreated her and Slate's chamber.

Chels lost track of the time, going in and out of trance until she could submerge within minutes after closing her eyes.

Slate's comm broke the silence in the room. "Chels, I've got you passage. The *Crossed Swords* will barnacle in two hours."

"I hope Rowland lets us leave," she replied.

"He should, your barnacle passage is on one of his scouts."

"How the hell did you manage that?"

"Treaty terms. He wants to pretend he's following the peace accord. And I had to make one or two commitments. Nothing we can't live with if the Confluence backs up Rowland."

Atone asked, "Will she be safe?"

"As your deputized agent, yes. The one agency the admiral apparently respects is the brotherhood. This is your last chance to back out, Chels. We can always try to find someone in the Eddy to chaperone Altman."

"Thanks, but I'm all in now. Just promise me you'll have a warm bed and lots of love waiting when I return. I'll need it."

"Done. Love you, Chels."

"Me too."

"Get rolling, Altman's in transit to the *Crossed Swords*."

She stretched her legs and stood. "Whoa, I'm woozy."

"You'll feel that way coming out of jump. Take your time."

"Time we don't have at the moment. See me to the *Crossed Swords*. Any message for Pious?"

"Tell him I'm trying."

"I'm sure he knows you are." Chels prayed she would be in condition to pass the message when she emerged on the other side.

Chapter 30

Penance made its first contact after a long push from the Eddy 'yard. Pinpoint lights flickered through the missionary ship's viewport. Carver was taken back to his one-man prospecting days in the Eddy. Prospecting for show, gathering intelligence for Admiral Rowland for go. Contacting small settlements like the one they approached now to exchange information and to hear a fresh voice.

"Have you been here before?" DualE squeezed in beside him.

"No. This one's new to me, but I know how they work. Extracting minerals one crystal at a time from the looks of those arc lights."

"An independent mining cooperative, Brother Cardinal tells me." Pious spoke behind the pair. "They've requested we halt some distance away while we explain our intentions."

"Suspicion comes with the territory," said Carver. They were ten days out from the shipyard. Ten days stuck in a small ship with nothing to do but eat, evacuate, sleep and run out of things to discuss. Carver envied Pious and Cardinal's ability to sink into meditation every day on schedule to reduce the boredom. Carver's ennui frustrated him but trumped the nightmares of spookspace.

Pious said, "Your insight will be appreciated to gain their trust, Carver."

Carver squirmed to face DualE. "We start earning our pay. I volunteer to transport myself to them if they'll agree."

"Can we ask for both of us?" she asked.

"Not you; a brother. Two armed spacers could do a lot of damage. Or so they could fear."

"More damage than one crazy one?"

"I'm not crazy," said Carver.

"How do they know that?"

Carver slid back beside Cardinal. "I'm ready to talk when they are."

Cardinal adjusted retro-fire and *Penance* completed deceleration. Carver telescoped the operation. He saw movement on the surface. "We're too far out to discern individuals."

"Would you explain the process," Pious asked.

"The front teams burrow like ants through the irregular moonlet, chasing surface veins deep until they run out. They tag any possible offshoots for the follow-up units and move on to the next lead."

"Time consuming." said DualE.

Carver did some calculating. "For a rock this size, six months minimum, depending on how many diggers they have. Those lights are on surface." He spoke to Cardinal. "Have they said how long they've been here?"

"A month."

"Significant time left," said Pious. "They'll be needing spiritual release."

Carver nodded. "Agreed. Their labor's intensive, exhausting and marginally profitable." What message could Pious bring to these toughened men and women?

"Let me talk to your contact." Carver replaced Cardinal at the console.

"Ahoy colony. This is Willie Renfrew aboard the *Penance*. We bring a message from The First Expansion Brotherhood to the Eddy. We'd like the chance to commune with you. Brother Pious has been spreading his counsel in the Realm, most recently at Slate's Progress and the Eddy shipyard. It's important to their cause to reach as many outlying settlements as possible, no matter how small. I'd be grateful if you could allow me and one pilgrim to transfer over to your rock and meet face—to-face."

A roughened face, creased by hard work, answered. "Have to run it by the chief. I'm just following protocol by ordering your stand-off. I'm not the usual comm hand but I twisted my back and I'm subbing while I recover. We don't get many visitors and don't trust the ones we get."

"Your claim's solid, though, right?" Carver asked.

"Of course. That doesn't stop 'jumpers. Give us time to check your identity with the 'yard." The face grimaced. "Don't call me. I'll call you."

Carver addressed his shipmates. "It's like I said. They can be a bit paranoid. We wait. This won't be the last time in the big beyond that we cool our heels."

P ious wondered if he should have talked to them before Denz. "I should have gone with him, despite their instructions to allow only one visitor for the initial contact."

"Think how I feel," said DualE. "You hired us to run handle first contact for you. If anything happens to him, I'm going in full attack mode."

Pious put his hand to her arm. "I appreciate your sentiment but that's not how the brotherhood reacts. Violence is not a precedent I will allow."

"It wouldn't be for the brotherhood. It'd be for my partner."

"Nevertheless, we won't initiate aggression. We monitor, we learn, we adapt. Besides, I have faith in Denz."

"So do I. Just no faith in these miners. They're unpredictable."

"This is all premature. Let's watch and listen. Cardinal, do you have Mr. Renfrew's feed ready?"

Cardinal tilted his screen so Pious could view the shoulder cam view where Denz pointed.

"This is Renfrew. Open the 'lock please."

"Enter hands raised and prepare to remove your suit."

The camera view moved inside the miners' factory-cargo-shelter-space craft. A large 'X' decorated the inner 'lock door. Pious heard the order to stand clear when the outer door sealed, then Denz's camera jumped around as he removed his suit. The view was restored as he settled the cam back on his waist.

"What's that on your belt?"

"Camera," answered Denz. "I'm linked to the *Penance*. It allows Brother Pious to comment on anything I can't answer in real time. Safer for both parties, don't you think?"

"We'll examine it. Pass it through the aperture in the door."

Again, the view jumped around, then the grizzled face from Cardinal's first contact focused before it went black.

"Shit," said DualE. "We're blind and deaf."

"Give them a moment," said Pious. "If it doesn't come back, we'll rely on Denz's memory."

They heard sounds before the picture returned. The view was at waist level. "I'm back," said Denz. "This is Mr. Coyle."

"Coyle is sufficient. Your man's unarmed but it doesn't remove suspicion. Why would anyone who isn't a prospector want to come here?"

Pious examined the rock wall behind Coyle. Rough-hewn by miners in a hurry to get past the dross and find the veins they hoped would be there. Men and women unused to down-time except to sleep and eat. "In a way," said Pious, "I seek what you seek, only on an emotional basis rather than material wealth. There is wealth in the souls of people like you, Coyle. An indefatigable spirit absent in established settlements and stations. I find your pioneer ways refreshing. If I can reciprocate a fraction of that reward back to you and your fellows, my order's function is fulfilled."

"Fancy talk. What's it really mean?"

Denz took over. "It means we're not here to disrupt your routine but we're here to render the routine a little less soul-draining, if we can.

I know how these operations work. I wish I had the drive to do what you do but I don't. I tried prospecting with mixed success."

Pious thought that a bit of a stretch. The man hiding behind the Willie Renfrew disguise was the most successful prospector in the last twenty years.

Denz continued, "Consider us 'entertainment'. *Free* entertainment."

Coyle appeared to digest the offer.

"You said you've been here a month?" Denz asked.

"More or less."

"Long enough to grow tired of each other, am I right? Long enough to forge, dissolve and make new alliances and friendships. It's natural. Brother Pious' message and counsel can take you back to day one and show you better ways of handling the stress going forward until you're done here. Lessons to last a lifetime out here scratching for every credit the hard way. His message can also carry you through the tough times when there's nothing to mine."

Pious was impressed by Denz's appeal. "I couldn't have put it better myself," he whispered to Cardinal and DualE.

"I still have to run it by the team," said Coyle.

"All I ask is one hour of your time," transmitted Pious. "I can make my way over while you arrange it with your people. We'll be gone before you know it and you can return to task. But returning with a renewed mental and physical energy."

"Your colleagues are listening and watching this, Coyle, if I'm any judge of how your security should operate. Ask them now?" Denz didn't plead but his voice carried authority.

"I'm suiting up," said Pious. He moved to the airlock and opened the suit locker. Once he was sealed up and the outside 'lock opened, he said, "I wonder if you could be so kind as to guide me in, Renfrew."

"Coyle's got the infrared beacon turned on. Let your suit-nav system tie in and it'll get you here."

Pious took the first push away from *Penance*, activated the suit guidance and propulsion module and felt the gentle acceleration away from the brotherhood's protective cocoon.

— ✝ ‖ ⇄ —

D enz and Coyle helped Pious from his EVA suit. Carver winced under Pious' grip into his shoulder.

"Welcome to their humble operation," said Carver. "Coyle is our guide and guard."

"Follow me," said Coyle. "You can speak with half our crew during mealtime."

"Best compromise I could arrange, brother," said Carver. "Time is the essence here. The sooner they're done with this rock, the more chance the next one will be a bigger strike."

"I understand. Thanks for the tip."

They trailed the limping Coyle along rough-hewn tunnels. Carver heard the conversation buzz before they turned into the mess.

A group of a dozen men and women sat around tables eating, drinking and chatting. Pious nudged Coyle before he could shout for attention.

"I think it would be better if I mingled," said Pious.

"Suit yourself. I'll introduce Renfrew around while you do."

Pious dropped his robe's hem to brush the ground and moved away, inserting himself in a quartet of diggers.

Carver and Coyle took two emptied seats on the other side of the mess.

"This here's Renfrew, one-time prospector, now expeditor for Brother Pious over there."

"Are you a religious man yourself, Renfrew?" One asked between bites.

"Fair question. I don't know. I've witnessed the brother's skill in helping conflicted souls reach a balance with who they are and who they'd like to be. Pious' philosophy seems to provide him internal balance. I respect his faith in God's guidance whether I embrace it or not. If that makes any sense." He tried to sound neutral until he could read the crowd.

"Well," said the man, "I know we'd most like to be rich. Let's see him pull *that* from his robe."

Carver chuckled with the rest. "Brother Pious would tell you wealth is a subjective thing. You might have it and not know." He examined the mess's drab interior and imagined what a day's work was like for them. "Though I'm not seeing non-monetary riches lurking in the background here."

"Toil for its own sake, right?" said Coyle.

"Something like that."

"You rich?" The lone woman at the table scrubbed her plate with a black bread.

"No," Carver answered. "I have been. Now I find I'd rather work for a living than have it drop in my lap."

She nodded. "Your current living's safer than ours, I grant. Still, you look like you can manage a pneumatic hammer. Lots of work here if you tire of spreading God's message to the infidels."

"I'm flattered," said Carver. "If this mission burns me out, I'll look you up at your next port of call." When he'd been prospecting, his thoughts were dominated by wishing he wasn't prospecting. Always chasing the 'after this' brought disappointment and heartache. Maybe there would come a time to return to the miner's life in earnest. Effort for its own worth.

Coyle dragged him to another table. "We'd need a lucky charm more than strong arms, Renfrew. And you don't appear to have much luck surrounding you."

Carver had apparently played the Renfrew role well. "Too right, Coyle. My luck could change."

They sat with a pair of miners almost indistinguishable from each other. "The Wellspring brothers," said Coyle. "See, we have brothers too. Though these two wouldn't qualify for the cloth."

One belched and grabbed Coyle by the shirtfront. "We heard there's a woman aboard that ship. Why didn't you get her over here?" He glanced at Carver. "He's not much to look at."

Coyle pushed the man's clutching hand free. "I showed her your picture and she fainted."

"Perfect. Imagine the effect I'd have in person."

Before Carver could inform the man DualE'd likely cripple him, Pious arrived at their table.

"You gentlemen have the most interesting skinwork." He sat. "What's this one's significance?" Pious pointed to an ornate jewel-encrusted tattoo ringing the man's neck. "Where did you get the work done?"

The man was off before Carver could catch his breath, spilling a story of love, hate, conflict and glory. It was quite a tale and impressive if only half true.

By the time Wellspring had finished, the crowd was breaking up. Pious spoke. "People. I thank you for the chance to meet you and talk with you." He pulled a handful of memory chips from his pocket. "I'll leave you with these. A recording of an address I gave aboard Slate's Progress some months ago. You may find a kernel of advice to help you reach the end of your labors here with a fresher body and mind. I won't be the last missionary you'll encounter. The Eddy attracts more spacers and settlers as it attracts space flotsam of all kinds. Be generous with your time and patience as you've shown me today. The *Penance* will be nearby for another few days should any of you wish to speak with me further. Good day and good digging."

The chatter rose as they filed out to their next shift, be it mining or sleep.

"Thank you, Coyle. We'll let you return to routine."

The miner escorted them silently back to the exit. As they suited up, he said, "More of you to come?"

"Eventually," said Pious. "Consider us a bellwether. My sect is stretched thin in these times but the Eddy calls us."

It had called Carver twice so far. The first call led him to material riches. This second encounter's result was still in question.

Chapter 31

Rowland was the last aboard to cryo. The growing nightmares tormented him. It was a weakness he resented. Last under, first awake. Give him time to compose himself, if required. The escort ship's crew were insignificant to his overall plan but soldiers talked and any idiosyncrasies displayed by a commander could undermine that command in a critical moment.

The *Crossed Swords* was barnacled and as far as its occupants were concerned, a jump ahead of Rowland from Slate's Progress to the Eddy shipyard. In truth, they were a jump ahead of the *Rickover*. Rowland jumped with them inside the cruiser class *Neptune*.

A last thought as he drifted into deepsleep was the debt owed to Carver Denz. The purity of his Schoenfeldium discovery allowed smaller jumpspace tech to be viable for spacecraft like the *Neptune*, though the psychological risk increased with the decrease in generator size. The distortion zone enveloped the entire ship, including its barnacle. It was a good thing he had the mental discipline to endure the risk. His psyche was robust. When not in jumpspace.

Chels focused on the outside view monitor. Their transport, the *Neptune*, accelerated past the first jump beacon. She absorbed the fact and integrated it with spookspace experience from her old life. How many jumps? Dozens? A hundred? They blurred into a continuum of nightmares and regrets.

The second beacon evaporated in a blink. Third, fourth and more coalesced into a luminous string. The light wavered as the distortion core expanded. She repeated her mantra through half-lidded eyes. She changed her focus from the starry void to a point directly in front of her chest.

Beside her, Altman's breathing rasped. The pressure on her wrist from his grip lessened. He twitched. She pulled back from her companion to imagine her breath carrying tension away from her body into the bypass universe.

The transition to jumpspace flickered in her consciousness but Chels continued her slow exhalations. Nausea battered her stomach. Her insides tried to balance the differing accelerations pummeling her head and her toes. The sickness should retreat as she kept her concentration focused on the cone of energy streaming away from her. But what about the nightmares?

A peripheral niggle wormed into her subconscious. The life she'd left years before slammed through her mind. Like a stray asteroid loosened from stable orbit to crash into a habitat, memories annihilated her carefully planned survival trajectory through jump.

The asteroid had been real. Its orbit was destabilized for efficient access. A veteran prospector had committed a gross error and instead of opening the rock up for mining, the explosive charges had sent it awry, ending its trajectory in a refining habitat. Chels felt the tears sting down her cheeks and tasted salt on her tongue. Four killed, three crippled. She knew all of them. She'd been related to two of the dead. Her brother and his wife.

Subsequent investigation revealed she hadn't been the one who misplaced the charges. But she hadn't refused orders to detonate before triple-checking. Pressure from command to increase productivity had driven the mistakes. Plenty of blame to go around but the worst was the absurdity that it was deemed an accident. Death a risk the victims accepted as part of the life. She never accepted the rationalization.

Meditation clarity and thoughts of Slate and Pious finally drove the repeating past away. To be replaced with a realization it was the guilt, not spookspace itself, which ended her ability to endure jump.

Altman moaned and she realized her fingers dug into his forearm. She relaxed but didn't release her grip. She dared open an eye. The viewport swam with photon bundles howling past the barnacle. Ghosts of previous ships, they said. She believed them ghosts of something.

She saw the jumpcarrier in two realities. One with *Crossed Swords* firmly barnacled, the other with *Swords* losing its purchase and tumbling away like the rogue asteroid. A shadowy figure piloted the jumpcarrier. She could distinguish the profile but couldn't see the face. A man. An officer of the navy. High rank, judging by the shoulder decorations. Admiral Rowland? Now she knew she hallucinated. Rowland was back near Slate's Progress; she wasn't barnacled to the *Rickover*. Chels viewed a future. The race was on to complete her mission in the Eddy before the admiral made his next jump.

A figure trailed them, its time-stream leaving a wake in the free-drifting molecules in this side-universe. The figure never closed nor passed them. It was attached to her and Altman. Perry? His ghost in death or his alternate life? He would always be in her essence. Another spookspace nightmare.

Chels retreated into the mantra, knowing she'd have to face the fatalities again and again. This meditation didn't stop the nightmares. It allowed release which cryo couldn't and she gave thanks.

Altman trembled and moaned but she wouldn't let go. His presence assured her there was an exit point to the agony. Whatever demons he faced, she hoped her presence helped him through them.

She slipped into her past for the second time, knowing it would not be the last. Time in spookspace held no relevance. Milliseconds seemed like weeks and days could compress into a single heartbeat. Her shoulders dropped and the tension in her neck dissipated.

Get me through. I need to find Pious and confess another sin.

The transition from jump to normal manifested as an ascent from an aspic ocean into sweet air. Chels breached the interface gasping for breath. Warmth against her side reminded her she wasn't alone in the ship. "Pious?" she blurted before she realized it was Altman sharing the barnacle. Brother Pious was somewhere in the Eddy by now.

Altman coughed, rolled onto the deck and dry-heaved for a minute.

Chels used the cabin walls to brace herself and open the food locker. She found the recovery flask and drank deep, energy and heat coursing through her system. She knelt beside Altman and passed him the flask. "Hope you don't mind cooties," she said.

He phlegmed and snorted before taking a drink. "Not bad. Whisky would be better."

"You'll have all you need after we locate the artifact. I promise. Slate's special blend. Until then, you stay sober. If not for me, for your late partner. Okay?"

She moved to the console to guide the *Crossed Swords* across the gap to the Eddy shipyard. The *Neptune* had moved away from the 'yard.

"The escort cruiser won't want to risk encounters with any Realm spacers before Rowland and his gunship arrive," she muttered.

An hour later, the *Crossed Swords* was docked, locked and ready to stock provisions for the journey into the Eddy's backwaters.

"I'll go," Altman offered. "I know where we can get the best deals."

Chels said, "We go together. I need to find out where Pious has gone. If anything happens to you, I need to know what you know." She also wanted to ensure Altman kept his word and stayed sober.

"Let's move. Sooner begun, sooner done."

Chels followed him out.

The Eddy shipyard was a tangle of connection cylinders and spherical joints, evolved since her last visit. Once she had the changed layout pictured, she memorized the path they took to Prospector Supplies and Stores.

The array of shopfronts here dwarfed the market alleys on Slate's Progress.

"This has grown since I mined." She noted 'Sale' and 'Bargain' signs everywhere.

"They keep saying business declines but Denz's Schoenfeldium strike created a new high." Altman walked past the promises of 'No better deals to be had' and turned down an unlit side corridor.

` "Aren't we buying back there?"

"We would be if we were green to the Eddy." Altman leaned close and winked. "I know a guy."

Altman's guy was an ancient spacer, eyes bloodshot and the veins in his inflated nose a bright match. Too many jumps and too many impairing pharms to do anything else.

"Hey Rory. I need a month package."

"Geezus, Altman. Thought you'd given it up. Saw your ship being carved up for scrap. Bought the spectral analyser myself. Want to buy it back?" Rory cast a rheumy glance toward Chels the whole time he spoke.

"Naw, just the nav'cube I left. Keep the analyser for me until I get back, if you would. Add five percent to the bill to remove it from your shelf for three months."

"Who's your friend?"

"I'm Chels." She gave him the spacer handslide. "Pleased to meet you, Rory."

"I'll hold it for free if you and the lady would join me for a drink or two at Eddie's Dive tonight."

"Rain check," said Chels before Altman could respond. "We need to roll."

"The package?" reminded Altman. He wrote a code on Rory's status board. "Here's our slip. Have it there in an hour." He nodded to Chels.

She unrolled her credit stash and peeled notes until Altman stopped her.

"Thanks Rory. Anything going on?"

"Heard the Confluence is on its way."

Chels answered. "Some of them are already here. You can have that info gratis. We barnacled with a navy cruiser from Slate's. It's standing off but it's here to evaluate the accord. No Realm frigates in 'yard?"

Rory shook his head. Strands of unwashed hair brushed his face. He ran a hand on both sides of his head, pulling them behind his copious ears. "The Confluence won't hold target practice here."

"What about a missionary ship. *Penance*. Know it?"

"I might. Friends of yours?"

"Colleagues."

Altman had moved away from the pair, examining various barter goods on the shelves of Rory's shop.

Rory pulled out a stack of flimsies from under his counter. "What was the name? Announce?"

"*Penance*. As is why you're here and not spacing any more."

He laughed. "I'm doing that all right. Paying for my sins. And girl, I wouldn't take back one sin to leave this place. My memories are intact and full of guilt."

"The best kind for a spacer."

It was the right thing to say and he soon tugged a yellowed sheet from the wad. "*Penance*. Left seventeen, no eighteen, shifts ago. Just under a week, 'yard time."

"Bound where?"

"Manifest would be logged with 'yard master. I can get it for you and deliver it with the supplies." He looked to her belt where her cash had retreated.

Chels peeled off a generous portion as Altman returned.

He put a hand on Rory's fist full of Chels' funds. "That should be enough for your information and a bonus to keep our intel to yourself."

"You got it," said Rory. "For a month I keep quiet."

"Fair enough." Altman released his grip. "Don't forget to wipe our slip code after delivery."

They stood in the narrow, dim passage outsider Rory's shop and hearing.

"Anything else you need to know?" Altman asked.

"If you buddy's telling us the honest, then no. Is there a way we can confirm his timetable about *Penance*?"

"His intel is solid."

"Then let's head back to the ship."

"We could nip down to Eddie's Dive for a jolt of his finest."

"We'll grab a half sphere to calm you down. And we take it with us."

Three hours and two Altman shots later, The *Crossed Swords* slid free from the 'yard and began her journey to one of the many eddies within The Eddy.

━━┼┼╫╲╲┼┼━

Admiral Rowland watched the screen. "They're pulling out. Any navlog from the yard master?"

The *Neptune's* communication officer shook his head. "The *Crossed Swords'* registered astrogation plan is vague. These outposts don't get all worked up about details. Some prospector goes missing, doesn't return to station, it's considered a trade risk. I could invoke your status to demand information they likely don't have."

"Until the *Rickover* arrives, Lieutenant Cappis, I'm not here. We'll rely on what you can find. Any hints at all?"

Cappis nodded. "I've got one clue. A delivery ticket from stores to the *Crossed Swords* ten hours ago. Judging by mass and size, enough food and water to provision two for three to five weeks."

Rowland watched the light trace on the screen. "They have a specific destination a week to two weeks distant. Allowing time for exploration there, I'd guess on the lower end. Is the transponder working?"

A short-short-long ping sounded from his screen. We can track them at a distance outside their normal detection range. Do we follow?"

"Not yet," Rowland replied. "Deploy a relay drone. We'll remain here until the *Rickover* arrives. Or until the *Crossed Swords* stays in one locale for more than two days. Then we'll send a recon ship to see what they've found."

"You sure about them, sir? She could be going back to her previous career. Slate's partner, I mean."

"No. Slate and Chels are a permanent couple. She wouldn't leave Progress without a strong reason. Doubled on that, the fact Slate told me she's jump-shy. Pathologically so. My radar's up." He turned to Cappis. "I won't chase them on a hunch. Wait until they find what I suspect they seek. Then we'll move in and expropriate."

He watched the *Crossed Swords'* signal track away on the holo view. "Keep me apprised of their progress. Any stops, any communications or rendezvous with other ships. But don't reveal our presence. The Confluence's future may ride on this seemingly insignificant craft and crew." Not just the Confluence's future, Rowland thought, but his as well.

Chapter 32

Zofie rose reluctantly from the cryo coffin. Even the disturbed sleep of jump had been a welcome escape after her frantic leave-taking from the Eddy. The real universe was a cold consort.

The *Whisper's* heater growled but she wrapped two blankets around her shoulders and rubbed her arms. She tucked her legs under and checked the astrogation log. They were in Bohr. Neither she nor the *Whisper* had been sabotaged or diverted. All good.

Zofie extracted Marshall's coffin and initiated thaw. "Time to rise."

Zofie kept an eye on her shipmate while monitoring radio traffic. None. The *Procyon* crew were no doubt having their own revival party. Marshall's head appeared, then torso, followed by a series of phlegmy coughs.

"Welcome back from the half-alive," said Zofie. "Or is it the half-dead? *Procyon* should be releasing us soon." She passed one of her blankets to Marshall.

"I'll brew us a drink," offered Marshall.

"Grateful beyond words." Zofie made contact with the machine parts pod. It too remained barnacled. Contrary to the chartered agenda, it had not been released near Argosy Station. "Kondradt's influence overrode the Reds' plan. Now we just need to contact your liaison and provide Kondradt's proof backing your intel."

Marshall handed her a steaming mug. The aroma filled the cabin with a cheery sense. "Simple. And keep from being blown up if the wrong people determine our real mission."

"I'm sending out standard resale messages for the shipment. The Confluence Administration post is twelve hours from here. Minimal military presence and no navy ships close."

"So far, so good."

"Hailing *Procyon*, this is *Whisper*. We're awake and intact. Request de-barnacling for *Whisper* and my freight pod. Thank you for not losing it in jump." In case anyone was listening and there was a pretty good chance they were. "It's my ticket home and funds for my next, bigger, shipment."

"Acknowledged, *Whisper*. Anchors disabled. You may release."

Zofie transferred trajectory data to the pod's onboard guidance system and ensured the pod was free before tripping the *Whisper's* releases.

"I'll swing around to tug it with us. Strap in."

The acceleration pushed Zofie sideways in her seat. Soon they locked onto the cache pod and nudged toward their target haven. Zofie had Marshall's trigger phrase memorized so they'd both need to be present when they contacted the proper authority.

"I hope this center has someone with enough clout to act on your intel," she said.

Three hours into their burn, Zofie cut the acceleration. "We'll drift on course for six hours, then commence decel. You want a nap?"

Marshall undid her harness and floated free. "I'm ravenous. Post-jump rations are looking attractive. Join me in a wafer feast?"

"I will. While I monitor the space chatter. There's a flask of the Realm's fourth-best brandy in the cupboard marked Emergency."

"I'm on it."

━━━┼┼║╎┼┼━━━

Sated and slightly buzzed, Zofie initiated the retro-burn and began transmitting to the station, requesting diplomatic audience.

"State the nature of your inquiry?"

"Not an inquiry. A shipload of information from the Realm."

"State the nature of your information."

"In person only."

"State the nature of your cargo pod."

Zofie turned in disgust to Marshall. "This is getting repetitive."

She re-opened communications. "Again, in person only."

"We cannot allow unknown cargo any closer until inspected. Please release your pod in a stasis orbit and come ahead. Our security will examine and grant clearance."

"Shit. What do we do?"

Marshall shrugged. "My intel should be enough. Lock pod access for now. If the arms are discovered, who'll know we've taken them from navy agents in the Realm?"

"They'll just arrest us for smuggling." Zofie shifted to accommodate the altered circumstance. "The pod contains surplus refining machinery. As a cover for weapons destined to arm guerilla action the Realm. We prevented the pod's release mid-jump to bring them here, beyond the reach of underground forces. Can you ensure your naval representatives don't destroy the pod until we meet face to face with your diplomats?"

"Release the pod as instructed and prepare for escort."

"Escort? I'm sure I can pilot my way in without help."

"Consider yourselves under protective custody."

"I hate that phrase." Zofie banged her fist against the console. "We're under arrest."

Marshall took another generous swallow from Zofie's flask. "Not unexpected."

"You say that like you have a contingency plan." Zofie took the proffered flask and drank.

"We'll see if Kondradt anticipated correctly. If not, then we're no further behind."

"Not very comforting."

T he women passed time in the featureless prison by exchanging stories of love, success and failures. After one of Zofie's longer, more excruciating tales, Marshall raised her hands in surrender.

"I win?" asked Zofie.

"For all time."

The wall began to slide open.

"About time." Zofie moved from direct sight.

"Stand down, ladies." Chancellor Mekli acknowledged Zofie's previous association with a nod. "Follow me, please."

"How are you here?" Zofie asked when they'd settled in the debriefing chamber. They couldn't have hoped for a more influential confessor but was their luck too good?

Mekli studied her. He was as physically unimpressive as the first time she'd met him. Not a man you'd tag a leader but he was as politically savvy as anyone she'd ever met. He shifted his attention to Marshall. "I haven't been back to the Realm since the accord was signed. I'm in safekeeping."

"You're a prisoner? Like us?"

"I could leave anytime, I suppose. But it would threaten the accord. I'm a performance guarantee. My subordinates are more than capable of running our government and our military. This may be the most important function I've ever performed."

Zofie's doubts escalated. Did he have any influence?

"I'm one of your subordinates, Chancellor," said Marshall. "I have important information from Gar Kondradt. A more important cog in your team."

Mekli leaned close and studied her eyes, then nodded. "An information-mule. He told me to expect one or more at some point." He glanced at Zofie. "Do you carry her trigger?"

Zofie nodded.

"The intel I carry is as much for the Confluence government as you, Chancellor. Will it get to them?" Marshall drummed her hands on the table.

Mekli gestured to the wall and ceiling. "It will. We are monitored."

"By who?" asked Zofie. "Not the navy."

"By all parties concerned."

"Not good," said Marshall.

Mekli's twitch showed he grasped the problem. "I don't see how it can be avoided. You reveal your information and let the Confluence sort it out amongst their factions."

Zofie just wanted Marshall to dump her mind load and get the hell out of there.

"I can't tell you what's buried in my head, Chancellor. But Kondradt did impress upon me the need for discretion when it came to disclosure to the navy. I'm afraid you and the Confluence won't learn any of it under these circumstances."

This was her contingency plan? Zofie could utter the trigger phrase but would Marshall comply? Under tough questioning, likely. Zofie wouldn't expose Marshall to any rough interrogation.

"I see." Mekli put a finger to his ear and listened to some external source. "Return to your ship. I and one other will join you."

"A diplomat?"

"Someone unaffiliated with the navy, yes." Mekli stood and walked to the door. He accepted two identity discs from the guard outside and passed them to Zofie and Marshall. "These will guide you. I hope your information is worth the risk you're taking. Admiral Rowland's power and support is not to be underestimated."

━━━┼┼╷╷┡┱━━

"At least we're out of custody," said Zofie. "Though the *Whisper* is disabled."

Marshall chewed a wafer. "Food's better in the station."

"If I gave the trigger, would you be able to withhold your sudden knowledge influx?"

"Please don't test it." Marshall dusted the crumbs from her hands and opened the suit locker. "Let's check these over."

Zofie nodded. The *Whisper* was bugged no doubt by now. If they could cleanse the hard and the thin suits, they'd have four. Outside the docking bay, they could communicate in private with Mekli and the Confluence rep.

They'd finished removing all eight bugs found on the suits and secreting masking bugs of their own supplied by Kondradt when Mekli arrived. He introduced his companion. "This is Raddam Shoop, Sector Governor."

"Slight change of plan, Chancellor," said Marshall. "We're going for an EVA."

Zofie's attention switched back to Marshall. Her companion was losing composure, the download drugs were wearing off. It was like addiction withdrawal, Zofie supposed. They needed to get on with it. "Let's suit up," she said.

Zofie didn't think Shoop looked military. He was soft in the face. Puffy in the waist. They had to stuff him into the hard suit designed for someone Marshall's size.

"I think this is overly cautious," said Mekli. "Under terms of the accord, your information will be shared by Governor Shoop as he sees fit. And I'm sure it has some strategic value to the navy."

"Kondradt only told me to use my best judgment in keeping it out of their hands as long as I could. Once you hear it, you may agree." Marshall tugged Zofie's sleeve. "Once you give me the trigger phrase, shut down your suit comm. What you don't know shouldn't kill you."

Zofie uttered the trigger words Kondradt had given her. Through the flimsuit faceplate, Marshall's eyes fluttered. The info-mule spasmed from head to boot then relaxed. "I've got it, Zofie. Thank you."

As curious as she was, Zofie was more concerned with her survival. She switched off her radio and watched Marshall's faceplate blacken. No spy would read her lips. Zofie kept scanning their surroundings for any sign of others present. She spotted four and guessed more were beyond her sight. The ones she spied weren't moving and their backs were to the group. Not eavesdroppers, protection. There were peace opponents everywhere.

Twenty minutes later, Marshall moved to her side and touched helmets. "Let's go inside."

The four of them sat in the *Whisper*. Governor Shoop spoke first. "Coupled with your transparency regarding the cargo pod which accompanied you through jumpspace, and the questioning of the *Procyon's* captain, I'm giving credence to your report."

"You don't mind other ears listening to this, Governor?" Mekli surveyed the *Whisper's* cabin.

"It's important they do."

"Do you feel safe, Governor?" Marshall asked.

Shoop nodded. "I've already contacted my allies. Not with your details, of course, but some misgivings have been previously raised regarding our naval emissaries to the Realm. Rowland will be recalled. Chancellor, it's time you and I left for Bohr. Might I suggest we use your security for our escort?"

Rowland being recalled. Marshall's info must have been significant and verified. "What about us?" Zofie asked.

"I think the sooner you return to the Realm, the healthier it will be," answered Shoop. "Your incoming freighter has undergone turnaround and is ready to leave shortly. I suggest you barnacle."

The men left Zofie and Marshall alone. "*Whisper's* back on line. Do you trust them?"

"My job's done," said Marshall. "Revenge execution isn't naval style. I hope."

Zofie sealed the 'lock and prepared for departure. "Me too."

Chapter 33

D ualE monitored the comm while Carver and Pious drowsed. Their first encounter in the frontier had wearied both men. Pious had been pleased with the reception, though Carver indicated the miners were a pragmatic lot, not pre-occupied with matters of the mind or soul. The *Penance* hadn't been fired upon, so, small victory.

"Cardinal, I've found another operation." She let the comm focus itself based on signal strength. The tuner scrolled and locked on four distinct wavelengths. "Make that more than one."

The navigator commenced active triangulation. "It's hard at this orientation to be certain but the similar strengths indicate to me they're close to one another."

"Lots of background static," she said. "What is that place? No asteroid worthy of the name I can see on the mass-density detector."

Cardinal changed his screen to nav chart. "According to this, they call it Little Sargasso. An eddy within the Eddy. Three dimensional."

"We'll approach until hailed not to."

DualE listened to the chatter, broken up and from different sources.

"...shipment ready three shifts from now."

"...watch derelict A-14, anchors broken loose and heading..."

"Where's that fuel cannister? You promised..."

DualE said, "There's an outpost of some kind in there." She'd gone into military mode at first, evaluating strategies from defensive and attack points of view. She had to consciously override her instinct and remind herself that job prime was looking out for the *Penance's* mission, not Rowland's. With that restored to mind, she concentrated on defense. "When we're within ten thousand klicks, change approach to tangent. Until we're certain the natives aren't hostile."

"Should we wake them?" Cardinal tilted his head toward the slumbering pair.

"Not yet. Let them doze. Pious especially looked drained. EVA on top of his visit took a toll."

Cardinal's reticence was enough to convince her there was more to it. Pious hadn't looked robust since they'd left Gamma Hub. She'd put it down to the strain of preparation and multi-faceted orders from the Church but he hadn't stabilized. The man was sick. Too far advanced to treat in the time he'd had in Gamma.

Or he'd chosen not to, placing this mission first. Leaving Atone and Remorse on their own to test their leadership skills. She doubted either had them. DualE'd seen enough potential officer material wash out in the field that she trusted her instincts. How much did Cardinal know? Their navigator was the logical candidate to succeed Pious in her estimation. But his astrogation skills were needed for this mission and he couldn't be risked off-ship.

She'd ask Pious straight out when she accompanied him on his next foray. Her turn to step up and her need to have all the data going in. His health could affect the operation and protecting him was her duty.

Penance altered course. Cardinal brought them to an orbit around the concentration of matter and operations.

"Not much to look at in normal light," she said. "I'm switching to infrared." A globe of mottled violet, indigo and blue danced on her viewscreen. "Relatively cool. Nothing hotter than 500 nanos." She zoomed in until four red-yellow pinpricks appeared. "There's our audience. Who wants to talk? Or do we let them come to us first?"

"I suggest we continue to listen until Brother Pious wakes," said Cardinal. "Nothing to gain by stirring an unknown nest, though the fact they appear to co-exist suggests a willingness to cooperate with external groups."

"We convince them we're not a competitor if we're addressed while Pious sleeps. Agreed?"

"Yes. We'll choose who responds depending on the tone of their contact."

DualE marvelled at the image of the gravity sink. A slowly turning morass of junk, some visible, more not visible she guessed. An unseen attractor lurking in the dark center. Not unlike her life at many times; whirling priorities surrounding an enigmatic core she rarely had the desire or courage to expose to herself or others. Ever dynamic, the thick disc had to be a navigational challenge for the operators within. "If we're invited in, your nav talents will be tested, Cardinal. Are you up to it?"

"The Gamma Hub refit software is supposed to be top-shelf. I will put it to the test. My own skills will be a supplement, not a requirement."

"You wish. Don't place all your faith in the refit based on cost. We go in slow when we go in."

A snort from Carver alerted her one of their sleepers neared consciousness.

"We have arrived at a new gathering?" Their leader's voice. Pious was awake and more alert than her cohort.

"See for yourself, Brother Pious." DualE doubled the screen to visual and infrared. "We found a few for you. I think I should be the one to accompany you this time. Give Carver the chance to monitor remotely."

"I leave it to your judgment, DualE," said Pious. "Unless I judge differently."

A reminder she wasn't in complete charge. More than one boss was no way to run a campaign. Or a crusade.

———✝✝╲╲╲╱╲✝✝———

C arver linked to DualE's helmet camera. He sat safely within *Penance* while she and Pious threaded into the whirlpool. He kept quiet, it took concentration not to tear a suit open on a jagged rock or machine part clustered around the nexus. A gray ovoid came into view.

"We're at the first ship," said DualE. "Though 'ship' is inaccurate. It's a small factory."

Pious' introduction had been acknowledged by the largest of the four facilities.

"You should enter one at a time," said Carver.

"Unlikely," answered Pious. "I promised I would come to them and I don't imagine DualE wishes to remain outside the 'lock."

"He's right," said DualE. "They've opened the outer bulkhead."

Carver and Cardinal monitored the feed, knowing there was little *Penance* could do against hostile action except run. Their armament was not intended to spread rumors throughout the Eddy of an armed and aggressive missionary force. Pious had been firm. Retaliation as a final resort only, and then only with full agreement. The cam frosted over but cleared as the two entered the ship proper.

Two salvagers, armed, greeted them.

"I don't like their body language," said Carver.

"Amateurs," whispered DualE before she removed her helmet.

"We come bearing nothing but words and philosophy," Pious began. "You've no doubt been in touch with our last port of call and they would have assured you of our peaceful intentions."

"We value our privacy and protect what's ours." A woman's voice.

Confidence and broad shoulders put her on an equal level physically with DualE. Carver hoped his partner didn't underestimate the woman's capability. Amateur perhaps, but committed to preserving whatever operations went on here and the existence keeping them viable. Desperation could triumph over skill.

"We understand your misgivings," said Pious. "We are an ecclesiastical order with no commercial interest in your operation. I welcome the chance to speak with you and offer escape from your routine. I am Brother Pious and this is my associate, DualE."

"What's her function?"

"My protection," said Pious. "Now that we've met you in person, I'm certain she won't be needed. Shall we join the rest of your crew?"

"Certainly. I'm Lucienne, he's Andre. A precaution first."

Carver watched DualE's cam focus on her wrists which were tied in front of her. Carver nudged Cardinal. "I'm impressed with DualE's restraint."

"Pious won't let anything happen to her."

"He'll need sharp teeth to sever the tie."

"My brother is not without resources, Carver. We're used to aggression."

"He's packing?"

"I don't understand the term," said Cardinal.

"Packing. *Dressed. Carrying. Armed and dangerous.*"

"Quite a euphemism collection. He has *resources*."

"Remind me not to cross you or him."

"They've joined the others."

Pious' cam swept across a dozen tough-looking crew. "Thank you for allowing our visit. You exemplify the spirit of the Eddy. Hard work. Independence. I could add environmentally responsible if not offensive to you."

"Aye. We're the bloody universal cleaners," offered one, to the amusement of his fellows.

"Well phrased," said Pious, joining in the mood. "You cleanse. You leave behind a better place than you found. You don't exploit raw materials, that is so often waste. You extract marrow from the last morsel and repeat until nothing of value remains."

Murmurs of approval echoed in Carver's ears.

"Tell me more," said Pious.

Lucienne spoke. "We harvest and re-purpose tech. Flotsam others are too rich or too lazy to notice."

"My order, in its way, performs similar services," said Pious. "You deal with the material plane. I deal in the spiritual one. I see comradery amongst you and ask myself 'What can I offer these pioneers?'. Maybe nothing. Not this day. But someday my message may help." Pious paused and his cam covered the audience again. They appeared ready to listen. Carver was impressed but not surprised.

"'Live in the moment' is a credo you follow, right? Because the next moment could bring disaster."

Nods all around. These salvagers knew the danger they faced every shift. They worked in a barely stable gravitational maelstrom. Random collisions occurred all the time, creating a domino effect no computer could predict. The habitat could be on the receiving end of the chain reaction.

"With luck and vigilance, you have avoided catastrophe. Take the time to enjoy it, by all means. But take the time to consider a future where you're not in danger every minute. Not just between operations but in the next phase of your lives. Create a legacy to share, not a plaque engraved on a nameless rock 'Here toiled so-and-so', long forgotten and without bequest. It will make your existence richer now and, in that future, when it comes."

"We have visitors," said Cardinal. A flash of explosion scarred the entrance to the ship-factory.

Carver's gut clenched. "Your hosts have company," he said to DualE.

Her cam moved before he'd finished speaking. He saw Pious' sleeve in her grasp and both of them moving. The spacers were moving as well. Andre dropped in front of DualE with a leveled gun. "You brought them in."

"Who?" Pious asked.

"Raiders," said DualE. She didn't deny the conspiracy. The salvagers wouldn't believe her if she did. Though their visit may have created a distraction.

DualE's camera feed died.

"Pull us back," Carver said to his pilot.

Cardinal initiated the drive.

"*Penance*. Remain where you are and you won't be holed. Move and you're dead." The voice shut off as quickly as it came. It wasn't from Pious' hosts.

"I guess they don't expect us to argue or disobey," said Carver. "Okay. We wait this one out. While DualE and Pious talk or fight free."

Carver and Cardinal waited and watched. Light bursts revealed active small fire upon the facility holding their shipmates. Return fire was equally modest. A raid or merely blowing off steam from some previous misunderstanding?

"What's going on at your end, Renfrew?" DualE's voice was welcome after an hour's silence.

"You're free?"

"They let me reconnect. It became apparent we weren't involved, except to serve as a distraction. Lucienne said this attack has been brewing for some time and they anticipated the timing when we showed up. Security breach here was an internal breakdown, not our fault. Though we don't have safe conduct through the lines. Looks like Pious and I are stuck here for a while. What's your status?"

"Under strict command not to move or we'll be shelled. 'Holed' and 'dead' were also mentioned in passing. What do the attackers want?"

"Like everyone out here, more."

"Suggestions? From a strategic view, assuming the attackers can hear us."

"Wouldn't make a difference. The main 'lock is in both parties' crosshairs. They can't get in; we can't get out. You can't run for aid. At some point, the situation will destabilize. Then one or more parties will act."

"Got it." Carver slumped in his seat.

"Destabilize. I don't care for the implications," said Cardinal.

"In this circumstance, I agree. By the time one of us reacts, it could be too late to save the others." Carver looked out the viewport. "Let's backtrack the sensors. See where the attack originated. Is it one or more of the other three operations?"

Cardinal keyed his console. "The destabilizing factor could be one of the other two if they chose to be neutral in this foray."

"I'll monitor their comms while you look for origin clues."

It turned out the attack originated from two of the operation hubs combined to equal the size of their target. The fourth, and so far, neutral, party was radio silent. Either preparing for an assault from the victor, readying to run or considering their own attack. The destabilizing factor.

Carver did not want to wait to find out. He hailed DualE. "Any sign of a thaw?"

"No."

What more wasn't she allowed to share? Carver came to a decision. "I think it's time we enacted that destabilizing threat. Give the parties concerned an indication of *who* they're dealing with."

"Give it more time, *Renfrew*." DualE knew where he was leading.

"How's your life-support?"

"We're good for months."

Whether that was true or for the sake of the besiegers' ears, Carver couldn't be certain. "I'll give them twenty hours, then I talk to the neutrals." He changed frequencies to ensure everyone heard. "Attention non-hostile salvage operation. This is Willie Renfrew aboard the *Penance*. As you know, two of our people are being held hostage by your fellow salvagers. I suggest you ready an armed shuttle to rendezvous with us in twenty hours if the situation hasn't resolved by then. It will be to our advantage and everyone else's disadvantage."

"What are you planning, Carver?" Cardinal asked. "Why should the attackers let such a ship approach us?"

"Because then they would have a two-front battle on their hands they can't be certain they'd win. I'm guessing they didn't attack the other operation out of fear, not for lack of greed. The neutrals are better armed."

"Another guess?"

"Maybe. We'll know in less than twenty hours. If we see a shuttle headed our way."

"And if our guards don't decide to take the *Penance* out of the equation."

"Did Pious tell you this mission would be easy? Without risk?"

"No," said Cardinal.

"We'll find out if his faith in your escort agents was justified. I need a short rest."

D ualE chafed at the lack of action. Lucienne brought Pious the tea he'd requested. DualE stood.

"What?" Lucienne's hand drifted to her side-arm.

"I'm ex-navy," said DualE. "Maybe I can help."

"You're not Realm navy."

"No. Confluence. I've seen my share of action, large and small. Are you just going to wait them out?"

"None of your business."

DualE held up her hands. "I'm available. For opinion, insight or an extra fighter."

"Noted." Lucienne turned her back and left.

"I'm not sure I like you volunteering for another's battle," said Pious.

"They're too passive. Something's brewing. I'd rather be in the middle of it than stuck here as unwanted baggage. Or battle fodder."

He sipped his tea. "It's possible this isn't a first."

Pious put a finger on it. The absence of immediate defensive response before the transition to offense. Lucienne and the others were waiting. Perhaps offense was already underway. The attackers may have left an open flank.

"Renfrew, still holding tight?"

"Bored but stable. You?"

"Same. Watch your perimeter. Out."

"A necessary warning?" asked Pious.

"For me as much as *Penance*." She rolled her back against the wall. "Would you refresh my meditation skills? We could be here a while."

Pious put down his flask and sat before her. He took her hands in his. Pious was cold to the touch. Right, she thought, I meant to ask about his health.

He led her into the initial relaxation.

DualE's mind emptied.

Chapter 34

Rowland's shuttle from the *Neptune* docked into his freshly-arrived frigate. Glad to be surrounded again by significant armory, he hurried to the *Rickover's* command deck.

His bridge crew were ready for him. "Captain Siebe, our course is with my escort ship. We move out, half speed but long-range sensors engaged."

"We have the signature for the *Crossed Swords* logged. It won't elude us, sir."

Rowland activated the holographic display for their surroundings. Schoenfeld Eddy twisted Euclidean order. It was chaos but he wasn't arrogant enough to assume that meant vulnerable. 'Bring order to chaos and introduce chaos to order'. His battle formula brought success more often than not. His planned subversion near Argosy Station would be most effective. Disorder at the Realm's brain would galvanize the rebel muster out here. Then the Eddy could be taken.

Two environments, two strategies. The duality of his existence resonated along a hundred battles fought and yet to come. Was there a third set? The skirmishes revealed in spookspace dreams? They were the ones he repressed. Defeat and victory overprinting each other. Not in this universe. Here, he would win.

Chels loved piloting the *Crossed Swords*. This was her kind of space travel. Not spookspace. Real space, the universe she was born into. The ghosts here were real.

"Change vector to up twenty, port fifteen." Altman looked up from his charts.

"You recognize the area?" Chels checked the view on their new heading.

"What's that?" She touched a fingertip to the screen where a spherical density anomaly glowed in the infrared.

"A salvage eddy. It's near where Perry and I worked. Once we're closer, I can line up our target and calculate the recoil trajectory, though I've no idea how far it could have traveled in the weeks since we fired it."

Chels tasked her console with more data monitoring. "Bit of chatter from that ball. How likely is it you know anyone out here?"

"Likely as not. Listen but don't broadcast or respond. Salvagers, like prospectors, don't welcome uninvited guests."

"How does one get invited?"

"One doesn't. Every guest is uninvited and therefore a threat. Fire first, dispose of the evidence second. And keep quiet."

"'Shoot, shovel and shut up.' Good survival mantra," she muttered.

Chels recognized the voice over the comm and cut their burn. "That's Brother Cardinal." More voices. Unknown. "The *Penance* isn't alone."

Altman scanned the noise. "Do we have armament?"

Chels activated the *Crossed Swords'* arsenal catalog. "DualE and Carver did not enter the brothers' service casually. We outgun anything our size I've ever run across in the Realm short of full-military."

"They won't know that. Keep drifting toward the *Penance* and prepare for hostile reaction."

Reaction came swiftly. "Attention approaching ship. You are invading our claim area. Leave or be fired upon."

Chels raised an eyebrow. Altman responded. "We are a non-salvage vessel."

"Turn around and leave."

"It's coming from the ship close to *Penance*," said Chels.

"We're having trouble initiating vector change," Altman announced. "We'll comply as soon as we can."

How much time did that lie buy them?

"There will be no warning shot. You will change vector now."

Altman shrugged. He switched on the broadcast link. "I'm out of ideas. You?"

"Ahoy second vessel," said Chels. "Is that the *Penance*? Thank goodness we found you. The navy's looking for you."

"Ahoy *Crossed Swords*. This is Willie Renfrew. Thought you'd got lost. Sorry we can't rendezvous at the moment, we're in a situation here."

Renfrew. Denz pre-empted any giveaway. "Tell us where to target and we'll have you free."

"Try it and your friends are vapor," the outsider warned.

"Try us or them and you are scrap for future salvagers," said Chels. "Except there won't be anything bigger than my fist to reclaim."

"You must think we're naïve. You're outnumbered."

"And you're overmatched." To prove her point, Chels targeted a decent-sized, unoccupied rock and vaporized it. "That's one. The next one's coming at you."

"We have hostages."

"And I've got a bigger cannon. Want to trade?"

Denz broke in. "As much as I want to give you carte blanche, *Crossed Swords*, Pious and DualE are under siege with the salvagers on the location dead ahead. A struggle for limited resources being exploited by too many salvagers."

"I can change the second part of that equation," said Chels.

"Give us an hour. I've made an offer already to our 'hosts'. The time isn't up but your arrival changes the power balance enough to accelerate my plan."

"An hour. Then I start eliminating threats." Chels switched off.

Altman huddled over the astrogation display.

"Familiar?" she asked him.

"I think so. My memory's usually better. Two jumps so close together is jumbling my neurons. But it'll come back."

It better or she'd risked sanity for half a mission. She still had to alert Pious and the others about Rowland. Later, they had enough worries.

DualE's voice was audible but cloaked in static. "Renfrew, Pious is reminding me of our mission. A shooting war won't endear the brotherhood in the Eddy."

Carver weighed his options. "And harming Pious won't endear the Eddy to the brotherhood at large. The order has a long reach and a longer memory, right?"

"Follow your original plan until no longer practicable."

Carver nudged Cardinal. "Any response from the neutrals?"

"Nothing. Your assessment of them waiting to salvage the pieces when this goes sideways is accurate, in my opinion."

Carver hailed the attackers. "Less than an hour. I want the ship behind us to begin withdrawal. *Crossed Swords*, hold your fire."

Fifty-five minutes later, the nearby ship moved, its course heading to the second operations center. "Good choice," said Carver. "Now for the trickier part." He opened the comm to the first aggressor. "This is Renfrew, I have a proposal for you, an incentive offer you shouldn't refuse. I'm broadcasting to your colleagues and competitors. First one in gets the goods so I suggest you don't hesitate."

"What's this wonderful offer we can't refuse, Renfrew?"

"I have information on the Carver Denz Schoenfeldium discovery which no one else has. I will share this information when you withdraw and my shipmates are back aboard the *Penance*."

"You must think we're fresh off a jumpfreighter. That con has been circulating for months. We're staying put until your shipmates' life support runs out."

"Well, despite Brother Pious' request not to initiate fire, my backup plan is to allow the *Crossed Swords* to open up her barrage on your base and then you. Pull out now."

A private message came through from Chels. "*Penance*, there's a bigger ship on the edge of our detectors. Our adversaries likely see it too."

"A freighter? Mobile refinery?"

"Can't be certain but unlikely. Moving faster than either."

"Reinforcements for someone. Let's get this done." He switched back to open hailing. "*Crossed Swords* is lining up your base."

"Give us more on Denz, then we'll discuss withdrawal."

"Do you know who found the lode before he did?"

"Denz was first. Legitimate claim. We're salvagers, not prospectors."

"By default, or by choice? Ask your full crew who'd like a chance at duplicating Denz's find?"

"Who got there before him?"

"Nev Mox," said Carver.

"Never heard of him. Why should that make any difference?"

"Because Mox kept a log of his explorations. He missed the main deposit and allowed his claim to lapse. But he was in a quadrant which could hold more before his last stop, twenty-five years before Denz re-discovered his lode."

"How the hell did you come by this log?"

"I'll tell you when you're back in your own hole." Carver cut the transmission. He exhaled. The beginnings of a headache tightened his forehead.

Cardinal passed him cold tea. "You're taking a risk. I see what you have in mind. How can you be sure they won't attack in unison and accept some losses?"

"Because they can't risk killing me."

"You know this for a fact?"

"No. But my charter is to protect Brother Pious. If revealing my true identity is the only way I can do that, then so be it." He opened the comm. "You have twenty minutes. Oh, and if you check your long-distance sensors, our real backup is closing." He switched off before they could reply.

"We don't know that," said Cardinal.

"Neither do they."

P ious followed DualE into the 'lock. He turned to Andre. "I know what Renfrew plans to do. I'll try to include your people as well."

Andre shook his head. "No thanks. We salvage. Prospecting is for the greedy and the desperate."

Pious held out his hand. "I'm impressed by your restraint and commend you. I don't need to prolong my message or my presence."

"You are welcome anytime, Brother Pious. We won't underestimate the value of your words nor underestimate our rivals' dishonesty."

"Good luck. I look forward to my next visit."

"Let's go while we can, Pious." DualE's plea reminded him time was essential.

They jumped back to the *Penance*. He couldn't see the *Crossed Swords* until DualE pointed it out but he was thankful for their appearance.

"Welcome home," said Carver.

"We're not home yet," said DualE. "Where are the attackers?"

Cardinal tapped the console screen and a 3D hologram outlined positions.

"We kept our bargain, *Penance*. Time to fulfill your promise."

Pious addressed Carver. "Are you okay with this?"

"I can't hide forever. It may be worth nothing but it got you out of a jam." Carver opened the external comm. "You're right. I'm sending you the location of Denz's lode's original orbit. It was huge, as you will see. The only reason Denz found it was due to it's return inside the survey quadrant. It has a decades-long periodicity but subsequent calculations added another factor. The moonlet's ellipse was distorted. It was part of a dual system." He waited for the implication to sink in.

"A companion? Why didn't Denz check it out?"

"Other priorities. One bonanza was more than enough."

"Sounds like a fable."

"Are you willing to risk it isn't? No guarantees, but if the companion came from the same origin, it too could be loaded with Schoenfeldium. Enough to satisfy the Realm's jumpspace drive requirements for a generation."

"I think your void happy, Renfrew. Why haven't you gone after it?"

"I told you. I was satisfied with one. Willie Renfrew is Carver Denz."

There was silence for many seconds. Pious glanced at DualE. Her lips were compressed. Carver hadn't cleared this move with her. Were they compromised throughout the Eddy now? The truth had to be the better course. He put a hand on Carver's shoulder and squeezed reassurance.

"We'll evaluate your data."

"I expect a royalty payment to the brotherhood if you strike," Carver added,

"Is that a joke?"

"Hardly. We know where you'll be. Give me your word and I won't broadcast my information throughout the Eddy."

DualE nudged Pious to his seat. "We should leave." She took Carver's comm. "Chels? DualE here. What's your plan going forward?"

"If you're okay with us using the *Crossed Swords*, Altman and I have our own treasure hunt."

DualE looked at Pious. "They're looking for the alien artifact. Better they find it than some nutter."

"Or worse," said Carver. "The military."

"Agreed. Should we set a rendezvous?"

"Chels. How long before you need to resupply the ship?"

"A month."

"Plan to meet us at the shipyard in one month."

"Sooner if we're lucky."

"Leave word."

Cardinal tugged Pious' sleeve. A low frequency wave swept across his screen. "What is it, Brother?"

"A beacon. Locator signal. I wouldn't normally scan this low a frequency but I thought the attackers might be using off-scale comm links."

DualE asked, "Where's it coming from?"

"The *Crossed Swords*."

"Hell and over again," said DualE.

Pious didn't see the problem. "What does it mean?"

"They're being tracked. Chels, did you know you're sending a low-frequency locator signal?"

"What? No. We are?"

"Cardinal will send you the frequency. See if you can find it and shut it down. It could be outside."

"Too late," said Carver. "The other ship is still closing. That's no freighter tracking you."

Chapter 35

The *Whisper* de-barnacled and held a parallel course with the diplomatic ship and its naval escort. Zofie engaged the handshake protocol with the Eddy shipyard's harbor-master software to find a berth.

The small ship eased automatically into dock. Marshall looked worse than Zofie felt from the jump back from the Confluence. To be fair, the info-mule had been running half-empty after her debriefing. "Are you up to hunting up a real meal and drink?" Zofie asked.

"Oh Lord, am I ever."

"I thought Kondradt would be waiting for us. Want to contact him before we hunt and gather comestibles?"

"Screw him," said Marshall. "He can find me."

"I want to alert Brother Remorse as well. And I want to know where Pious and team are." Zofie queried the harbor-master. "Is *Penance* in port?"

"The *Penance* left ten standard days ago."

"Is Brother Remorse on station?"

There was a delay in the answer. "He is. The brother is not body-linked to the station communication. Would you like a message delivered to his berth?"

"Thank you, yes. Tell him the *Whisper* has arrived and Zofie will be in Eddie's Dive for the next two hours."

The pub was nearly empty. Zofie and Marshall downed a rejuvenation elixir before proceeding to select protein and alcohol cocktails. Remorse arrived simultaneous with their food.

"Can you join us?" Zofie asked. "Kondradt's picking up the tab."

The brother's robe was cinched tight and looked like it could go around him twice. "My ministry hasn't garnered much compensation thus far, sister. I would welcome the chance to share a meal."

Once he settled into food, Remorse asked, "How was your mission?"

"Successful so far. We've only initiated a first step. Higher powers can take it from here. We're out of it."

"We hope," added Marshall.

"Any word from *Penance*?" Zofie asked. "Their mission goes well?"

"Mixed success," Remorse answered between chewing and washing the food down with diluted wine. "They ran into some trouble with a salvage cluster but plan to regain traction soon. The *Crossed Swords* showed up to aid them but I gather from Brother Pious it was Carver whose ingenuity settled the problem."

"I've missed a lot in my absence," said Zofie. "Who's crewing *Crossed Swords*?"

"Two people from Slate's Progress. A woman named Chels Harte whom the brothers and I met the first time we visited Progress and a salvager named Altman. My colleague, Atone, remained behind."

"That leaves Brother Atone alone on Slate's," said Zofie. "Abandoned. Like you." The missionaries spread themselves as thin as Remorse's waistline. At least DualE and Carver bolstered Pious and Cardinal. Zofie took pride in her role in freeing Carver.

"I'm not abandoned," said Remorse. "This is a challenge to create a new congregation. It's a battle but I'll rise to that challenge. As will Atone on Slate's Progress."

A fourth voice hailed them. "Didn't take me long to figure out where you'd be."

"Kondradt, join us," said Marshall. "Do you know Brother Remorse?"

"By reputation. Your presence aboard the 'yard is a benefit, brother." Kondradt didn't sit down. He addressed Marshall and Zofie. "If you would finish up your meal, we have a briefing to attend. Your association with me was sufficient to have you included."

"There goes my plan to get well-decompressed," said Zofie. "Are you sure you want me?"

Kondradt nodded. "Your input and future actions could be needed."

Zofie passed her mug to Remorse. "Yours to finish if you like. You can access the *Whisper* if you want a change from your berth. I know the cubby-tubes here are a bit confining. We'll catch up later."

"Most appreciated," said Remorse. "A scene change might be in order."

"Bring your navigation records for *Penance* and *Crossed Swords*," said Zofie. "I've a sense they could use more resources on their mission."

Zofie and Marshall followed Kondradt out and onto a waiting scooter.

———————✠✠⎟⎟⧗⧗———————

The briefing was underway when Zofie and company were ushered inside. To Zofie's surprise, Chancellor Mekli was present. Mekli co-chaired the meeting with his Director General Shoop and an Admiral Bakken, a toughened, crewcut naval officer. The two diplomats and female commander looked grim, and not just from jumpspace hangover.

"Admiral Rowland's flightplan wasn't registered with the 'yard but we know he tracked a small ship called The *Crossed Swords* out into the Eddy." A junior officer handed a flimsy to Bakken.

"We don't have anything more specific? Can we track this *Crossed Swords* from its plan?"

"No sir. They filed a typical prospector plan. Time and general quadrant only."

"We've got to locate Rowland without alerting him," said Bakken. "That means no public requests for sightings amongst nearby operations. Suggestions?"

Zofie nudged Kondradt. "I might be able to help," she whispered.

Kondradt stood. "My associate may have relevant information, Admiral."

Mekli leaned and spoke into Bakken's ear. The admiral stared at Zofie, then nodded. "Proceed."

Zofie approached the three. "You said Rowland was tracking the *Crossed Swords*. I have friends aboard another small ship, a missionary craft, the *Penance*. *Penance* and *Crossed Swords* were or are still, in the same area. I believe *Penance* did file a more specific plan and Brother Remorse, one of the missionaries who is aboard this station, has their most recent location."

"You will contact Remorse, find out where they might be, and relay the information to me," said Bakken.

Zofie realized from Bakken's tone this was not a request, this was an order.

Bakken turned to the two men beside her and spoke too low for Zofie to hear. Nods from Mekli and the Confluence representative triggered a gavel hammer from Bakken. "Admiral Rowland has entered Eddy space without authorization for aggressive purposes. He has breached the terms of the peace accord by engaging in espionage at Realm facilities. He attempted to arm seditious uprisings within Argosy Realm. Rowland is hereby declared 'Rogue' and all steps necessary to recall him are invoked as of this moment." She pointed to Zofie. "You will accompany my fleet, Miss or Ms..."

"Ked. Zofie Ked, sir."

The meeting had finished. The diverse coalition wasn't wasting time or effort in prolonged debate. Zofie hadn't anticipated joining the navy.

Certainly not the Confluence Navy. She wondered if it came with a pension.

Chapter 36

C arver confronted Altman in the cabin of the *Crossed Swords*. "You're the reason I was jailed on Argosy Station."

Chels inserted herself between the two men. "Look past it, Mr. Denz," she said. Her voice soothed.

Carver's shoulders slumped. "Easy to say, tough to do but you're right, Chels. Now isn't the time to revive old anger. His is too crazy a story not to be appreciated for its legend-capable telling. I've made mistakes as well but mine usually turn out on the good side of luck." He pointed at Altman. "You found the bad side of the coin. I was arrested. Your partner paid with his life. Chels paid with a potentially lethal jump. For her. Anything I do or say is wasted."

"For what it's worth, Denz, I'm sorry," said Altman. "I overheard what you did to save your colleagues. I should have done the same for mine and I didn't. I was too late for Perry."

Chels said, "Altman went outside and disabled the tracking beacon."

"I hope it wasn't too late. What's your next step, Chels?"

"We've established the location where Altman and Perry fired the weapon. We begin backtracking recoil trajectories from there. The navcom's already given us locations within a day or two's flight. If you're comfortable, we'll be moving on before we have to recalculate."

"You'd better send Cardinal your plan. We'll join you for a fortnight at least. This ship belongs to DualE and I, we wouldn't want anything to happen to it. We separated once against our plan." Carver gathered his helmet and stepped into the lock. "I suggest you divert from the real target on your initial course, just in case the beacon wasn't the only choice to shadow you."

Outside, Carver clipped the safety line to his belt. "*Penance*, you can reel me back."

The tug drew him away from his ship toward *Penance*. He'd have to tell Pious about the schedule change. Safety was the main selling point. They didn't need another volatile encounter like the last.

"How's Chels?" Pious asked when he was inside.

Carver removed the rest of his EVA suit. "Her attitude seems solid. I saw no visible sign she's jumphappy. Whatever she did from Slate's to the shipyard worked. Once, anyway."

"She has a mental strength perhaps greater than her physical prowess. I hope she doesn't try the return trip too soon. I wish I could monitor her."

Pious' concern fit Carver's plan. "I think we should stay with them until they find the artifact. It keeps the two ships together as we originally chartered and allows you to keep watch over her. Altman is more salvager than partner and we've witnessed how they can lose moral direction. We'll log any potential audiences while we track with *Crossed Swords* for return visits."

"I'm with Carver on this," said DualE.

"Very well, we'll accompany them. Brother Cardinal, I leave astrogation in your hands. I need some time to recover from this experience."

DualE cornered Carver as the ships departed the salvage enclave. "You're an amateur astrogator, what do think of the peripheral signal?" She scrolled the second screen and identified the blip.

"Beyond my expertise. Could be another prospector following the *Crossed Swords*. Piracy isn't unknown in the Eddy. Let someone else do the heavy lifting, then scoop it. Or someone who stumbled across our signals and figures we're not who we say. Paranoia, laziness and greed motivate more than one indolent prospector out here."

"*Crossed Swords*, this is DualE. Keep a watch on that signal bearing fourteen hours twenty RA and six degrees declination. Initiate your burn, we'll follow in a few hours and see if it shadows either of us."

"Got it," Chels answered. "Thanks."

"I'm not going to wait on an empty stomach," said Carver. "Cardinal, can I fix you something to eat?"

"Thank you, yes."

DualE helped him pull food from the larder. "It's quite the wild show out here, Carver. Surprised a thrill-seeker like you retreated after his big find."

"Rowland was pulling my strings, remember?"

"Rowland and Helena."

The hurt hadn't fully diminished from his fiancé's abrupt desertion before he'd returned to the Confluence. "And Helena," he confirmed.

"Does Pious' meditation routine help?"

"Sometimes. What were the salvagers like? Did they appreciate his message before the hostiles showed up?"

"Yeah." She handed Cardinal his food. "They're eking out a hard living here. But it's relatively unencumbered by oversight. The kind of freedom you and I could only wish for."

"I'll take comfort and authority over austerity and the illusion of freedom. They have to rely on some infrastructure to resupply resources and buy their bounty."

"The ghost is moving," said Cardinal.

"Following the *Crossed Swords*?" Carver looked over the astrogator's shoulder.

"Too far away to be certain. They are getting closer."

"Hide us on the other side of the biggest rock," said DualE. "Periscope a monitor."

Rowland's patience strained. The *Rickover* retraced the *Crossed Swords'* path for days until it's halt at a small salvage aggregate. Was this their destination? The artifact left in the hands of allies? More witnesses to dispose of but the prize was worth it.

The ship had joined another small vessel. A rendezvous to the next step or the final location.

"*'Swords* is moving, Admiral."

"Nudge us back, Captain Siebe. Now that we've a fix on the other ship, monitor its movements as well and relay to the escorts. If the targets split up, so will our ships. The *Rickover* will shadow the *Crossed Swords*."

He'd sacrifice one or more of his own craft to capture the weapon. If they used it on a fighter, so be it. The *Rickover* would retaliate. He would possess the weapon and reset the balance of power between the Confluence and the Realm. And the balance between the do-little politicians and the navy. He tired of being an enforcement tool. He was ready to command the government. Stratocracy was his goal. Such a government required a strong head. The Realm could do worse than him at the helm.

DualE sat beside Brother Cardinal.

"They're definitely on *Crossed Swords'* tail. I'm getting more than one signal. Appears to be three distinct sources." The brother looked worried.

"Numbers alone say we can't fight them if they're Confluence or Realm Navy," said DualE. "We need leverage."

Carver remained silent. Come on, partner, she willed. *Help out*.

"What do you suggest?" asked Pious. He lay prone on the deck.

"We know where Altman and Chels were going to start their search. We go straight there; we're not the ship being tracked. If we can find the artifact, we'll have a negotiating position."

"*If* they don't track us," said Cardinal. "Your assumption could be wrong."

"It's a risk we need to take," said DualE. "For us and Argosy Realm if Rowland's hunting for that weapon." She turned to Carver. "What do you say?"

He glared. "Are you working with Rowland?"

"I was supposed to. As a trade for your release on Argosy Station. When Zofie spirited you off, my obligation ceased."

"I don't think so. You've been evaluating every step from a broader viewpoint. A tactical military viewpoint."

"You're right, Carver. But my interest was purely defensive. If battles arise, I don't want to be forced to choose a side but I will do what I can to ensure the safety of my former grunt-mates."

Pious rose, concern reddened his face. "I need to know whose side you are on at this moment, DualE. The brotherhood or your former colleagues aboard one or all of those vessels under Rowland's command?"

"We all need to know, DualE," said Carver.

"If I wasn't on this side, Rowland wouldn't have to track the *Crossed Swords*. He could wait for me to signal him."

"You still could, if we follow your plan."

"Then make certain I don't," she said. "I appreciate that your trust wavers. Cut my comm access but we need to get moving."

"Are you certain we're not broadcasting a beacon, Cardinal?" asked Carver.

"I can't be one hundred percent sure but there's nothing I can detect."

"Pious? This is your commission and your call," said DualE.

The brother gripped her hands. "They weren't tracking you. Despite the dual role you've played, you have my faith and trust. I agree with your plan."

"Thank you, Brother Pious. I won't let any of you down."

The *Penance* moved slowly beyond line-of-sight contact with the fleet ships before initiating a burst to set it on its way to hunt for the artifact. DualE planned to use the time to determine how she would regain Carver's trust.

Chapter 37

Zofie dosed on and off for hours before finally settling into proper sleep. The disruption was sudden and disorienting. It took her a minute to climb from the dream realms into shipyard reality. The *Whisper* had a visitor. Zofie recognized her right in the external light.

Zofie cracked the airlock and pulled on a shirt over her head then looked for pants.

"Keep dressing," said Marshall. "We've been invited to join Admiral Bakken and company aboard the *Marlborough*."

"Now?"

"Twenty minutes before 'now'. My scooter's outside. We need to move."

Zofie sat on the deck, pulling on shoes, then stopped. "What if I decline the invitation?"

"If you ever want to broker again in the Confluence or the Realm, don't consider it."

"Okay, that's my motivation. What's theirs?"

"I can only speculate. Keep you out of circulation? Exploit your acquaintance with Carver Denz and his people?"

Marshall was on edge. Zofie's resistance wouldn't help her or her new possible ally. "Why you?"

"I'm included at Kondradt's request. Another witness to whatever occurs when we catch up to Rowland. I'm afraid our choices are currently down to one, Zofie."

Zofie sealed her flimsuit. "I'm glad they sent you instead of a couple of muscle-bound marines. I could've got myself injured by gut reaction."

She secured her ship and climbed on the scooter.

Zofie looked through the viewport of the *Marlborough*. During Zofie's admission interview onto the warship, Bakken herself had reinforced Zofie's potential value as an intermediary with *Penance* and *Crossed Swords'* crews. The role wouldn't generate immediate credit but if she looked at the long game, perhaps new commercial opportunities could be negotiated with the Confluence and the Realm.

"Kondradt tells me they've located the *Rickover*." Marshall came up behind her.

Zofie's former cargo claimed to be here at Kondradt's request but Zofie had seen her speaking alone with Chancellor Mekli when she emerged from her interview with Bakken. Dynamics between Mekli and Kondradt were hard to follow.

"Is Rowland still tracking Chels and Altman?" Zofie settled onto a hard bench.

"If he is, we're too removed to pick up their signal so we follow him."

"When do we pursue?"

"Momentarily. Kondradt suggested we buckle in. Navy ships don't follow passenger liner protocol when it comes to acceleration limits. Come on, I've found a more comfortable set of recliners."

Zofie and Marshall hurried down a catwalk and entered a door marked 'Wardroom'. "They won't be using it while we're in pursuit."

Zofie strapped into a cushioned chaise. Marshall fiddled with the comm until they could hear the bridge chatter. "We'll travel in comfort and not be blind to what's happening outside."

"Does Kondradt anticipate armed resistance?"

Marshall shook her head. "I don't know what Kondradt expects. From what I hear, Rowland's unlikely to stand down without a scrap.

He's already crossed numerous lines in the sand. Admiral Bakken sounded pretty pissed. She might be the one to start shooting."

Zofie wasn't sure she agreed. Bakken showed no emotion during their chat. This commander wouldn't show that much of a crack in the Confluence's solidarity in front of Chancellor Mekli. On the other hand, such a move might convince Mekli the Confluence wouldn't hesitate to fire on any perceived enemy if they'd act against one of the their own.

The chair pushed into her as the cruiser began its chase. She hoped her value as go-between with *Penance* and *Crossed Swords* would be needed. She didn't want either to be caught in Rowland and Bakken's crossfire.

"They're closing," Chels said.

Altman scanned the screen. "Do we run?"

"Not much chance we can lose them and I don't want to make us a target. We continue our current heading until we're hailed." She clenched her hands on her chair to stop the tremors coursing through her muscles.

They didn't have long to wait.

"Attention *Crossed Swords*. This is the *Rickover*, Confluence Naval Frigate under the command of Admiral Rowland. Stand by to be boarded."

"Haven't got your identification handshake confirmed," Chels replied. "State your reason for request, if indeed you are who you claim."

"You will allow us to match vector and prepare to be boarded."

"I..." She coughed to clear the lump rising in her throat. "I repeat. No identity confirmation. There's plenty of false ID's out here, looking for naïve prospectors to rob."

"Take a good look out your portside, *Crossed Swords*. Do we look like a vandal?"

Chels and Altman both stared at the now illuminated frigate. It wasn't large compared to a naval dreadnaught but it dwarfed their ship. "No. Why do you need to board us? The Confluence has no authority in Schoenfeld Eddy. Has Argosy Realm transferred policing to the Confluence while I wasn't listening?"

"Our armament provides all the authority we require. Further questions can wait until we are aboard your vessel."

Chels closed the link, letting the ship drift on course. "He must believe we found what we sought at the last outpost." She'd endured jumpspace to end the search too soon? "We need to buy time, Altman. Any suggestions?"

"I could claim you kidnapped me and demand a hearing. Or we could bluff a race to lodge a claim."

Or I could launch Swords into their flank and destroy all evidence of what we're doing. Chels wasn't ready for self-immolation. Not yet.

She had to control her nerves. Pious' teachings? No time to meditate out of this. "They'll be searching for any sign of the artifact if that's why they tracked us." She opened the astrogation log. "First thing I delete is where we're headed."

"I spent a lot of time calculating that course." Altman blocked her fingers.

"We have backup. *Penance* may already be there if they concluded we were first target for Rowland."

"Okay. Wipe it. Better it gets lost for good rather than the Confluence acquiring it. I need a drink."

"Help yourself. What are we prospecting for?"

"Same as everyone. Schoenfeldium."

"Too late to falsify logs," said Chels. "We tell them it's in our brains so no one can claim jump us."

Clunk. The *Crossed Swords* shook once. They heard the telltale noises of cables being anchored to the hull.

Chels had one desperate card to play before they were restrained. "Mayday, mayday. This is *Crossed Swords* out of Eddy Shipyard. We are being boarded by personnel claiming to represent Confluence Navy." She put it on repeat and waited for punishment.

"That was unnecessary," said the first of the two men through the 'lock.

A Lieutenant by insignia. Followed by a higher rank. Admiral Rowland.

"Unnecessary?" said Chels. "Then why are you armed?" she shrunk back from the marine.

The Lieutenant patted down both Chels and Altman, then holstered his sidearm. "Precaution."

Rowland examined the cabin. "Where is it?"

"What?" asked Altman.

"Don't be stupid. I don't have the time nor the patience." Rowland answered. "The artifact you came looking for."

The officer was combing their navlog. "It's been erased, sir. I think I can retrieve what's missing." He inserted a black strip of plastic in a port and waited.

"It's legally mine," said Altman.

"You will sign it over to the Confluence Navy," said Rowland. "I saw what it could do. Such a weapon is not to be left in the hands of someone like you. It isn't salvage. It's a guarantee of lasting peace between the Confluence and Argosy Realm."

"In your hands, it's safer? Peace only with the Realm subservient as we've always been." Chels regretted leading them close. Maybe they wouldn't find it. Altman's treasure would remain a myth to future searchers.

"Got it, Admiral. This was a decoy path."

"You will remain on board, Lieutenant. Pilot ahead. These two will accompany me back to the *Rickover*."

"You're hijacking my ship?"

"Not yours, Ms. Harte."

"I have charter from Brother Remorse at the Eddy shipyard."

"The brother isn't here and my mission takes precedence. We leave now." Rowland picked up his helmet. "If you don't want to vacuum freeze, I suggest you suit up."

Chels was out of options. She took as long as she dared to don her suit, pretending to have trouble with the seals. Every minute gained could bring help or put the artifact further from Rowland's grip. A grip now holding both her and the only man who could operate it.

Aboard Bakken's pursuit ship, Zofie listened to the mayday call and the subsequent denial by the *Rickover*. "*Crossed Swords* is under Rowland's control."

"We're overtaking them," said Marshall.

"Catching up is one thing," said Zofie. "How do you plan to stop him? Rowland's doing what he thinks is right. If he's a fanatic then it's worse."

Kondradt stood in the doorway. "There's enough authority with Bakken and Mekli to justify any argument or force required."

Zofie had her doubts. The temptation of the alien weapon could be too great for either side to destroy it or clues leading to its recovery. *Crossed Swords* crew, her fellow Realm citizens, would be small collateral damage. What action could she take?

Chapter 38

"Mayday, mayday. This is *Crossed Swords* out of Eddy Shipyard. We are being boarded by personnel claiming to represent Confluence Navy."

Carver lowered the volume. "Do we try to help?"

DualE shook her head. "I vote no. Reaching the artifact becomes even more important now. We're in a race and our only advantage is we're closer."

"What if we do get it first but the navy wants to trade? Pious? Thoughts?"

"Will they harm Chels or Altman?"

"I don't think so," said DualE. "Rowland will extract their course and place them under protection. He may need Altman's expertise with the artifact."

"How can you be sure he won't eliminate them?" asked Carver. "He's shown little restraint to date about inciting reaction."

"We couldn't do anything if we did go to their aid. We'd be in the same situation as the *Crossed Swords*." DualE's expression pleaded to all of them. "If we find the artifact, if gives us bargaining power."

Carver wanted to be convinced. "To give it up regardless. Or he decides to destroy us and it. If Rowland can't have it, I'm sure his second strategy will be to ensure no one else will."

"He won't want us to destroy it."

"If we find it and he's on our trail, I say we dismantle it and scatter the pieces."

"If we have time," said DualE. "Cardinal, how close?"

"Two hours to Altman's last known location when he and Perry fired it. An hour to align with the jumphole the *Orson* opened. After that, a guess as to how long to catch it, if all our assumptions hold."

Carver tapped the screen. "The big unknown being the weapon's recoil velocity."

"Can we catch up?" asked Pious.

"Our refit included revised power," Cardinal answered. "If it's out there and on line, we'll catch it."

"Needle in the void," Carver muttered. "I hate abandoning Chels and Altman but I agree we continue on."

"Thanks, Carver."

DualE's gratitude didn't reinforce his decision.

"I'm sorry, Chels," said Altman. "I shouldn't have involved you. I should have had the guts to come out here quietly and alone."

"We're not done," she said. "I've overcome my fear of jump thanks to your confession. They haven't found the artifact yet and maybe they won't. Or if they do, maybe they won't have your insight to make it work."

"I don't know if I could keep my knowledge from them, if Rowland was determined to extract it."

"Consider a stronger faith. The brotherhood will sustain you."

Their door opened and two guards signalled. "Come on. You're wanted on the bridge."

The *Rickover* was cramped inside and Chels had to duck under a few tight ceilings and conduits before they entered the command center.

Rowland beckoned them to his side. "We're near your target, Altman. Recognize anything?"

A holographic display churned with detritus. Rock, ice and manmade refuse spun slowly around a center point.

"I can't be sure. Orbits change."

"But this is where you found the artifact," insisted Rowland.

"My partner was the astrogator. I just input what I could recall from our trip back to the shipyard."

Chels had to give credit to Altman's courage. How long would it last?

"Recall? You stashed a copy of the log before you left the 'yard for Slate's Progress to hunt and kill your former partner."

Chels moved in front of Altman. "He didn't kill Perry. Perry killed himself. If anyone's to blame for his death, it's me. I was the one who counselled him and likely the last person in Slate's to talk to him."

"Enough blame to share," said Rowland. "Fact is, both of you can make up for your mistakes by helping me now."

"Helping *you*? I thought we were being recruited by the Confluence." She tensed inside. Rowland was the immediate threat. Not just to her, but to Pious. Her fears had been confirmed.

"Do not test me, Harte. I *am* the Confluence as far as you are concerned. As far as the Eddy is concerned." He turned to Altman. "Show me where you found the artifact."

Chels watched Altman tremble. His determination wavered. He immersed into the holo, reaching out with a hand to pass through the flotsam, turning his head to view from differing angles.

A bridge officer called to Rowland. "Admiral, we're being followed."

"Idiot," said Rowland. "You do not relay such information in front of outsiders."

Chels pushed him with both hands. "You're stretching your mandate, admiral. Intimidation's no good on me. I'm no threat other than to myself."

Rowland gripped her wrists in one hand. "You're correct. You are no threat."

She struggled uselessly, even tried to kick him. He swept her feet from the deck and dropped her.

"Take them back to quarters," Rowland ordered. "The rummy's useless. We'll complete the search of the quadrant ourselves."

Inside their holding cell, Chels rested her back against the wall. Her sudden attack against Rowland had been lunacy. Maybe her jump demons still rode inside her. She tried to calm and thought about what Rowland had been told. Who pursued the pursuer? Foe or ally? Was a foe to Rowland necessarily a friend to the Realm? Would it affect their fate?

———————— ⧧⧧⧵⧸⧵⧩⧩ ————————

Carver spelled off Cardinal on the pilot console. DualE seated beside him, the two protectors scanned ahead of the *Penance* for any unnatural object. Behind them, Pious rasped in meditation. How relaxing could labored breath be?

"Got something," said DualE. "We're barely catching up but it's the right trajectory." She fine-tuned the echo. "Linear. Tumbling. Make it twenty meters long, give or take another ten."

Carver confirmed her readings. It was their artifact. "Bigger than I expected somehow."

"Give us a burn," said DualE.

His finger hovered. "We catch up, then what? We don't have a way to grab on."

"I'll EVA."

"It's too big for the airlock. I don't see how we can do anything with it out here."

"A pessimistic view, Carver. What's really on your mind?"

"A thousand negative outcomes," he said.

"You pushed to chase it. Second thoughts destroy missions."

"I've had time to think. Reconsider. Whatever we do with it, whoever we give it too, it changes an already fragile balance. We've got enough power in the small laser cannon to wreck it. Make it useless. Render it unsalvageable and so screwed up it can't be reverse engineered. We melt it and send it further on its way from the Eddy, the Realm and the Confluence."

"I don't know what to say," said DualE. "You've turned pacifist?"

"I've turned realist. Do you honestly want it in Rowland's hands?"

"No. That's why you need to accelerate now."

"Grab it for the Realm? How do we know Chancellor Mekli et al would be any different in exploiting it for advantage?"

DualE looked over her shoulder. Pious had coughed wetly. "Catch up, Carver" she said. "We'll take a vote once we know it's the artifact. I'll bow to the majority."

Unless she was still loyal to Rowland. Then her bow would be followed by action. Carver held no illusions she couldn't take out the three of them in two blinks.

He initiated burn.

Chapter 39

"We're being hailed, Admiral," said Captain Siebe. "On navy frequency."

"Ignore it," said Rowland.

"There's more, sir. We're ordered to decelerate and stand by. From Admiral Bakken aboard the *Marlborough*."

"I don't care if it's Julius Caesar. We are on a critical mission. Expedience and removing a threat to the Confluence supersede Bakken's orders."

"A new burn, sir. Small ship signature on this heading." The astrogator highlighted a new holo.

Rowland peered into the display. "It's the *Penance*. The ship Altman and Harte rendezvoused with, I'm certain. Maximum acceleration. And scan ahead of them for any object."

"We're being ordered again to slow, Admiral."

For an answer, Rowland opened comm to his two escort ships. "Disengage from us and distract the *Marlborough*. Give me time to get clear." He didn't wait for confirmation. "*Crossed Swords*, give me flanking coverage but stay out of our way." He took control of the navcomm. "All hands prepare for maximum acceleration starting in fifteen seconds. Get secure." He buckled in and locked onto the *Penance's* course.

"Its surface appears seamless," Carver observed. "I thought Altman said it looked like a communication beacon."

Penance closed on the object. DualE's first description was accurate. A bar, rotating end over end. He spun his chair to face Pious. Cardinal huddled over his leader. "We could use your guidance, brothers," said Carver.

"I'm afraid Brother Pious has taken a bad turn," said Cardinal.

"He's terminal, isn't he?" Carver turned to DualE. "I suspected there was more to his weakness than jump-reaction. The three of us will have to decide."

"At least it won't end in a tie," she answered. "You know how I feel. Cardinal, do we destroy a unique alien artifact or attempt to use it for good?"

"Weapons and human good intentions rarely go hand in hand," said Cardinal.

"I agree," said Carver. "My experience with finding the lode reinforced my feeling about altering the status quo."

"The status quo is a myth, Carver," said DualE. "I've been through enough battles which prove the status quo is anything but. You need to progress to reach stability. Stability through forward momentum."

"Is that you talking or Rowland?"

Before she could answer, a new presence made itself known. "Ahoy *Penance*. We have your identity signature. This is Admiral Rowland. Shut down your propulsion systems or face fire. Prepare to be boarded."

"That was quick," said Carver. He fumed at DualE. "One last time, did you lead them here?"

"No, believe me. They must have been looking for us and saw our burn. They don't want us; they want that object. I'm sorry Carver. This isn't my doing, I swear."

"Is it too late to fire on it, destroy it before they get it?"

"If you want to die quickly, no it isn't," said DualE.

Cardinal spoke. "Brother Pious needs their medical services."

DualE repeated, "Destroy it and we all die. Are you making that decision for all of us?"

Carver lowered his hand. "No. They're here. Is there anything you can do?"

"Attention Admiral Rowland. This is DualE. We're on a salvage hunt requiring our engines to engage and match velocities. I was not aware the Confluence Navy had authority to board freelance Realm ships."

"I claim such authority. You will brief me on your activities after our first order of business is complete. In the meantime, obey my command."

"They're taking it," said Carver. "Look." An EVA team on an open skiff blasted free from the naval ship. Light from their bow revealed the artifact spinning its way through the void. Grapnels shot forward and the skiff rocked with the artifact's motion. "It's more massive than they assumed. It'll tear the skiff into pieces." Carver repressed a grin. If their situation had been less dire, he'd have laughed aloud.

"No, there's a second team," said DualE. "That's *our* ship, Carver. The *Crossed Swords*."

"The mayday was no bluff. They've captured Chels and Altman. The gang's re-united."

Within minutes, the object was wrangled back to Rowland's frigate. Then they heard the thunk of the boarding team outside *Penance's* hull.

DualE knelt next to Pious. "I won't betray the brotherhood. I will do what I must. Have faith in me regardless of how my actions appear."

Pious gripped her hand. "I will."

Carver spoke, "We have an emergency medical evac required for one of our crew."

"Understood. Stand away from the inner airlock."

The 'lock opened and an armed marine lifted his face shield. A second marine stood behind him, weapon resting on the first's shoulder.

"Suit up," ordered the closest man. "The patient and DualE will go first." He pointed to Carver and Cardinal. "You two will wait with me for the 'all clear.'"

DualE said, "Help me with this, Carver." She'd caught Pious' arm in a sleeve. When Carver got close, she whispered, "I know where my loyalties lie. Be ready to follow my lead if we get a chance."

They finished suiting Pious and DualE and him cycled out. Carver and Cardinal were left alone with the marine.

"What's the deal with Rowland?" Carver asked. "Seems a bit stretched beyond his mandate."

"The standoff with the Realm was too unstable from a military view."

It hadn't been a standoff; it was sane minds backing down from mutual conflagration. "Is that your opinion or his?"

"The Admiral's opinion is my opinion, sir."

Carver couldn't blame him. It was less stressful to follow commands than make your own decisions. And the next step was allowing Command's ideas to become your own. Saves wear and tear on the brain. Would DualE succumb once Rowland got close to her?

Carver heard the outer 'lock cycle. The inner door re-opened for their escort. "Your turn," said the marine. "I'll take charge of your ship now."

"Come, Cardinal. The conversation's getting as stale as the air in here."

Chapter 40

DualE waited in the wardroom. The door opened and Chels was ushered in, followed seconds later by Carver.

"Where's Cardinal?" she asked.

"Escorted to Pious," said her partner. "They wouldn't let me see him." Carver turned to Chels. "Where's your salvager?"

"Helping them with the artifact." Her voice was bitter.

"That's why I'm waiting for Rowland's summons," said DualE. "He's prioritized the weapon before my debriefing."

"You planning on giving him anything useful?" Carver's tone was a challenge.

"I'd like a shot at demonstrating my utility. Before I take a swing at him."

Chels stepped between them. "The *Rickover's* being pursued."

DualE shifted focus. "Who?"

"Rowland dropped his escort to buy him time. I'm guessing no one friendly."

"God, I hope he isn't preparing to start a war with the Realm." DualE had to see him. Convince him this course was wrong.

The door opened again and Altman came in, supported by a marine. Altman bled from a gash on his cheek.

Chels made a sudden move toward the marine. He lowered his sidearm and shook his head. "Behave."

She changed tack and put an arm around Altman. "What happened to you?" she asked.

Altman collapsed into a chair. "The Admiral wasn't pleased with the outcome of my work."

DualE accosted the marine. "Striking a civilian is an offense. Did you witness this?"

"I saw nothing. This man is no civilian, he's a Realm partisan."

DualE stuck her face close to the marine's. "Your commander is unfit." She faced Altman. "Why?"

Altman pressed a towel to his face. "The artifact's junk. A fused mess. It must have burned out when Perry and I fired it. A one-shot deal. The Admiral took exception to my 'incompetence, irresponsibility and traitorous actions against the Confluence'."

DualE addressed the marine again. "Tell Admiral Rowland I must see him. I have information crucial to his mission. Mr. Denz must come with me. He is my colleague and partner fulfilling my role for the admiral."

The marine stepped back and whispered into his lapel comm. He nodded, then spoke to the pair. "Follow me."

Carver feared the fluid, uncertain situation. He had no idea what DualE planned, if any concrete plan was in her mind. 'Follow my lead' she'd said aboard the *Penance*. As far as he could tell, she was leading them into confronting a very angry, very powerful man.

"Admiral Rowland's cabin." The marine stood aside, allowing them to enter.

Rowland had aged a decade since Carver had last seen him. The stress from dissonant thinking would do that.

"This had better involve some way to restore that artifact," said Rowland. "DualE, if you damaged it in your clumsy pursuit, your alliance with me won't save you."

Rowland's attention flashed from one place to another. He moved around the room, unsettled. The man was unbalanced in thought and action.

"We'd have to examine it for ourselves but I assure you we didn't interfere with it," said DualE. She was on the offensive. "We wanted it intact as much as you did."

"Altman says it's useless. Why would you think different?"

"We aren't reliant upon Altman's opinion," she answered.

"Altman's a drunk," added Carver. He backed her up, though he didn't know where DualE was headed.

"My technicians support the drunk's view."

"They haven't seen what we have in the Eddy."

It dawned on Rowland's face. "More alien artifacts?"

"We're not certain but it's a possibility," said DualE. "Carver's Schoenfeldium lode had signs of unnatural orbit tinkering deep in its past. Before humans arrived."

Now she'd left Carver far behind. What possible advantage could such a lie gain?

Rowland's comm lit up. "Ahoy *Rickover*." A woman's voice. "This is the *Marlborough*, Admiral Bakken speaking. I am accompanied by Chancellor Mekli representing Argosy Realm and Sector General Raddam Shoop on behalf of the Bohr Confluence. Rowland has been declared 'Rogue' and is hereby notified of his formal 'Relief From Command'. Ranking officers will assume *Rickover* control and surrender immediately."

Rowland lunged for the comm. "This is Admiral Rowland. I remain in full command under my charter to enforce the peace accord by whatever means necessary. *Marlborough* will draw away. I have control of the alien weapon system and will not hesitate to fire upon your ship. Ask Chancellor Mekli if that's how he chooses to die."

DualE gave Carver the head signal. A moment later, she launched herself at the marine. Carver grabbed Rowland in a Full Nelson. By the time he'd spun Rowland away from the comm, DualE had the now-prone marine's sidearm.

"This is ex-commander DualE, Rowland's bluffing. The alien device is garbage."

"Relieved and disappointed in the same breath, DualE. What is your situation aboard? Hold that response, there's another..."

Rowland laughed. "My backup, I would say."

"One fighter escort isn't much backup," said DualE.

Rowland continued to grin. "No, but the *Indefatigable* is. The dreadnaught follows my orders. You can release me now and I'll ensure your sentencing is swift."

Carver remembered the ship from Argosy station. The balance had changed. "Bakken's cruiser...?" His question was drowned in a chorus of threats over the comm.

"They're engaging," said Rowland. He twisted in Carver's grasp. "Your question is about to be answered, Denz. No, Bakken can't. Captain Siebe, fire on the *Marlborough*. Escort fighters attack."

"Fighters are out of the fight, Admiral. We're spidered."

Carver raised an eyebrow in query. "Spidered?"

"Trapped eight or more directions with the *Marlborough* and her escorts and drones," DualE explained.

There were more command-response exchanges, then silence.

"Siebe, commence fire. This is an order." Rowland dragged Carver around the cabin.

Carver tried to put a hand over Rowland's mouth and got bit.

"Siebe here, Admiral. I'm not going to sacrifice my ship in a friendly firefight."

DualE spoke. "Admiral Bakken. We have Rowland restrained in his cabin. I don't know the status or mindsets of his officers listening to this. What is your situation?"

"This will be interesting," said Rowland. He'd relaxed under Carver's restraint. "Their situation is one of choice. Support me or be declared traitors to the Confluence."

"This is Admiral Bakken. Situation is under my control. We will continue our approach. DualE, you are re-commissioned and in command of the *Rickover*. Senior staff aboard acknowledge."

Slowly assents pinged the comm.

"What happened?" Carver asked. "What happened to Rowland's dreadnaught?"

"Not his," answered Bakken. "I had my own loyalists aboard. Rowland's allies were few and quickly subdued once the situation was clarified for them."

Rowland resumed his struggle. "Idiots. They'll settle for half when we could've had it all."

"For how long?" asked DualE. She removed his belt and secured his hands behind his back.

Carver used his own belt to bind Rowland's feet. "You'd create resentment which would eventually boil into a full rebellion."

DualE addressed the *Rickover* crew. "This is your interim commander. I want to see all senior officers in the wardroom in ten minutes." She lifted the marine to his feet. "You heard Admiral Bakken. Are you on the navy's side or his?" She pointed to Rowland.

He stood at attention as best he could. "Navy."

"Good. Me too. Lead the way." She kept the marine's weapon in her hand. "Carver, would you keep an eye on our former commander?"

He rummaged in the desk until he found another sidearm. "Glad to. Glad you chose the right loyalty, DualE."

"It took a long time to sort out my mind. But the mission helped. I hope you can find your singularity."

"My time out here blurs my choices. Am I Realm, Confluence, both or neither?" Who was he? Carver wasn't certain whose philosophy he followed. Did he have his own buried inside? One revealed in spookspace but repressed?

———————+++||+++———————

Epilogue

Pious sat up in the bed, two tubes running beneath a bandage on his arm. Brother Cardinal dozed in a chair beside him, chin resting on his chest.

Carver nudged Cardinal. "Take a break, brother. I'll spell you."

Pious opened his eyes. "Denz. Glad to see you. We are all sound? Chels came by to apprise me of your and DualE's heroics in avoiding armed destruction."

"Mayhem seems to follow us around, brother. I'm not certain we're the ideal team to run protection for your mission after all. DualE's considering resuming her naval career. Officer candidate. Wants to command something larger than either *Penance* or *Crossed Swords*."

"What about you?"

"I don't know. I'm missing clarity. Maybe I can find it our here. Nothing's tugging me back to Bohr."

"We often miss it when it stands directly before us."

"That's typical Pious enigmatic counsel. You're recovering, then?"

Pious' attempted smile was more grimace than grin. "No. I am...terminal. Don't mourn me in advance, Carver. Look at me and tell me you don't see your future."

Carver racked his brain. What did Pious mean? He looked at the brother's face, then past him. Unfocussed. "Me?"

"You'd make a fine replacement, Carver. A secular leader for now if you choose. You'd have three disciples to guide you through our religious mission as they've guided me. And one more, a sister to compliment the brothers."

"Not Zofie."

Pious chuckled. "No, she is committed to fulfillment through economic endeavor. Chels has indicated her choice to remain with us rather than return to Slate's Progress." He sighed. "My disciple has suffered a setback with her attempts to conquer jumpspace trauma. I fear she will be bound to normal space."

Carver paced, mind whirling. "I've never considered myself a man of the cloth, Pious. I have no history with your order. I'm more friend than adherent."

"That is why you struggle to find direction. This is your path. Embrace it and you will be rewarded more than you can imagine."

"I'll think about it."

Pious lifted his arm trailing the IV tubes prolonging his existence. "Don't take too long."

Chels entered the room. She hugged Pious, tears in her eyes. "Carver, DualE told me you voted to destroy the artifact and remove its temptation from existence. It was the right choice, even though unnecessary. I think the 'Denz luck' Zofie told me about is developing into a deeper connection to the universe."

Carver gripped Pious' hand. "Who am I to argue with the universe?"

"You are *Brother Denz*," said Pious.

The end

Other ebooks by Al Onia

Javenny

Transient City

Rogue Town

The Sixth Helix

About the Author

Al lives on Vancouver Island with his wife Sandra. Shadowed Passage is his eighth novel following Javenny, Transient City, Rogue Town, The Sixth Helix, The Fourth Vertex, The Third Redux and Barnacle Passage. Read more at ajonia.com.

Lightning Source UK Ltd.
Milton Keynes UK
UKHW010628260722
406393UK00001B/209